King Tut and the Girl Who Loved Him

King Tut and the Girl Who Loved Him

The Strange Adventures of Johanna Wilson

Robin M. Berard

iUniverse Star
New York Lincoln Shanghai

King Tut and the Girl Who Loved Him
The Strange Adventures of Johanna Wilson

iUniverse Star
an iUniverse, Inc. imprint

iUniverse books may be ordered through booksellers or by contacting:

iUniverse
2021 Pine Lake Road, Suite 100
Lincoln, NE 68512
www.iuniverse.com
1-800-Authors (1-800-288-4677)

Because of the dynamic nature of the Internet, any Web addresses or links contained in this book may have changed since publication and may no longer be valid.

This is a work of fiction. All of the characters, names, incidents, organizations, and dialogue in this novel are either the products of the author's imagination or are used fictitiously.

ISBN: 978-1-58348-477-7 (pbk)
ISBN: 978-0-595-86341-9 (ebk)

Printed in the United States of America

For my mother,
Beatrice Mitchell Martin,
with much love.

With many thanks to
Terry Campanella and Trudy Wasserman;
without you this book never would have been started.
To Carol Jones,
for reading about a million times;
without you this book never would have been finished.
To Jeanne Krauss,
for coming into the process at just the right time and providing great feedback
and moral support.
To dozens of my sixth-, seventh-, and eighth-grade students
who read this book and made helpful comments.
To my husband, Tony Berard,
for his unending patience.
To Carey, Kyle,
and Diana Haneski for their thoughtful comments.
And most especially to Nova Jones,
my first official fan.

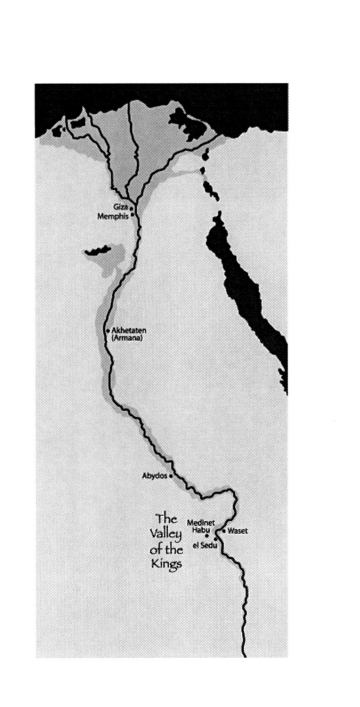

Giza
Memphis

Akhetaten
(Armana)

Abydos

The
Valley
of the
Kings

Medinet
Habu
Waset
el Sedu

CHAPTER 1

It all started with Tommy Nystrom.

Of all the slimy reptiles slithering around Southglades High, Tommy was the worst. Oh, it wasn't like he was the meanest kid in school; there were at least a hundred guys who were bigger and badder. Tommy was just the most annoying. He knew how to get under Jo's skin and exactly when to do it. In fact, he'd been giving her grief for years, ever since they had been in elementary school together.

"Hey, Anthill!" he yelled at her over the noisy crowd between third and fourth period. It was just another inane reference to her freckles.

"Buzz off, Butthead," she yelled back, just as Mr. Julian, the uptight band director, rounded the corner.

It wasn't the verbal retort that got her into trouble; it was the gesture that accompanied it.

"He started it," Jo tried to explain as Julian scribbled the detention form.

"Hey, I don't know anything about that. All I saw was you flipping him the bird. We don't do that here at 'Glades."

Right. And the sun doesn't shine in South Florida, either.

So it was Tommy who started the whole chain of events that day; although, if the truth be known, it didn't take much to shove Jo over the edge. And here's another truth: her run-in with him was only the first of many incidents that would make this day one she would never forget. Nonetheless, because of Tommy, Jo was in a truly bad mood when she arrived in Ms. Foster's social studies class.

Foster was sporting her usual uniform: a long, baggy dress and tiny wire spectacles, but she had also added GI boots laced up to midcalf and a camouflage vest she'd purchased from the local Army-Navy surplus store. Her style of dress, along with her tendency to forget what she was saying midsentence, made her a favorite target for ridicule among Southglades' students.

Jo dropped into her assigned seat and whispered to a couple of friends who sat nearby, "She looks like she's been lost in a time warp. Hasn't anyone told her that the sixties are over?"

This brought giggles, although Jo would have placed bets that most of her classmates didn't get the joke. She was on a roll, though, so she continued, "You'd think a history teacher would know what decade she's living in."

More giggles.

Foster shot her the evil eye, surmising that Jo was working the crowd again. She closed the classroom door and began her routine: attendance, review, lecture, lecture, and more lecture. Her voice droned on and on, and Jo tuned out. She put her head down on her desk and tried to pretend she was somewhere else.

"Miss Wilson, am I boring you?" Jo heard the question but thought it was rhetorical, so she didn't answer.

"Miss Wilson!"

"What?" Jo snapped to attention. Foster meant business.

"Am I boring you?" Foster asked again.

Does she really want me to answer that?

"Perhaps, if you know all this already—if you think you can just sleep through class and still pass the test—well, maybe you'd like to take the test right now?"

"Ummm ..."

"Ummm? Just exactly what does that mean? Could you be a bit more articulate?" Eyes were on Jo now, and she could tell by the snickers that some of her classmates were enjoying her discomfort.

She lashed out the only way she could, with her mouth. "I just don't get what we have to know all this stuff for."

That remark accomplished what Foster's endless lectures never had: it caught the attention of the entire class. The room went so silent Jo thought she could hear her own blood forcing its way through her arteries. Even Foster—capable of talking nonstop for hours, probably days—was at a loss for words. Sliding her glasses down her nose, she gave Jo the long, hard teacher-stare.

In deep now, but too stubborn to back down, Jo glared back.

After a century, or what seemed like it, Foster spoke. "Miss Wilson, do you like movies?"

"Yeah, I guess so," Jo replied.

"Did you ever flip on the TV to a movie that was almost over?" Jo continued to stare without answering. "Did you have a hard time understanding the ending?"

"I guess."

"Well, that's why we study the ancient civilizations, Miss Wilson, to understand the ending." Foster paused. "You no doubt think this world revolves around you, but really, you are but a microscopic blip on the time line of civilization." She narrowed her eyes and spoke in a decidedly condescending tone. "You are as insignificant, historically speaking, as a gnat."

"Ooookay," Jo said. Out in the hallway, a door slammed, and someone shouted an obscenity. In the classroom, no one so much as flinched.

"Nonetheless," Foster continued, "all of you will eventually be required to make decisions—cast votes—that will determine the future of this nation, this world." She spoke to the class but kept her eyes on Jo. She continued, "If we don't understand what went on before, how can we expect to appreciate the present? How can we make good decisions for the future?"

"Weeelll," Jo replied, "I just don't see how anything that happened five thousand years ago could possibly be of importance to me. Besides, we studied Egypt to death in middle school, and it's *ancient history*, for crying out loud. You know ... over ... pointless ... and *so* boring."

Her classmates sat in stunned silence. Too late, Jo realized she'd gone too far. After another long, breathless silence, Foster said, "Miss Wilson, do see me after class."

"Ooooohhhh," her classmates teased in unison.

"Way to go, Anthill!" someone yelled from the back.

Whatever. Jo rolled her eyes, crossed her arms over her chest, and tried her best to look unconcerned—despite the large lump that was growing in her throat. The rest of the hour flew by at warp speed, and before Jo could say *I'm in real trouble now*, class was over.

"Tomorrow we will begin our investigation into the death of King Tut," Foster called over the noise of the students gathering their belongings. "Our question: Did he die of natural causes, or was he *murdered*?"

Unimpressed, the other students filed out of the room, and Jo was left standing alone in front of Foster's desk. Foster just sat there, with her head in her hands, not saying a word. For a few minutes, Jo thought the teacher had forgotten about her.

Finally, Foster looked up.

Jo expected about a week's worth of detentions to add to Julian's, so she was astounded when, instead, Foster pulled an enormous book from the shelf behind her desk. *Life in Ancient Egypt*, Jo read silently. "Oh, I get it," she said. "I have to read the entire book by tomorrow and write a ten-page report, right?"

"I can do without the sarcasm, young lady."

Jo rolled her eyes.

"And the eye-rolling. One page will do. On the religious significance of the celestial alignment of the Great Pyramid at Giza pyramid.

"The *what*?"

"Don't play dumb with me," Foster snapped. She paused for a full ten seconds before continuing. "I was hoping that you would enjoy our study of ancient Egypt. You have such a good mind ... such a bright and talented student ... and I would so much value your honest participation." That was a line many teachers had used on Jo in the past, ever since she'd been labeled *gifted*. "If you just gave it a chance instead of always having to play the wise guy. The ancient civilizations are so fascinating—"

"For you, maybe."

"For anyone with intellectual curiosity." Foster paused, as if waiting for a response. "Look, just take this home. Write a brief report. A page will do, and see if you can't find *something* interesting. You just might be surprised by what you discover."

"Okay. One page. Typed or handwritten?"

"I ... don't ... care!" Foster said, completely exasperated. Standing, she pulled her long graying hair into a rubber band. "I'm going to lunch. You are dismissed."

Jo stuffed the book into her backpack and trudged off to math class.

Later, after letting herself into the second-story apartment, Jo dropped her book bag by the door and headed straight for the refrigerator. The cool blast was a welcome relief, as the walk home from school had been especially arduous on this September day, the height of the humid hurricane season in Miami. She grabbed a bag of chips from the cupboard and headed for the other end of the apartment.

"Mom?" she yelled. "Mom, you here?"

No answer.

She nudged open the door to her mother's bedroom and stuck her head through the narrow opening. "Mom?"

Still no answer.

In her own room, she pulled off her school clothes, leaving them right where they hit the floor, and shimmied into a pair of shorts and a tank top. She ran a brush through her long, blond hair and glanced in the mirror.

She didn't much like the looks of the girl that stared back. She hated the freckles that were splattered across her nose—more of them seemed to crop up every day. An almost two-mile walk in the afternoon sun hadn't helped any.

"Thanks, Mom," she said aloud with a good bit of sarcasm. "I can always count on you." Her mother had promised to pick Jo up from school, and she had hung around the parking lot for thirty or forty minutes, all the while believing that her mother's rusted-out Chevy would be the next car to come careening around the corner.

Instead, Jo had watched as the parking lot emptied. Even the geeks from the Latin Club had left the building, slid into the back seats of their parents' expensive cars, and been carted home.

She had finally heaved on her backpack and trudged home.

Now, disgusted, she flopped down on the unmade bed. Her room was always a total disaster, and this day was no exception. Coke cans littered the desktop; clothes were strewn everywhere. She thought briefly of cleaning it all up. Very briefly.

Instead, she threw the crumpled chip bag into the pile already accumulated on the floor. That was when she noticed the note pinned to her pillow:

Jo,

Sorry, got called to work. I know we planned a special night together, but I couldn't say no—need the extra cash. Do NOT leave the house. NO company! Dinner in the freezer.

Love ya,
Mom

Just what I wanted, another frozen dinner, thought Jo. She stretched out across the bed, folded her hands beneath her head, and squeezed her eyes shut. *Another night, just like the rest. This sucks. I wish I were anywhere but here.*

She rolled over, pulled open the drawer to her nightstand, and dug through the debris until she found the framed five-by-seven photograph she kept hidden away there. Using the hem of her tank top, she dusted the glass and stared at the family in the picture. Slim, dark-haired mother; smiling, sandy-haired father; little girl who looks a lot like Dad. The all-American family, or at least they had been, complete with a big house and new cars and all. Not rich, exactly—it wasn't like somebody died and left them a whole lot of money—but life had been pretty good.

Then, one day, Jo's father left, and that was that.

"Trust me," he had told her. Jo sat crossed-legged on her parents' bed and watched him throw his clothes into a suitcase. Big tears rolled down her cheeks, but he hadn't noticed.

He snapped the suitcase shut and slowed down just long enough to plant a token kiss on the top of her head. "I'll call ya. You'll see. Nothing will change between you and me. We'll go up to Orlando next weekend."

For a long time all she could remember was the snap of the locks on his suitcase and his voice echoing, *Trust me.*

"Right," she said aloud, "I trust ya, Dad."

He had disappeared like a puddle in the Florida sun.

She jammed the picture back into the drawer and slammed it shut.

She skipped the frozen dinner in favor of a bowl of chocolate ice cream, complete with chocolate syrup and chocolate chips. By eight o'clock she had already watched several reruns of her favorite sitcom, and none of her friends were online. She knew she should probably do her homework, but she didn't feel ready for algebra.

Deciding to take a bath instead, she took Foster's book into the bathroom and poured a deep, hot bath. She threw in a couple of handfuls of her mother's bubble bath, enough to work up a really good pile of bubbles.

There was a wide ledge on the bathtub, so she set the book on the ledge and climbed in. Jo loved to read, and the tub was a great place for reading. Also, the truth of the matter was that something Foster said had struck a nerve with her. *Intellectual curiosity.*

She knew that she had some of that. Not that she'd ever admit it to Foster or any of the kids at school; she'd sooner confess to being born on Mars. But as much as she hated the term *gifted*, she could own up to some curiosity, and something about Foster's book, with its glossy color foldouts of pyramids and ancient temples, did intrigue her.

What went on in the bathroom behind all those bubbles, absolutely no one had to know.

She opened the huge book, being extra careful to keep it out of the bubbles, thinking all the while about how much trouble she'd be in if it got even the slightest bit wet.

She turned the pages carefully and then flipped to the table of contents to find the section on the Great Pyramid at Giza. On page seventy-two, there was a huge picture of the pyramid. It filled the entire left-hand side and spilled onto the facing page. Jo scanned the accompanying article, looking for any mention of *celestial alignment.*

But then something caught her eye. Way down in the corner of the picture stood a gray-haired, gray-bearded man wearing a long skirt with a sash at the waist. The rest of him was bare except for the virtual ton of metal jewelry he wore. She leaned closer … and he was waving at her!

"Not possible," she said aloud. Still, she could feel her heart thumping in her chest. She put the book on the ledge, climbed out of the tub, and wrapped herself in a towel. Returning to the book, she tried to convince herself that the old man had been a figment of her frequently overactive imagination. *Too much chocolate*, she reasoned.

But he was still beckoning to her, like he wanted her to come along.

She leaned closer again.

It was as if he could see her and was desperate for her to follow.

This is just too weird, she thought. She squeezed her eyes shut and shook her head, trying to erase the little old guy from her brain. But when she opened her eyes, he was still there. He picked up a handful of sand and threw it at her.

"Ahhhhh!" she screamed. The sand caught her right in both eyes. She covered her face with her hands and, much to her dismay, heard Foster's big, expensive book go *plop*, right into the bathwater.

But Jo didn't have much time to think about the book.

The room went dark, and then she experienced a gut-wrenching, sickening feeling, as if she'd just hit the fourth drop on that big roller coaster, the free-fall that seems to go on forever while your stomach ends up stuck in your throat.

And then she was gone.

CHAPTER 2

For a few minutes Jo felt as though she was hanging, suspended in some void, conscious but not able to see, alive but not able to move. The only thing still working was her brain, and it was in overdrive trying to figure out what the hell had happened.

Still, the coming out was slow, very slow, and the first thing she was conscious of was more sand.

Deep sand.

She was on her hands and knees in the sand, and it felt cool and damp beneath her.

She sat back on her heels and attempted to clear her vision. A pair of torches lit the cavelike chamber. She squinted. No one was in the room at that moment, but everything indicated that someone was in the process of painting murals—primitive drawings of strange people with long, dark hair and bronze skin.

She struggled to her feet. Tools lay scattered here and there, and clay jars of paint lay right where the artist had left them, wet brushes propped against the jars.

A shiver ran up and down her spine.

Jo had an idea of where she was, as incredible as it might be, and she knew she was wearing only a towel. Even worse, she knew that someone had been working in this chamber very recently. Chances were pretty good that someone would return soon.

The only thing she could think of was to get out of there—fast.

Clutching her towel around herself, she stumbled through a low door and then down a long hall so narrow she could touch the jagged walls on either side. One turn to the right and she could see a tiny rectangle of sunlight. Running, she made for the opening. The angle of the hallway changed, forcing her to run uphill.

She stumbled and fell.

She got up again and pressed on.

She reached the low doorway and came to an abrupt halt. She squinted. *What is this place?* she wondered. She saw nothing but light, as if she had stepped onto the sun itself. Finally, her eyes adjusted, and before her a short flight of stairs led downward. *What to do now?*

Behind her she could see nothing but a long, dark tunnel. *No way I'm going back in there.*

She hurried down the stairs and then, feeling every bit as though she had been pushed, fell to her hands and knees. Totally creeped out and shading her eyes with one hand, she looked over her shoulder at the building she had just escaped.

It wasn't so much a building as it was a pile of stones, and it was huge—so big she could only imagine where it ended high in the sky. Suddenly the whole world went dark again. Jo's stomach lurched, and she fought to keep from throwing up.

This time she was sure of it; someone or something pushed her from behind, and she fell face-first into the sand.

She gave up. She had no idea what was happening to her, but she knew it was all out of her control. So she just lay there and waited for whatever it was that was going to happen next. For a few minutes she wondered whether she might be in the middle of a nightmare, but the heat, the gritty sand that clung to her, and the quick beating of her heart were all too real. She knew she wasn't dreaming. That's when she heard them, voices coming from the other side of the building.

They were coming closer. Jo froze.

She realized that, in another minute, they'd round the corner and stumble right into her. Forcing her legs to move, she flung herself behind the only shelter she could find—a wide column, one of a pair that flanked the stairs she had just stumbled down. She wedged herself between the pillar and the rough stone exterior of the building until she was just barely out of sight and then held her breath.

She could tell that the group had turned the corner. Some of them climbed the stairs and entered the building, their voices fading away. Others stayed behind and, much to her alarm, were joined by still more. She thought she heard orders being given—something about splitting stones—and then all voices were drowned out by the constant hammering of metal on rock.

The huge column she hid behind was maybe four or five feet wide, but she remained standing so as not to be seen from either side. Tilting her head just slightly to the left, she discovered that she could see part of the stairway that led into the building, as well as the landing. Presently several men climbed the stairs and went straight to the entrance.

Panicking, she slid back behind the column. *If I can see them, then they can see me, right?* But then her curiosity got the best of her, and she tilted her head again—just enough to peek at the stairway. More men stood in the entrance to the building.

Like the others, these people wore little clothing—just loincloths, really—and were bronze in color, as if they had spent many hours in the sun. They all had black hair and the same haircut, shoulder length with bangs.

Most of the group entered the building, but two of them turned to go down the stairway. They were involved in some sort of debate and were not looking Jo's way. She couldn't take her eyes off them. The hammering let up just long enough for her to catch a chunk of their conversation.

"Pharaoh will be out here tomorrow, you know. He will not be pleased," said the taller of the two men.

"I say, what more proof do we need?" his companion replied. "Construction has been delayed at every stage. Clearly, the gods do not favor our young pharaoh."

"Don't be so quick to judge—"

"*Quick*?" asked the second man. "Is this not the ninth year of his reign? You are too gracious, my friend. That Aten-worshipper will never restore Kemet to her rightful glory—"

"You are wrong. The kingdom prospers and—"

"Ha!" the second man snapped. "The Hittites threaten from the north and the Nubians from the south. What good is prosperity when we are about to be overrun?" The two men passed from Jo's sight, and the conversation was drowned out by the noise of construction.

Stunned, she retreated behind the column.

Pharaoh? No freaking way. This can't be happening.

"Hey, you, what are you doing there?" asked someone standing very close, within a few feet of Jo's hiding place. She felt her heartbeat rise into her throat; her legs felt like cooked spaghetti.

"I said, what are you doing?"

"My name is Ahmose," another voice answered. "I have a message for you from the foreman."

The conversation faded. Jo started breathing again. It was all just like she'd seen in books and movies and heard about in social studies.

Kemet, she knew, was the ancient name for Egypt. It meant *black land*, because of the black soil that was left behind by the floodwaters of the Nile. Everything fit together and made strange, whacked-out sense.

And, of course, it didn't make any sense at all. Time travel was only for movies and sci-fi novels; that much Jo knew for sure. And something else didn't make sense: if this *thing* beyond comprehension had happened, if she was truly in ancient Egypt, why did she understand all the conversations she heard? Certainly they must be speaking in some ancient language.

Jo remained out of sight, just a few yards from the doorway to the building, and her hiding place continued to serve her well. Despite the dozens of people who passed just feet from her, she was able to remain undiscovered for the rest of the day. All the while she stood, still dressed only in her towel, afraid her slightest movement would change a shadow and catch someone's attention. All the while, too, she was trying to figure what had happened to her. Was it possible that this was all some kind of a joke? Maybe she had been drugged and carted off to a movie set. As ludicrous as that idea was, it made more sense than traveling through time.

The afternoon dragged on, and Jo could not hide from the sun, more powerful, even, than the South Florida version to which she was so accustomed. It crept around the column from all directions and pursued her relentlessly, leaving her thirsty to the point of near-delirium. Her legs throbbed from standing, and the sharp edge of a stone cut into her back. Finally, stiff, sore, and desperate for water, she decided to risk it all, to step from her hiding place and beg someone—anyone—for help. But just then, the afternoon sun slid behind the pyramid, leaving a sliver of shade. The noise of construction dimmed; Jo thought she heard someone talking about being finished for the day. *Hang in there*, she thought, *just a bit longer.* Despite her confusion, or maybe because of it, she was convinced that asking for help from these men would be a dangerous thing to do.

She was quite sure she would have given her towel for a Coke.

Her thoughts turned to Foster. Who was she, really? Was she the one who had caused all this to happen? It had to be her. What kind of person is capable of sending someone through time? What kind of person would actually do this to a defenseless girl? And what about the book? The old man in the picture? Jo knew that all of it was tied together somehow; she just couldn't figure out how.

I ticked Foster off, and this is payback, she reasoned. *Could it really be that simple?*

The sun had been high in the sky when Jo first escaped from the pyramid, but the end of the day arrived, finally, and she was still too scared or too stiff to move. She just stood there for a while longer, not sure which scenario was more frightening: hearing strange men working just a few yards from where she cowered, or the absolute and total silence that enveloped her once they left. The night grew large and ominous, but still she didn't dare budge.

"Hello?" she asked, tentatively. Even the sound of her own voice, unfamiliar in the empty desert, frightened her as it floated through the eerie stillness. She peeked out from behind the column. The night was as still as a tomb. Jo stepped out of her hiding place and sat, no, fell, on the ground.

She was alone, more alone than she had ever been in her entire young life.

You might be surprised at what you discover, Foster had said.

"Okay, I'm surprised; you win," Jo said out loud. "I've done my time in this weirdo detention. Now get me home!"

But no one came to rescue her, and Jo was left sitting there in the sand, on her own. She thought about her mother, who had obviously returned from work to find her little girl missing. No doubt her mother had been royally ticked off, at least initially. But how long had it been? Had her mother reached the point of panic yet? Had she called the cops? She longed to reach out, across space or time or whatever it was that separated them, and tell her that everything would be okay.

I'll figure it all out, Mom.

She knew she couldn't stay where she was much longer. She needed to get away before the work crew came back in the morning. They had overlooked her for one day, but she knew she had been lucky. Finding her way home was imperative—she was very much looking forward to having Foster fired—but for now she needed clothes, food, and most urgently, water.

None of which she was likely to find where she was, in the desert.

She had an idea, one that had been nagging at the back of her brain all afternoon and through the evening. She remembered enough Egyptology to know that the ancient Egyptians built most of the pyramids on the west side of the Nile River. This was the case with the Great Pyramid, the one in the picture she'd been looking at when she made her leap through time. Jo figured that if she *was* in Egypt, and if she walked due east, she would eventually reach the Nile. But exactly how far away was the river? And what dangers lay between here and there? Scorpions? Snakes?

Those were questions Jo couldn't answer. If the Nile was within walking distance, she knew, it was not within *easy* walking distance. *Doable*, she told herself, *but not easy*. She was exhausted and suffering from dehydration, but she decided that she had to find the strength to reach the river before sunrise. She figured she'd find water and a shady spot to hide in until she could come up with a plan.

Brushing the sand off as best she could, she stood and stretched her cramped, sore muscles, and, as if the desert had eyes, pulled her pink towel closer. From the afternoon shadows, she had determined that the sun had set directly over her left shoulder. Under the cover of night, her heart pounding wildly in her chest, she proceeded cautiously in the opposite direction.

A bright moon filled the night sky, providing just enough light to guide her through the desert. Jo noticed a dim star hanging low in the sky to the east and used that as her compass, making certain to walk directly toward it. With every step, she dreaded what might lie ahead, but she also knew what might happen if she was caught by the morning sun.

The deep sand made walking difficult. Jo had walked miles on South Florida beaches, but this sand was deeper. Also unlike the beach, the desert was not flat. The dunes were huge, so she spent much of the night walking uphill and downhill. Every time she reached the top of a dune, she pointed herself toward what she hoped was the same eastern star.

She trudged on, but it didn't take her long to regret her decision to set off in search of the Nile. She started to think about all the stories she had read about people dying in the desert, crawling on their hands and knees toward some oasis mirage. Visions of sun-bleached skeletons—mouths open, full of spiders—danced through her head.

She really wished she hadn't watched all those late-night mummy movies.

Problem was, she couldn't turn back. She had a star to guide her in an easterly direction, but she'd never thought to devise a way back to the pyramid in the dark.

She just kept going.

Finally the land leveled, and the sand under her feet became firmer. She could see well enough in the moonlight to know that she had stumbled onto a road of some sort, one that led directly east.

She thought she heard running water.

I'm delusional, she thought. *This must be what happens right before you die.*

Then, almost before she knew it, she was wading into the cool water of the Nile River.

CHAPTER 3

There she was, splashing around in the Nile like it was the pool at her apartment complex, not giving any thought at all to staying out of sight or even being quiet about it.

"Who are you?" asked a distinctly male voice.

Jo stopped breathing, again.

"I demand your name," he said. She turned to face the riverbank and saw the man who went with the voice standing a mere twenty feet away. Try as she might, she couldn't get anything to come out of her mouth.

The man waded toward her. In the dim light of the early morning, he looked much like the others she had seen out in the desert—tall, dark, and scantily dressed. She couldn't see his face very well.

"I … I … I am Jo," she stuttered.

"Jo? That is not a name used in this kingdom. Where are you from? How did you come to be here?"

Good questions.

She tried to figure out how to answer them. How do you explain to an ancient Egyptian that you just blew in from the twenty-first century? While she attempted to figure that out, the sandy river bottom began to slide away under her feet, and it seemed as though the once-friendly river was now trying to pull her under. She struggled to keep her balance.

"Speak! Explain yourself!"

"I come from a place far away. I was taken from my home … kidnapped … now I'm lost." Jo could tell by the way he stood—feet planted wide in the river, arms crossed—that he wasn't ready to buy her story. "Please, you're scaring me." She hadn't planned for that to slip out, but it did, and she could see that it softened him a bit. She wasn't above begging. "I'm tired and thirsty, and I need help."

The young man was almost as startled by the turn of events as Jo was. He'd left camp for an early bath in the river, quite confident that he was the first to rise. He hadn't expected to run into anyone, much less a girl, certainly not a girl with golden-colored hair.

He stepped closer, trying to get a better look at her.

He knew his duty; he should turn her over to the *medjai*, the pharaoh's elite guards, for she had wandered far too close to the king. It was their job to interrogate intruders and determine their fate. What would the *medjai* do with a girl? Jail her? Sell her as a slave? Marry her off to one of the cruel, old generals?

Maybe so, and that was too bad, because she was unusual, exotic even, with her long, golden hair and fair skin. Having seen very few girls like her, his curiosity was piqued. The young man, a royal scribe and assistant to the pharaoh, made a decision of his own and stepped into the chain of events that would change his life, Jo's life, and even the course of history.

"Come," he said. "I will find you something to drink." He turned and strode toward a line of trees in the distance. Jo clutched her soggy towel and struggled to keep up.

They walked along a sandy path, and in the dim light Jo could see a cluster of small huts not far from the river's edge. He led her to one of the huts near the rear of the group, lifted a curtain over the only door, and motioned for her to go inside.

She dared not do anything else.

"Wait here," he instructed. "Do not leave. The others will wake shortly, and you must not be found wandering. I will bring you food and drink." He let the curtain fall, and Jo was left alone. The hut, not even as large as her bedroom back home, had narrow windows near the roof that let in just enough light for her to notice a rough-looking blanket on the dirt floor. She sat down, not knowing how long it would be before she saw him again.

As it turned out, he wasn't gone long, and when he returned he dropped an unwrapped loaf of bread beside her on the blanket and handed her a clay jar.

"Here." he said. "You will be safe in this hut until evening, when the pharaoh's men go back to Waset. Rest, and I will find you when I return from the temple." He turned to leave.

"Wait," Jo said. "What is your name?"

"I am Nekhare." He left, letting the rectangle of cloth fall behind him. She took the lid off the jar and took a long swig, fully expecting water.

It was beer, or so she guessed. She'd never tasted beer of any kind before, much less Egyptian beer, and she spit that first mouthful about halfway across the hut. She knew she should drink something, so she drank more, much slower this time. The bread was heavy and gritty, as if it had sand in it, but she was starving, so she ate as much of it as she could.

She polished off the beer, lay back on the blanket, and fell asleep.

The hut Jo slept in was part of a tiny village called el Sedu, little more than a few uninhabited clay brick huts and a campsite, nestled in the narrow band of green between the Nile and the desert. The river grew wide here, and engineers had constructed a dock large enough to tie down several boats. For this reason, and because it was en route between Waset (the city that would later be known as Thebes) and the Valley of the Kings, el Sedu served as a pit stop for all those traveling between the two.

On that particular day, the king of Egypt, complete with royal entourage, passed by her hut not once, but twice, first on his way out to inspect the construction site in the desert, the very same one in which Jo had hidden the day before, and then again on his way back to the palace in nearby Waset. They had arrived in two large ships and then disembarked with enough noise to wake the long-dead pharaohs in the nearby tombs. Captains barked orders, and the river valley echoed with the sound of marching feet. But Jo was so exhausted that the pharaoh himself could have ridden into her hut on an elephant, and she wouldn't have known it. In fact, she slept the entire day, wrapped in her towel and blissfully unaware of the men who marched by just a few hundred feet from where she slept.

While she was sleeping off the shock of recent events, and the beer, Nekhare was out at the construction site with the pharaoh, inspecting every inch of the building, transcribing every word spoken between the pharaoh, the architects, and the engineers, and all the while wondering whether the golden-haired girl would still be in el Sedu when he returned—and wondering what he'd do with her if she was.

Late in the afternoon, the pharaoh's party returned to the village to rest and reorganize before boarding and sailing back to Waset. Nekhare waited as long as he could, watching to be certain that no one entered *that* hut. Then, when the others were aboard the barges that had been waiting for them, he returned to the hut under the pretense of collecting his personal belongings.

Jo woke up with a gasp. She was still a little groggy and having a hard time remembering where she was. A man stood in the doorway, but with the blinding sun behind him, Jo couldn't see who he was. Frightened, she clutched her towel and scooted away from him. He stepped into the hut and let the curtain fall behind him.

"Ssshhh. Make no noise, or the others will hear you," he said.

"N … N … Nekhare?" she asked, remembering slowly.

"Yes." He moved away from the door, closer to Jo, and dropped down on one knee. "Have you seen anyone?"

"No," she whispered. The afternoon sun filtered through the windows high in the walls, and this little bit of light allowed Jo to study him. His skin was smooth and clear, without stubble, and his body was long and lean. *He's not much older than me*, she thought. *Not so scary.*

"The pharaoh will be departing soon," he continued, "and with him all his men. It should be safe for you to leave in a short time, if you so desire. I must return to the palace with the pharaoh. He will be looking for me soon."

"You can't leave me here by myself! I don't know where to go or what to do."

He looked at her long and hard. "I wonder. You said that you were kidnapped—brought to this kingdom against your will. Yet you speak our language perfectly."

"I do?"

"And I am not sure what you would have me do for you anyway. Especially wearing … that." He motioned toward her pink towel. She pulled it tighter.

"Don't you have anything I can wear?"

"No."

"Or some way to get something for me to wear?"

"Not without going all the way to the palace and back." He stood, leaned against the doorframe, and continued to stare.

She thought about her freckles and the sunburn and how totally grungy she must have looked. She knew he had absolutely no reason to help her.

He thought about all the things that could happen to a beautiful girl who was lost and alone in this kingdom. He knew he could save her if he could keep her away from the others. He was, after all, a very resourceful young man. And then she would be *his*, not that he couldn't have any girl he wanted.

"Yes, yes," she said finally. "Don't you see? You could go back to the palace and get some clothing. Bring me clothes, and I swear I won't bother you anymore." She didn't know where the palace was or how long it would take for him to get there and back, but she was desperate.

Suddenly, there were voices outside the hut. Nekhare leaned out the door and spoke to someone. "I'll be right along. Just let me pick up my things." He let the curtain fall again, entered the hut, and began folding the blanket.

"Please," Jo whispered.

He nodded and continued in a hushed voice. "I will be awhile. I'll have to go back with Pharaoh and his party, make some excuse to leave, and paddle back across the river …"

"Thank you, thank you, thank you," she said, not believing her luck.

"My sister will have a dress you can borrow."

"You'll tell her about me?" asked Jo nervously.

"Don't worry," Nekhare replied, "Meritaken and I take care of each other. I can count on her to help us out."

Jo nodded.

"You can't wait here," Nekhare said.

"I can't?"

"Not unless you want to be found. Workers from Der el Medina use these huts on their trips to and from Waset, the Holy City. It's late in the day now, and sometimes they spend the night here on their way to one place or the other."

Der el Medina? The Holy City? "Where should I wait?" she asked aloud.

"It won't be long before we weigh anchor. Behind the village, you will find a line of sycamore trees. Follow them to the river's edge and stay in the shade there by the river. It is high ground, so you will be able to stay out of sight while keeping an eye on those who come and go from the river landing. I will find you when I return."

"Are you sure that's safe?" Jo asked.

"As safe as any place, I'm afraid. And Jo …" Her name sounded funny as it rolled off his tongue. "Be careful; don't let anyone see you."

She nodded, her eyes filling with tears.

"One last thing."

"Yes?" A tear broke loose and rolled down her cheek. He stepped close and wiped it away with his thumb. The gesture was tender and unexpected.

"Don't get too close to the river."

She just looked at him, unable to speak.

"Nile crocs." He let the curtain fall behind him as he left.

Jo decided to wait about fifteen minutes before leaving the hut, so she counted to sixty fifteen times, marking each minute in the sand. Then, nervously, she stuck her head out From behind the curtain. The valley sparkled with green.

Now or never, she thought. She held her breath and scurried out of the hut and around to the back. Running, staying low, she made her way to the line of trees that wound toward the river's edge and then followed them just a hundred yards or so, constantly looking over her shoulder, until she came upon a group of trees that stood on slightly higher ground. Tall grass grew under the trees, providing perfect cover; she knew she'd found the spot to which Nekhare had directed her.

From her position, she could part the grass and see northward, down the legendary Nile River as it snaked its way through the lush river valley and disappeared in the distance. She also had a clear view of the west—the temporarily empty village and the sand dunes beyond it.

Just as Nekhare had predicted, over the course of the late afternoon and early evening, several long wooden boats—their bows curled toward the sun—pulled alongside the dock a hundred yards or so from where Jo hid. From those boats came men, young and old, most carrying large sacks on their backs. As she watched, they trudged up the sandy road to the huts. Before long, a bonfire blazed in the general vicinity of the village, and Jo could smell the rich aroma of something being roasted.

Her stomach growled; she hadn't eaten since she had forced down Nekhare's gritty bread that morning. She longed for her frozen dinner and a Coke. The sun set over the desert, painting the western sky with glorious shades of red, orange, and pink. As nervous as she was, Jo was still awed by the spectacle of it all. The colors deepened, and a pale moon so large she thought she might reach out and touch it replaced the sunset. It was all so incredibly beautiful, yet so surreal.

The bonfire died, the village quieted, and Jo tried to make herself comfortable. She curled up in the grass and thought about sleep, but she didn't dare close her eyes in case those crocodiles, or something more sinister, tried to sneak up on her. Try as she might, she couldn't see how any of this could end well.

Her only hope was Nekhare, and he was taking his time getting back to her. Jo thought she had sensed some kind of *thing* happening between the two of them, but then again, she wasn't very experienced with guys. Still, if he had a crush on her—and she didn't know what other reason he could have for helping her—then perhaps he would find her clothes, food, and a safe place to stay until she could figure out how she had arrived in Egypt and how she could get home.

Yes, that was what she needed: a safe haven from which to assess the situation. *C'mon, Nekhare, find me safe haven.*

CHAPTER 4

While Jo was hiding in the tall grass, Nekhare was back at the palace, trying to find an excuse to get away. The pharaoh, unhappy with the inspection of his mortuary temple, called his closest advisers to an informal evening meeting. They gathered in the pharaoh's opulent office while the rest of the palace settled in for the night.

Dressed casually in a simple kilt and a leopard-skin tunic, the pharaoh sat behind a large table in a golden chair. Two older men sat across the desk from him. One was Ay, vizier of Upper Egypt and close friend of the royal family. The other was Horemheb, General of Pharaoh's Armies. Nekhare sprawled on a settee in one corner of the room, close enough to hear the conversation. A single lamp, placed behind the pharaoh, left the largest portion of the room in shadows.

Nekhare had other things on his mind, but despite the hour, he could hardly say, "Excuse me, I have to go rescue a strange but beautiful girl I found wading in the Nile." So, he sat through the meeting, restless and uneasy, while the pharaoh and his advisers debated the intricacies of temple construction.

"I still think we would get better stone from the Abydos quarries," Ay insisted.

"No doubt," agreed General Horemheb, "but the cost! Abydos is another two days' sail north. How can we afford to bring stone from there? We have already exceeded our budget …"

"Yes, yes. I've heard all about it. We are overspent, and you're afraid we'll have to dip into the military budget," said Ay.

"It's a matter of priorities …"

"General Horemheb, what could be more important than the construction of the pharaoh's eternal home? *Ma'at* must be preserved at all costs."

"Even at the cost of being overrun by our enemies? Look at him! He's a young man. We have many years to finish this temple—"

"Maybe," interrupted the pharaoh, "and maybe not." The two older men turned to look at the young pharaoh.

"Yes," said Ay, the more grandfatherly of the two. "Your brother died young, but your father lived well into his fifties. There is no reason to doubt your longevity."

"Precisely," said Horemheb.

And so the two old men continued to argue as the pharaoh watched. He had grown accustomed to their constant quibbling, and he had heard it all before. It was a never-ending debate, one that none of them would win. There was never enough money, not even in this, the greatest kingdom on earth.

"Do you have those figures, Nekhare?" asked General Horemheb.

Nekhare was thinking about the girl again.

"Nekhare!"

"I'm sorry ..."

"You are not paying attention," said Horemheb, his tone sharp. The two of them, Horemheb and Nekhare, had a long-standing distrust of each other, mostly due to the fact that neither of them liked the other's closeness to the pharaoh. "I asked for the cost estimates of shipping the remaining stone from Abydos."

"Of course." Nekhare turned to the pharaoh. "Your Highness, may I get them for you in the morning?" The two older men stiffened, surprised by Nekhare's bold request.

The pharaoh laughed. "Nekhare is right," he said. "We are all tired. We'll continue this discussion in the morning." With that, the four men filed out of the room.

Three of them went straightaway to their beds.

A few minutes later, on the other side of the palace, Nekhare tapped on his sister's bedroom door and waited for her to answer. He knocked again, a little louder this time. Finally, Meritaken opened the door just wide enough to see her brother standing outside. "What?" she asked.

"I need to borrow a dress."

"Excuse me?" Meritaken stared at her brother in amazement. "A dress?"

"Look, I don't have time to explain now, but I need a dress for a girl. She's slim like you, about your size."

"Nekhare ..."

"I found a girl ..." He searched for the right words. "Let me in."

Meritaken stepped aside, and Nekhare entered the candlelit room. "She's out at el Sedu, and she needs help. She's waiting for me there."

"Who? Who is at el Sedu?"

"I really can't explain right now. Just let me borrow a dress, and I'll tell you all about it later."

"You can't row across the river in the middle of the night. Not by yourself."

"I've got that all figured out. I promise, it will be all right."

"Nekhare, this sounds very dangerous. Perhaps I should go with you."

"Absolutely not. You will just slow me down. I need to move quickly in order to be back before sunrise. Just give me the dress."

Never one to refuse her brother, Meritaken dug into a deep chest and pulled out a long white tunic.

The Nile runs south to north, and el Sedu lay just south of Waset and the palace. Nekhare knew that rescuing Jo would require rowing upstream in the dark, a dangerous and time-consuming trip. It would be daybreak before he found his girl; he formulated another plan. He left the palace and jogged upstream several miles through Waset and then another mile or so, until he was well south of Jo's position. Then, commandeering a small boat, he paddled downstream.

Nekhare knew the Nile well; he had grown up on the river, hunting in the tall grass on either side and swimming in its lazy current. As part of the royal family, he'd enjoyed a leisurely childhood, free from the work and worry of other young Kemetans. He'd sailed and rowed all manner of boats, big and small, and he knew every twist and every sandy landing spot. It didn't take him long to find Jo's hiding place, even in the dark. As he approached, he could see her sitting with her back to him.

He snuck up behind her, wrapped his arms around her so she couldn't move, and clamped his hand over her mouth.

Caught by surprise, she fought back with surprising strength.

"Ssshhh! It's me, Nekhare. You must be quiet." He hung onto her until the information sunk in and he felt her relax. She nodded in understanding, and he could feel her heart begin to slow to its normal rate.

He released her. "I'm sorry, but I couldn't take the chance that I'd startle you and you'd scream," he whispered.

"It's okay," she choked out.

"I have a boat. Let's get out of here." He grabbed her hand and pulled her along, Jo still wearing her towel, holding onto it for all she was worth. "Stay low," he cautioned. "They're probably asleep or too drunk to be much of a problem, but I'd rather not be noticed."

Aided by the moonlight, they found the boat. Nekhare reached in and pulled out a cloth bag, and from the bag he removed a white garment. "Meritaken is about your size, so this should fit. You'd better put it on now."

"Turn around," she said, and he did as requested.

"Have you got it on?" Nekhare asked, after a few moments.

"Yes ... except I can't fasten it." He turned and noticed that the dress reached almost to her ankles and clung to her body as if it had been painted there.

She fumbled with the long ties at the back of the dress.

"Here, let me." She turned her back to him and held her hair out of the way, and he tied the dress together. She flinched as his fingers brushed the back of her neck, and Nekhare noticed that her skin radiated heat from the sunburn he had noticed earlier in the day.

"I thought you'd forgotten about me," she whispered.

He thought about how impossible it would have been to leave her behind.

"Forgive me," he said finally. "I had some difficulty getting away from the palace. We must hurry—there is no time to waste. We must get back before daybreak." Nekhare shoved the boat into the river and held it steady for her.

"You're taking me to the palace?"

"Yes. I've told Meritaken about you. She's waiting for us. Let's go."

"Wait! What about this?" she asked, holding up her pink towel.

"Roll it up and hide it in the tall grass." She did as he suggested and then climbed awkwardly into the boat as though unaccustomed to the narrow dress that restricted her movement. Nekhare pushed the boat away from the bank with an oar. A few minutes later, they were moving with the current. She didn't say anything until they were well away from the river's edge and the men who slept in the village.

"What will you do with me when we get to the palace?" she asked.

"I haven't figured that out yet."

"But what will you tell people about me?"

"Look, let's just worry about getting there first," he said. "The three of us will come up with a plan. Pharaoh is a reasonable man. If we can get to him alone, without his advisers, I think he will help you."

"And if he won't?"

Nekhare didn't reply right away. Finally, he said, "We'll think of something. You'll just have to trust me."

Nekhare paddled downriver, and Jo listened to the sounds of the river at night—the oar in the water and the occasional splashes that told her that they were not completely alone. She wondered about the wildlife that lived in and around the river and remembered Nekhare's warning about crocodiles. For the first time, she realized how foolish she had been to wade in the Nile, especially in the half-light. *And now I'm letting a total stranger take me farther and farther from ... what?*

He had asked for her trust, but the last guy who had demanded her trust hadn't been all that trustworthy.

Suddenly she had a nasty sinking feeling, as though she'd just stepped off a very tall cliff. The feeling was so physical, so profound, that she reached out and grabbed both sides of the narrow boat. With every stroke of the oar, Nekhare was taking her farther from the spot where she had been deposited when she'd arrived in ancient Egypt. With every stroke of the oar, he further removed her from the possibility of rescue, or so she imagined.

But it was too late now. She wasn't about to ask Nekhare to paddle back upriver and take her back out to the worksite, and she had a feeling that he wouldn't do that anyway. Jo knew that her only course of action was to proceed with caution and focus on what lay ahead. She could just make out the banks on either side of the Nile, bathed in moonlight, higher in some places than in others. A cool breeze ruffled the palm trees and soothed Jo's sunburn but did nothing to relieve her anxiety.

They didn't speak at all.

After half an hour or so, she could see the silhouette of the city on the horizon: flat-topped buildings of two and three stories, taller buildings, and obelisks. It wasn't much like the familiar skyline of Miami, and Jo grew more and more anxious as she thought about the challenges that lay before her, here in this strange city. Again, she was struck with a sharp sense of being alone and on her own, despite Nekhare's presence. He had rescued her from the desert, and he seemed to have some connections with important people, but just how far would he go to keep her safe? And what would he expect in return?

Nekhare paddled for a few more minutes and then steered the boat to shore. When they were within a few feet of the bank, he jumped out, pulled the boat onto the sand, and held it steady for Jo. He grabbed her hand and pulled her out of the boat and up over a little hill. "A borrowed boat," he whispered. "The owner will miss it in the morning, but it had to be done."

They hurried down a narrow, sandy street, neither of them talking, Jo still struggling to keep up. The dark shapes of buildings loomed on either side; otherwise, she would have never known she was even in a city. There were no lights, no lamps, no fires—just the moon. And not a sound—not so much as a snore—came from those who slept as the two of them hurried by.

The sand beneath Jo's feet turned to stone, the streets widened, and the moonlight reflected off whitewashed buildings. She was tiring now, slowing down. She wished she could trade her dress for a pair of jeans and a tank top, clothing she could move in.

"Come," Nekhare said. "Just a bit farther." They rounded a corner and passed through a tall, arched opening in a huge wall.

"Halt! Who goes there?" Guards were upon them, bronzed men brandishing long swords, casting long shadows in the flickering lamplight. Jo let slip a gasp, but Nekhare pulled her close.

"'Tis Nekhare. Step aside." A huge man held a lantern high enough to ascertain Nekhare's identity. He cast a quick glance in Jo's direction and then smiled.

Jo shuddered as the guard continued to leer at her.

"So it is. And I see you've brought company." The guard laughed. "Go on, then."

They entered the palace's huge courtyard and turned right. They walked under another, smaller arch, and Jo suddenly felt damp grass beneath her feet. By the aroma, it was undeniably a garden.

The path skirted the edge of the garden before finally coming to a wooden double door. Nekhare pulled the door open and strode down a wide hallway. A lamp burned at one end, casting most of the hallway in long shadows. He let go of Jo's hand but continued to lead the way. Feeling relieved, Jo slowed to a more comfortable stride in her borrowed dress.

Suddenly a door opened, and a dark figure stepped between them. Gasping, Jo turned to run back the way she had come, but the man grabbed her by the arm.

"Who are you, and how did you get in here?" he demanded. Jo cowered, too startled to reply.

Nekhare backtracked up the hall to her rescue. "General Horemheb, please leave her alone. She's with me."

"Oh, it's you," the general said, sounding disgusted. "I should have guessed. What no-good are you up to tonight, Prince Nekhare?"

Prince Nekhare? Jo wondered. *He didn't say anything about being a prince.*

"I might ask you the same. Let the girl go," Nekhare repeated. "Pharaoh won't like it if you are rude to his cousin …"

His cousin? At first Jo didn't think she'd heard him right.

The general snorted. "His cousin?"

"Yes, this is Princess Johenaten, just arrived from the palace at Akhetaten."

"In the middle of the night?"

"Yes, well, there were some difficulties."

The general released his vice-grip on Jo's arm, but then he stepped closer still and lifted a lock of her hair. She could feel his stale breath on her face and throat. "Ha! You expect me to believe that? Even in the dark of night with my old man's eyes, I can see she's no Amarna princess."

"The third daughter of my uncle's second wife," Nekhare replied, sounding more certain every minute. "Come, Johenaten; Meritaken is waiting for you."

"Yes, yes. Go along now. But I shall see you in the morning. Count on it." With that, the old man set off down the hallway. Nekhare didn't say a word but continued in the other direction before finally stopping to pound on a wooden door.

"Meritaken, open up." The door opened, and Nekhare pushed his way in, pulling Jo behind him.

"*Princess Johenaten?* What were you thinking?" Jo asked, as soon as the door closed behind them. She couldn't believe Nekhare had told the general that she was a princess.

"Princess Johenaten?" repeated the girl who could only be Nekhare's sister. The room was dimly lit with candles, but Jo could see that Meritaken was slender and had long, dark hair. She wore a simple white dress, much like the one Jo was now wearing.

"Well, on the way over here, I was trying to figure out what to do with you once I got you here. There's been a flood of royals abandoning the Amarna palace lately, so when he asked who you were, *Princess Johenaten* just popped out. I knew that he would never allow you into the palace unless you had a legitimate reason to be here—unless you were actually part of the family."

"Who is *he*?" interrupted Meritaken.

"General Horemheb," replied Nekhare with a sigh.

"Oh no," gasped Meritaken.

"Oh yes," said Nekhare.

"I take it this Horemheb guy isn't a friend of yours? I'm Jo, by the way."

"I'm Meritaken. I've been waiting for you most of the night. My brother told me about you, but I had no idea he'd cooked up this ridiculous scheme." She turned to her brother. "You had to go and run into Horemheb. Of all the people—"

"I didn't exactly plan it that way," cut in Nekhare.

Meritaken ignored him. She turned to Jo. "Horemheb is the general of the pharaoh's armies. He's a mean old man who likes nothing better than to stir up a little trouble, so he'll be telling Pharaoh all about you as soon as the sun rises, if not sooner."

Jo knew her situation had gone from bad to worse. Wandering around the desert alone was bad enough, but now she had the general of the pharaoh's armies gunning for her.

"So, what then? What happens when the pharaoh finds out about me?"

"He'll want to talk with you. He has an obligation to take care of members of the royal family, but before he allows you to stay here, he'll want to make sure you are who you say you are," replied Meritaken, scowling at her brother. Nekhare was looking less sure of himself.

"Seems like he could leave all that to someone else," Jo said hopefully.

Meritaken continued to glare at her brother. Finally Nekhare said, "Pharaoh has a personal interest in members of the family who lived in Akhetaten, the city where he was born. His father built the city, and now it's being abandoned, much to Pharaoh's dismay."

"So ... what you're saying is that not only will he want to interrogate me about Ak ... Ak ..."

"Akhetaten," said Nekhare.

"Whatever. Not only will he ask me a whole lot of questions, but he'll be angry with me even before I get there?"

They both nodded. "Maybe," said Nekhare. "Probably."

"Well, that's it then; I'm dead. Look, maybe it would be better if I just left right now. Better for you, too." She glanced back at the door and, for a moment, wondered who might be listening on the other side.

"No," chorused Nekhare and Meritaken.

"You can't go now," explained Nekhare. "Horemheb has already seen you. If you disappear now, he'll accuse me of some crime. Kidnapping, perhaps. He's always looking for some way to malign me. I am, after all, just one more obstacle in his quest for the throne. Besides, what will you do? Wander the streets of Waset?"

Jo sighed.

"Where are you from?" asked Meritaken.

Not at all ready to explain, Jo replied, "A long, long way away."

"She'll have to stay here for what little is left of the night," said Nekhare, turning to his sister.

"Sure," Meritaken agreed. "But what are you going to do with her in the morning?"

"Not me. You."

"What do you mean?" she asked.

"You and the servants will have to turn her into a princess—or at least make her look like one." They both turned to stare at Jo, and she could see doubt written across their faces.

"I don't get it," Jo said. "Why can't we just confess, tell the pharaoh that I'm lost and need help? Tell him that you said I was a princess to get me by Horemheb in the middle of the night. You said he was a reasonable man."

"He is, but his advisers aren't always. And apparently you do not understand the politics of the palace. If we confess, in front of everyone in the Hall of Audiences, that you are not who I said you are, then Horemheb in particular will demand consequences … for both you and me. Never has a commoner been allowed inside this palace, this close to the pharaoh, without proper documentation. And Horemheb will demand that I be punished for lying to him. Pharaoh will be forced to align himself with one side or the other."

"You think he will take the other side? Aren't you his cousin? His friend?"

"Yes, but his whole existence is one political alignment after another. If he takes our side now and gives you permission to stay, he may have to give up something else, something far dearer to him, later on. Who knows what's on his mind, what battles he's planning on waging with Horemheb? The two of us may become pawns in some larger scheme. But, if we can put on a good show," he looked cautiously at Jo, "if you can do well enough to create some uncertainty, than we may be able to buy some time. We can talk to Tutankhamun later …"

"Tutankhamun!" Jo exclaimed.

They both stared at her.

"Your pharaoh is King Tut?"

"Who?" asked Nekhare.

"Tutankhamun. Your pharaoh is Tutankhamun?"

Nekhare frowned. "How could you not know that?" he asked.

CHAPTER 5

Morning came much too soon.

Nekhare and Meritaken had stretched out across the huge bed—Jo perched on one corner—and told her all about King Tut, or Tutankhamun as they always called him, and the other people Jo might encounter in the morning. They described how she would be expected to act in the presence of the pharaoh and the Great Royal Wife. Still, Jo knew she was in no way prepared, not for meeting the famous King Tut, and not for spending any amount of time in ancient Egypt. She just wanted to go home. She lay back on the bed, finally, and closed her eyes, falling asleep just as the sun peeked over the eastern horizon.

When she woke, the room was full of activity. Two very young girls, maybe seven or eight years old, were organizing Meritaken's sandal collection. Two more girls appeared to be dusting the room. All of them wore simple, straight skirts, held up by crisscrossed straps. Meritaken stood in the middle of the room, stark naked, while two more girls—these a bit older—rubbed oil into her body. Embarrassed, Jo couldn't figure out where to look. Finally she sat up, and all activity in the room stopped. The servant girls stared.

"Where is Nekhare?" Jo asked.

"Gone to try to get a word in private with Tutankhamun," Meritaken answered. "He says we'd better get ready, just in case. I've already had my bath. Now it's your turn. Here's your water now," she said as two more girls entered, each carrying two buckets.

A bath sounded like a great idea until Jo realized what they intended to do to her. Attached to Meritaken's bedroom was a small tiled room, not unlike a twenty-first-century shower. It even had a drain in the floor. But soon it became clear that Meritaken expected Jo to strip naked and stand in there while the servants poured water all over her. She managed to convince all of them that she could handle her own bath.

"Where's the soap?" Jo asked.

"The what?" asked Meritaken. The rest stared at Jo blankly.

"Never mind. I'll do without for now."

When Jo emerged, hiding behind the same dress she had worn the night before, Meritaken was wearing a pleated white dress clearly intended for formal occasions.

"Now the oils," Meritaken said, and Jo knew there was no way to avoid it. No soap, no shampoo, no deodorant … she could see why the scented oils were essential, and she hoped they would relieve her sunburn. She allowed the servants to dry her with muffs, and then they rubbed her all over with a variety of oils. She stood in the center of the room and tried to pretend that this wasn't the most embarrassing moment of her life.

Once she was acceptably oiled, the servants dressed her. Two of them took a long, rectangular piece of soft fabric, draped it over Jo's shoulder, and with a couple of twists and turns, wrapped her in a flowing, graceful dress. They cinched her waist with a belt made of gold links. Then came the makeup. They applied layers upon layers from the pots on Meritaken's bureau: a deep red stain to her cheeks and lips, and dark eyeliner—called *kohl*, she learned—in thick lines around her eyes. They applied gray shadow to her eyebrows and upper lids, and green to her lower lids.

Nekhare arrived just as they were debating what to do with Jo's hair. The color of it seemed to horrify them, and they were getting ready to stick one of Meritaken's dark wigs on her when he walked in. He hadn't bothered to knock.

For a moment or two, he just stood there, not saying a word, his masculine presence flooding the room. The servant girls tensed noticeably. Jo couldn't tell whether Nekhare approved or disapproved of the new her.

"I said no wig," he said finally, frowning in his sister's direction. "And keep it simple."

The hairdressers resumed work quietly, settling for a few braids on either side of Jo's face. They added beads and flowers, nowhere near as many as they had woven into Meritaken's hair, and scurried out of the room.

"Where you able to see Pharaoh?" Meritaken asked.

"Yes, but Horemheb got to him first. I think the general must have slept in the hall outside Pharaoh's bedroom. By the time I got there, he had told Tutankhamun everything." He turned to Jo. "They'll be calling you to the Hall of Audiences soon, right after Tutankhamun completes the morning rituals."

Jo's stomach lurched. "I don't want to go," she said quietly.

Nekhare walked over to her and pulled her to her feet. "You have no choice. We'll go with you, but there's not much we can do or say to help. Just answer his questions as briefly as possible. Don't offer any more information than you have to."

Jo could only nod.

Nekhare had dressed for the occasion. He was wearing a kilt—a knee-length, skirt-like garment—and he smelled of bath oils. Around his neck hung several heavily beaded necklaces, and his eyes were lined with *kohl*. He motioned to a servant who had followed him into the room, and the young man handed over a cloth bag. From it Nekhare pulled a pair of gold, snake-like armbands.

Sliding them up Jo's arms, he said, "These are yours. No Amarna princess would report to the Hall of Audiences without her jewelry."

With a wave of Nekhare's hand, the servants disappeared. Then another appeared at the door with a huge bowl of fruit. "Hungry?" Nekhare asked.

Jo shook her head.

A few minutes later, there was a heavy pounding on the door, and the three of them followed a tall, sturdily built man out the long hallway and across the manicured garden, a lush contrast to the Egyptian desert.

Jo had the same feeling she remembered from when she'd been sent to the principal's office for writing *Tommy Nystrom is an ass* in her math book: she knew that at the end of her walk there was a person with the power to make her life miserable—only this was way more serious than being sent to the principal. Her chest felt tight, like someone had stuck a hand down her throat and was squeezing all the air out of her lungs. Their escort led them up a sweeping staircase and threw open a pair of huge, golden doors. *Just get through this*, she thought, *and then you can work on getting home.*

The room they entered was like none Jo had ever seen before. It was at least the size of a football field, the high ceiling supported on two sides by a series of giant columns painted bright colors and inlaid with gold. The marble floor had been polished until it could have passed for glass. Everywhere there was color; the walls were painted with oversized murals of hunting and battle scenes.

Stepping aside, the man motioned for Jo to enter first. Her knees wobbled, but she forced herself to walk straight ahead. Nekhare and Meritaken followed closely behind.

At the other end of the room, on a slightly raised platform flanked by tall pillars, sat the queen, Ankesenamun. She wore a flowing white dress, belted at the waist with a wide red sash. Around her neck hung several thick necklaces. Her long dark hair had been woven in multiple braids with an assortment of beads and flowers. She sat with her legs crossed at the knees, her feet bare. Jo had never seen anyone so perfect; it was as though the queen had just walked off a movie set or stepped from the pages of an ancient fashion magazine.

Pharaoh Tutankhamun stood beside his queen. *So that's the famous King Tut*, Jo thought. From what she had read and heard about in school, she had expected a boy, but what she saw was a young man about Nekhare's age. His chest was bare except for a wide beaded collar, and he wore a white kilt. On his head rested the double crown of Egypt—a tall white crown shaped a bit like a bowling pin, cupped by a red crown that rose to a point in the back—just like Jo had seen in books. His eyes were ringed with *kohl,* and his cheeks were painted red. Strangest of all was the carved wooden beard that was attached to his chin with string. All of this Jo noticed on her slow walk to the throne.

Several important-looking men waited in line to talk with the king. Jo recognized Horemheb; he stood just to Tutankhamun's right. Seeing the three of them enter, the pharaoh waved away all of the others and directed his attention to the new arrivals. Horemheb, Jo noticed, remained close by.

"Kneel before the king and don't look up until he speaks," Nekhare reminded her in a low tone. Jo hurried to the carpet before the throne, knelt, and bowed her head to the floor, as she'd been taught was protocol in the Hall. She felt Nekhare and Meritaken do the same behind her.

She heard the pharaoh walk closer and then pause before her. Hushed conversations among others in the room continued, but it was still several long moments before he spoke.

"The general tells me that your name is Johenaten and you claim to be from the palace at Akhetaten," said the king. His voice was surprisingly deep.

"Yes," Jo said, raising her eyes to meet the dark eyes of Tutankhamun. She fought for control of her own body. Her hands shook, and her stomach did backflips.

"Who are your parents?" he demanded.

"My father was Paneb, and my mother was Naunakht, his second wife," Jo said, just as she had rehearsed. She dropped her eyes again, unable to meet his piercing stare.

"I was unaware that my uncle had a daughter your age—or a second wife, for that matter." The king seemed suddenly amused.

She looked up again. His face was smooth, and he had a long, straight nose.

Jo glanced at Ankesenamun, who frowned.

"But that is not so surprising. Your mother was not Kemetan, I assume." Jo realized that he was referring to her light skin and hair.

"No."

"I see. Who brought you here?"

She thought for a few seconds. "A bodyguard, Your Highness."

"He did not stay long enough to introduce you and himself? I find that rather odd."

"She was delivered to me, Your Highness," interjected Nekhare. That much was not exactly a lie. Jo had been delivered to him, so to speak, on the bank of the Nile. "She had a long and exhausting journey, and I promised to look after her until you had a chance to do so yourself. I assured the one who brought her to me that I acted with your authority and he need not trouble himself any further."

"I see," Tutankhamun said again.

"Forgive me, Your Highness, if I have overstepped my bounds. I am but your loyal servant." Nekhare said, bowing his head again.

"So you are," Tutankhamun said, with a smile. "Yes, Nekhare. You have done the right thing." The king directed his attention to Jo again. "So, another of the royal family abandons my father's dream," Tutankhamun said, his voice sad and sarcastic at the same time. "Soon Akhetaten will be nothing but a dusty memory. Still, I can understand why you would leave."

He paused.

"Have you had any formal training?"

"Training?" Jo didn't know what he meant.

"Reading, writing … how to figure sums. Most girls of the royal family have some education. Surely you know how to read the hieroglyphs?"

She weighed the possible answers. If she admitted that she couldn't read and write—and she certainly didn't have a clue how to decipher hieroglyphs—it would explose her lie. But what if she said she could do it? She might be called upon to perform tasks she couldn't do.

"No, Your Highness," she replied.

"Then perhaps you've been trained in the songs of the priestesses, like my grandmother?" he asked, sounding hopeful.

"No." Jo found herself staring at her own hands.

Horemheb interrupted, "You see, Your Highness. She cannot possibly be who she claims to be. Not only does she not resemble the other members of the family, but also she is not educated as one would expect. This girl is nothing but a lowborn imposter trying to take advantage of your graciousness."

Score that one for Horemheb.

Tutankhamun paused, as if considering Horemheb's words. "You have just come from the place of my birth. Perhaps you can give me some news of those few who remain there. How is Smenkare? Does Amun treat him well these days?" the king asked, looking Jo straight in the eye.

Smenkare. Now there was a name that never came up in Foster's lectures. Meritaken and Nekhare hadn't mentioned him either. Jo waited as long as she dared for a hint of some kind from Nekhare.

He didn't dare speak.

Jo knew she was in trouble.

The pause in the conversation became too long. A nasty smirk spread across Horemheb's face.

"He's …" Jo began.

The door burst open, startling the entire group. Glancing over her shoulder, Jo watched several burly men hurry across the room and approach the throne. "Your Highness, we must speak immediately. We have trouble on the southern border."

Tutankhamun shifted gears. "You have a message from Huy? Is he still in Nubia?"

"Yes, but he is asking for more troops. Several tribes have refused to pay tribute. The viceroy has a rebellion on his hands."

Still staring over her shoulder, Jo made eye contact with Nekhare. He glanced in the direction of Tutankhamun, who was focused on the new arrivals, and then back at Jo. "His brother is dead," whispered Nekhare.

"It is as we expected, then. Give me just a minute." Tutankhamun turned his attention back to Jo. "Smenkare?"

"Your brother is dead, of course. Why else would you be king?" She heard several in the room gasp and knew she had said something horribly inappropriate.

Tutankhamun laughed. "An honest girl, at least."

If he only knew. She forced herself to look into his dark, penetrating eyes. *Please.*

The king met her stare and nodded almost imperceptibly. To Horemheb he said, "Surely you would not turn out a member of my family?"

The old general protested, "You can't let her loose in the palace. We have no idea what she is trying—"

Tutankhamun cut him off with a wave of his hand, his decision made. "There is time for that. Nekhare, I entrust her to you and to Meritaken. See that she has all that she needs—a comfortable room and servants to tend to her. I suspect she will need to recover from her journey, and then we will begin her long-neglected education. Meritaken, you are released from your studies until further notice."

"Thank you, Your Highness," Nekhare and Jo said in unison as Meritaken nodded.

"You could have told me about Smenkare," Jo whispered as they hurried from the room.

"Ssshhh. Let's get out of here before he changes his mind," replied Nekhare.

CHAPTER 6

Nekhare, Meritaken, and Jo rushed into Meritaken's bedroom, slammed the door behind them, and simultaneously breathed a sigh of relief. It was a few minutes before anyone spoke.

"I can't believe he believed us," Meritaken said.

"He didn't," said Nekhare.

"He didn't?" Meritaken repeated.

"At least, I don't think he did. Tutankhamun is no fool." He turned to Jo. "Perhaps he gave you the benefit of the doubt, but more likely he's just toying with Horemheb. Either way, you are safe here, for now."

"For now?" Jo had hoped for more.

"Yes." Nekhare's face was grave. "Fortunately for you, Pharaoh and his advisers have much on their minds: the revolt in Nubia and the dwindling stash of gold in the kingdom's coffers, among other things. Frankly, I don't think you will be of much concern to him. If you lay low, he may even forget you are here."

"Great," Jo said, and yet she didn't feel any better.

"I must return to work," he continued. "I suggest the two of you get some rest."

"No! I mean, can't you stay a while?"

Nekhare smiled. "You are safe. The pharaoh has commanded that you be taken care of. So it will be. I must return to my duties. My absence would call too much attention to us. I will tell the royal housekeeper, Sitamun, to keep the servants away while you sleep. We can see about getting you your own bedchamber this afternoon or even tomorrow."

Jo really didn't want her own bedroom. It seemed much too permanent. "Nekhare?"

"Yes?"

"How will I find my way home?"

"I don't know," he replied. "I'll think of something." He turned to go. "For now, let's just get you settled in," he said from the doorway.

All Jo could do was nod. The whole idea of *settling in* scared her more than anything. More, even, than her presentation to Tutankhamun.

"We'll talk later. Meritaken, I don't want the two of you out and about the palace today. Stay here. Get some rest," Nekhare said, closing the door behind him.

"Nekhare is right," said Meritaken. "You need some sleep. So do I." With that, she stretched out across the bed, and it wasn't long before she was asleep. For Jo, sleep came much later.

When Jo woke, late-afternoon shadows fell across the unlit room. Meritaken sat cross-legged at the end of the bed, stroking a large gray cat.

"He's beautiful," Jo said.

"His name is Smoke."

"I've never owned a cat," Jo explained. "My mother is allergic."

"Allergic?"

"You know; her eyes turn all red, and she sneezes like crazy."

Meritaken gave her a strange look. "I should take him out?" she asked.

"Oh, no. I'm okay with cats. It was just my mother."

"Good," she said looking relieved. "There are several more in this wing of the palace, but I like Smoke the best. He keeps me company when there is no one to talk with." She turned the cat loose, and he curled up close to Jo.

Meritaken laughed. "I see the cat has *also* taken an immediate liking to you," she said.

"I'm sorry?" Jo asked, not sure what the other girl meant.

"My brother. Why else would he go to so much trouble?"

"Trouble?"

"He lied to Pharaoh. Not to mention the fact that he risked his life paddling across the Nile in the middle of the night."

Meritaken was right; Nekhare had gone to considerable trouble for her. "I'd probably be dead right now if he hadn't rescued me," she said, "but I'm going home. Someone will come looking for me tomorrow or the next day."

"Maybe so," said Meritaken. "But there's something you should know: my brother *always* gets what he wants."

"Does he have a girlfriend?"

"A *girlfriend*?"

"Yeah, you know. A girl that he spends time with."

Meritaken laughed. "Of course. Nekhare will be vizier one day. He has his pick of all the prettiest girls," she said, and then changed the subject. "Sitamun sent us a tray of bread and cheese. Hungry?"

"Starving," Jo replied. She dug in, not caring that the bread was gritty and the cheese smelly. They washed their snack down with warm goat's milk.

They stayed in Meritaken's room all afternoon, as Nekhare had directed. Jo wasn't ready to leave the safety of the room anyway, and she couldn't help wondering how people would react to her. The atmosphere in the Hall of Audiences had been openly hostile. Would she have to explain herself, justify her stay at the palace to everyone she met? And then there was Horemheb; he was one person Jo could do without seeing again.

"I don't get it," Jo said. "What is Horemheb's problem? He acts like he's Pharaoh."

"Well, he certainly wants to be," said Meritaken. "Tutankhamun was so young when he took the throne; Ay and Horemheb stepped in to make all the important decisions."

"Ay is the other old guy that was in the Hall of Audiences, right?"

"Yes. Now that Tutankhamun is old enough to assume power, Horemheb, in particular, hates giving up his authority."

"That must make life difficult for Tut. I mean, Tutankhamun," Jo said.

"Yes, and that's not all," continued Meritaken. "Many of our people agree with Horemheb. They think that Tutankhamun is weak, like his father, and incapable of leading the kingdom."

"Tutankhamun's father … what was his name?" Jo asked.

"Akhenaten," replied Meritaken.

"Ah-ken-AH-ten," Jo repeated. "He built Ah-ke-TAH-ten." Meritaken nodded. It was all so confusing. "He was some kind of a weirdo?"

"*Weirdo?*"

"You know … strange. Not like everyone else."

"Yes, a *weirdo*," Meritaken said, smiling. "He believed in the worship of only one god, and he started the Cult of the Aten."

"I don't understand. What's wrong with that?" Jo asked.

Meritaken explained, "For thousands of years, my people have worshipped many gods. Our great pharaohs built temples for the worship of those gods. The temple priests became very powerful. When Akhenaten disavowed the gods and shut down the temples, many people were offended—outraged, really. The priests and the thousands of Kemetans who worked for the temples called for a new pharaoh."

"They got a new one, didn't they, when Akhenaten died and Tutankhamun became king?"

"Yes, and Ay and Horemheb have worked to restore the kingdom. They moved back here to Waset, the City of Temples, to demonstrate their support for the old ways. They changed the pharaoh's name. It used to be Tutankh-*aten*, Son of the Aten. Tutankh-*amun* indicates loyalty to the god most honored here in Waset, Amun."

"And that's why you and Nekhare live here also?"

"Yes. Since both of our parents are dead, Tutankhamun is responsible for our well-being." She paused. "Now that Tutankhamun is older, he, too, works to restore the old ways. But there are many who see him as too much like his father. They are afraid he will return to the Cult of the Aten and the palace at Akhetaten—or Amarna, as some people call it."

Jo thought about the conversation she had overheard at the construction site, and she knew that Meritaken was right. There were also things that Meritaken couldn't possibly know, like the fact that Pharaoh Tutankhamun, King Tut, was most famous for his tomb of riches and for dying young. Of course, Jo didn't say anything about that to Meritaken. She also remembered Foster's words as the other students filed out of class: *Tomorrow we will begin our investigation into the death of King Tut. Did he die of natural causes, or was he murdered?*

I'd put my money on the murder theory, thought Jo.

Late in the afternoon, there was a tap on the door, and in came a tiny lady whose age Jo couldn't quite figure. Meritaken introduced her as Sitamun, Keeper of the Royal Household.

"I am honored," Sitamun said, without smiling, when they were introduced. Jo noticed that she kept her eyes averted. "We have prepared the room next door for you," she continued. "I think you will find it comfortable." With that, she was gone as quietly as she had appeared.

"She doesn't like me," Jo said to Meritaken after Sitamun closed the door.

"Pay her no mind. She's always like that—as sour as last week's milk."

The two girls laughed and went next door to check out Jo's new room. It was about ten times the size of her room back home and every bit as luxurious as Meritaken's. The floor and the ceiling were tiled, and the walls were plastered and painted white. Every inch of walls and ceiling was painted with vivid murals of Nile scenes. The huge bed was inlaid with ebony and gold, as were the three chairs in the room and the chest on the wall across from the bed. Tall vases filled with freshly cut flowers graced both nightstands.

"We could both do with some freshening," Meritaken said. "I'll get the servants." She stepped into the hallway and spoke briefly to someone there. Within minutes, the room was full, and Jo found herself going through the whole routine of bathing again.

Nekhare showed up just as night fell. "Come," he said. "I've ordered the servants to bring our evening meal."

"We'll eat right here?" Jo asked, relieved to think she wouldn't have to go to a public dining room of some kind.

"No." Nekhare smiled. "Let's go up to the roof and enjoy the breeze."

Jo let Nekhare and Meritaken lead her out of the room, down a long hall, and up a narrow stairway that led to the rooftop. A few of the palace courtiers were already there.

Courtiers were the ancient equivalent of groupies, or so they seemed to Jo. They hung around the palace, hoping to get in good with the pharaoh. Nekhare and Meritaken nodded at them politely but, much to Jo's relief, didn't invite anyone to eat with the three of them. Soon there was a flock of servants to fan them with palm fronds and to tend the dozens of colored, scented candles that burned all around them.

Dinner arrived, and the servants passed clay bowls filled with roast duck, several types of vegetables, including whole onions, and breads. Jo watched as Meritaken and Nekhare cut their food with tiny knives and ate with their fingers.

As soon as each bowl was emptied, the servants whisked it away.

She mimicked Nekhare and Meritaken as best she could, but some of the foods were unusual to her, and she felt uncomfortable eating with her fingers.

"You're not hungry?" Nekhare asked.

"Not really," Jo said. She had eaten enough bread to quiet her stomach, and the duck just didn't appeal to her.

They washed their dinner down with wine, and once again Jo found herself wishing for a Coke. Afterward, she merely watched as Meritaken and Nekhare munched on their dessert, a bowl of figs. After the servants removed the last remnants of the meal, the three of them sat a while longer, hesitant to leave the cool rooftop and to return to their rooms.

"Did the pharaoh say anything about me?" Jo asked Nekhare in a whisper so the others wouldn't hear.

"No. The whole day was a disaster. Tutankhamun wants to go to Nubia himself to lead the war effort there, but I think Ay has talked him out of it. At least, I hope he has. The civil engineers delivered reports on the flood levels. The water has not risen to the marks we would like. Crops will be insufficient and tax revenues low. That will set the priests' tongues wagging about disfavor from the gods, and Pharaoh will have to pacify them—send them wine or wheat or even gold."

Nekhare continued to detail all that had gone on during the day, most of which Jo didn't fully understand. She didn't ask many questions. The evening grew long.

"Well, I still have work to do tonight," said Nekhare. "Tutankhamun wants some of the inscriptions for his tomb rewritten, and with everything else going on, I won't get it done unless I work into the evenings. I'll walk the two of you back down."

"You'll be all right here now?" he asked as they stepped into Jo's room.

No, she thought, but she nodded anyway.

"I'm still exhausted," Meritaken said. "I think I'll go to my room and have the servants bring me my bath. I'll send yours in also, Jo."

"No, I'll pass for tonight," she said. "Thanks, anyway."

"Then I'll have them come in and prepare you for bed."

"No, really, I'm fine," Jo insisted. Meritaken gave her an odd look, and she left the room with Nekhare, closing the door behind them.

Jo was alone for the first time since arriving at the palace.

She wandered the huge room, amazed by the luxury of it—the overstuffed pillows on the bed, the colorful carpet over the tile, the delicate furniture inlaid with real gold. She paused to open the stoppers on several bottles among the toiletries that had been left for her. Exotic floral scents drifted across the room.

There was a scratching at the door, and when Jo opened it, in came Smoke. He headed straight for the foot of the bed and curled up into a furry ball. She blew out the candles and climbed between silk sheets, still wearing the dress that the servants wrapped her in that afternoon, her hair still in braids.

I should have let the servants in after all. I don't even know what I'm supposed to wear to bed. Tossing and turning, she thought about the old man with the beard, the one in Foster's book. He'd been here in Egypt; that much was clear. But where was he now?

She wanted to go home, climb into her lumpy bed in her tiny, messy bedroom, pull the sheets up over her head, and forget that any of this had ever happened. Sure, Meritaken was nice enough, and Nekhare was ... well, Nekhare was kind and gentle and sometimes dark and mysterious. Either way, he was the first guy other than Tommy who had ever paid her much attention. Despite all that, Jo was so homesick that it actually hurt, a dull ache that began down deep and threatened to overwhelm her.

The scene with Tutankhamun and Ankesenamun kept playing in her head like the trailer of an upcoming horror flick. The title? *A Slow, Cruel Death in Egypt*, perhaps, or *Tut Gets His Revenge*. She couldn't shake the image of the two of them sitting high above her as she knelt before them, fearing for her life. It was not a scene she wanted to experience again. Jo figured that it was just a matter of time before she found herself out on the streets—or worse.

What is the penalty for lying to the pharaoh? she wondered.

One thing was certain: she needed to steer clear of Tutankhamun and Ankesenamun until she could figure out how to get out of Egypt. She rolled over on her side and wrapped her arms around her stomach, which, by that time, felt hollow and sore all at the same time.

Tears stung her eyes, and then she began to sob; it was a long time before she finally cried herself to sleep.

Jo survived that first night in her own room but woke the next morning feeling disoriented. She'd been dreaming of horses, and she was back at the

Rocking R Ranch, where she had learned to ride. It should have been a happy dream, but there was something disturbing about it, something she couldn't quite recall. Rousing slowly from sleep, she stretched, rubbed the sleep from her eyes, and wondered what she'd done to make every muscle in her body sore.

Must be Saturday, she thought. *Mom didn't wake me up for school.*

And then reality hit like a freight train running at full throttle. It all came back to her: her long walk in the desert, meeting Nekhare on the riverbank, the Hall of Audiences with King Tut.

Egypt? Back in time … could it be true? Her heart sank all over again.

The early-morning sun had just begun to filter through the narrow windows, and with it came a cool breeze. The day had not yet turned warm.

"What now?" she said out loud.

She didn't have time to think about it. Presently, there was a tap on the wooden door. Jo sat up, and several servants entered, carrying buckets of water and freshly laundered dresses. One girl, a little older than the rest, introduced herself. "I am Sashri," she said.

Jo nodded.

Sashri frowned, obviously confused by the fact that Jo was still wearing yesterday's dress. "Come. We must begin your bath."

About an hour later, just as the girls were finishing her hair, Nekhare appeared.

He hadn't knocked, again, but Jo didn't care. The servants disappeared.

"Nekhare, thank God you're here," she said. "We've got to start looking for that old man right away."

He stared at her. "What old man? You never said anything about an old man."

"Yes, yes, I'm sure I did. He had a long white beard."

"No, you didn't. He brought you here? What is his name?"

"I don't know. I don't know anything about him, except he had a white beard."

"Then he wasn't Kemetan. Perhaps a Greek. They wear beards."

"Well, whoever he is, we have to find him."

"*We* do?"

"Isn't that why you brought me here, to help me?"

"Jo, I lied to Tutankhamun for you. I took risks … brought you to the palace. Is that not enough for you? I don't remember making any promise to help you search for an old man with a beard."

Jo gulped. "Of course. I'm … sorry. It just seems as though he's my only hope. But you're right: *I* have to find him, not you."

"And how do you think you are going to do that?" Nekhare asked.

"I … don't know."

"Well, you certainly cannot wander the entire kingdom looking for an old man with a beard. Nor should you ask too many questions. No, I think the best thing to do is just be patient—"

"You mean, just sit and wait and hope someone comes looking for me? I can't do that. I have to get home! Besides, how will anyone find me in the palace?"

"You must have patience. If anyone is going to have access to information—"

"Patience?"

"… it will be me. After all, I work for the pharaoh." Nekhare stepped closer and took both her hands in his. "I know you're anxious to go home, but trust me. I'll keep my ears open for any information about kidnappings or the black market slave trade. In the meantime, try to enjoy life in the palace. You're lucky, you know."

"I was kidnapped and taken from my home. How is that lucky?"

Nekhare smiled. "You found me. Besides, think of where you could be right now."

"I could be home …"

"And you could be wandering the streets of Waset," Nekhare reminded her. He was right, of course.

"Come. We must go to the rooftop to pay homage to the sun," he said.

CHAPTER 7

She didn't give up hope of going home, at least not right away, but Jo knew that in order to make it back to the twenty-first century alive, she'd have to *stay* alive. Her plan, for lack of a better one, was to remain out of sight until someone showed up to take her home.

She managed to do that for a while, but it didn't take long for her to become bored with staying cooped up in her room. Meritaken was not allowed outside the palace walls, and Nekhare had made it clear that the same rule also applied to Jo. But the two of them were free to wander the palace as they pleased, and so, little by little, she began to explore.

Back home, Jo had visited all the Orlando theme parks, and she had been to the White House on a class trip when she was in the fifth grade. The palace seemed like both rolled into one. It included an entire wing for the pharaoh and his queen, apartments for officials and administrators, royal workshops, and a village for the craftsmen who kept the palace well supplied with everything from furniture to pottery to jewelry. Several temples to Amun, the local god, had been constructed within the palace walls, and gardeners tended at least a dozen gardens with endless varieties of flowers and shrubbery, imported from all over the kingdom and all over the world.

Even the dirt in the pharaoh's gardens was imported.

Most of the people that she and Meritaken came into direct contact with were servants. Hundreds of them, maybe thousands, lived and worked in the palace. She and Meritaken each had dozens waiting on them, including two whose only jobs were to tend their sandals. The servants moved about the palace like ghosts, never speaking—at least not to Jo and Meritaken—unless spoken to first. Occasionally, Jo might run into a courtier or a government employee wandering the halls of the palace, and polite nods were exchanged.

Hundreds of people traipsed in and out of the palace every day for appointments with administrators, all of them carefully screened by an army of scribes who wrote down volumes of information about each one. Of course, none of them were allowed anywhere near the royal family's quarters, but sometimes Jo and Meritaken sat in the garden just off the main entrance to the palace and watched the comings and goings.

The palace was a very busy place, and as it turned out, a great place to hide. With all that went on any given day, Jo managed to blend right in. The person she considered most dangerous, Horemheb, left for Nubia, and that was a major relief. Neither Ankesenamun nor Tutankhamun ever came down to the wing of the palace where Meritaken and Jo lived, and there was no reason for Jo to go anywhere near their apartments. She was sure they had forgotten all about her.

The weeks stretched into a month, and still Nekhare heard nothing that would explain Jo's mysterious arrival in Kemet.

"You're listening carefully, right?" she asked Nekhare every time she saw him.

"Of course," he replied, but neither of them knew what he was listening for.

She discovered that there were no less than three swimming pools on the palace grounds. They were hand dug and kept fresh by an army of servants who carried buckets of water to fill them daily from the Nile. One of these marvels of ancient luxury was in the garden just outside the wing of the palace where Meritaken and Jo slept.

"Let's go for a swim!" Meritaken suggested one especially warm day.

"Great idea," Jo replied. "Do you have an extra bathing suit I can borrow?"

"Bathing suit?" asked Meritaken. "I don't understand."

"You know, to wear in the pool?"

"You would wear clothing in the water?"

It finally sunk in, but Jo wasn't ready to abandon her sense of modesty. She resigned herself to watching Meritaken glide across the pool, while sweat induced by the midday sun trickled down her own back and made her clothing stick to her.

Later that evening, after the sun had set, leaving behind an unusually stifling night, they lay across Meritaken's bed, complaining of the heat. They had been playing *senet*, a rather complicated board game that simulated the quest for eternal life after death. Meritaken had been patiently teaching Jo, but on that night Jo gave up after landing on the "House of Misfortune" square for the fourth time. Landing on that particular square required starting all over at the beginning, and the game had become tedious. She surrendered the *senet* championship to Meritaken, at least for the night. Their talk then turned again to swimming.

"C'mon," Meritaken pleaded. "No one will see you in the dark." Jo remembered how enticing the pool had been earlier that day, how jealous she had been of Meritaken as she splashed in the water.

"Let's go."

They tiptoed out of the bedroom and made their way down the darkened hallway, feeling the route rather than seeing it, all the while giggling like nervous conspirators. The palace, silent and still, slept under a blanket of oppressive heat, and the air was heavy with the pungent aroma from the gardens. The night, Jo noticed, seemed to intensify the fragrance from the pharaoh's extensive collection of exotic flowers.

Meritaken pulled her to the pool's edge and lowered her voice to a whisper. "See, everyone's asleep. No one will ever know." Moonlight skittered across the surface of the water but left the surrounding garden in shadows.

The two girls slipped their dresses over their heads and plunged into the cool water.

Jo dove under the surface, scrubbing at her hair and feeling sand-free for the first time in weeks. In Kemet, the sand permeated everything—clothes, beds, hair, even the food—and Jo couldn't remember a swim that felt so good, or that had been so long overdue.

She swam away from Meritaken toward the deeper end of the large pool. Reaching the opposite end, she dove under again, coming to the surface, finally, with a gasp.

That was when she saw him.

Sitting cross-legged at the edge of the pool, not more than six feet from her, was Tutankhamun himself. Even in the dark, she could tell it was the king by the silhouette of his body, slim and still, and by the way her own pulse quickened. He wore no crown, no golden collar, and no wooden beard, but still, there could be no mistake.

She stopped breathing. The whole world came to a grinding halt, as if so ordered.

He didn't utter a word.

Her hands flew up to cover her chest. Even though her body was under water and the night was dark, she felt exposed.

"The two of you should not be in the pool after dark," he said, finally. "You never know when a water snake might slither in, and without the daylight, you might never see it. Meritaken, you should know better," he said as Meritaken swam up behind Jo.

"Yes, Your Highness, but the evening was so warm—"

"And this swim was worth the risk?" They both shook their heads. "Go, and save your excursions in the palace pools for the light of day."

They swam back to the other end, climbed out of the pool, and headed back to Meritaken's bedchamber. Jo knew she'd blown it. She'd spent weeks staying out of Tutankhamun's sight and then sacrificed it all for one late-night swim in the pool.

Stupid. Really stupid.

Trouble was on the way.

Sure enough, the next day arrived with a message from Tutankhamun, delivered by Nekhare: Meritaken should return to the palace school, and Jo should go with her.

This is it, Jo thought. *I'll be exposed as a fraud, for sure. How do you go to school and avoid talking about yourself, answering questions?*

Sinuhe, the teacher, was about eighty years old. He walked with a cane and wore the black wig that, as Jo was starting to recognize, most wealthy Egyptian men wore after they began to bald. From his wig, his fine robe, and his jewelry, Jo could tell that Sinuhe enjoyed an important position in the royal household.

Classes were held in one of the palace gardens, under the shade of a banyan tree imported from the Far East. Sinuhe stood, leaning on his cane, while his twelve students—Meritaken, Jo, and ten boys who were all the sons of palace noblemen—sat on the ground with their *ostraca*, shards of stone or clay on which they practiced their writing, balanced on their laps. They spent hours practicing the hieroglyphs, copying from one dry old text or another. When Jo finished before the others, she watched the palace gardeners coax and plead with the pharaoh's imported plants. Sometimes she counted the buckets of water that a long line of servants carried from the Nile and splashed upon the dirt.

There were more than seven hundred different hieroglyphs, and Jo learned every one of them, in about a week. It was as if all the information was already loaded into her brain and all she had to do was dust it off. In addition, she'd acquired an uncanny ability to remember, word for word, everything she read. Jo knew that she was smart, even though back at Southglades she'd worked diligently at not showing it. Nothing was as uncool as a nerd. But the kind of aptitude she was showing in Kemet ... well, there was no logical explanation for it. Then again, there was no logical explanation for anything that had happened to her in the last few weeks.

When they weren't copying the hieroglyphs, they were listening to Sinuhe drone on and on about the value of an education.

"This is your chance to escape the drudgery of physical labor," he was fond of saying. "Study, and you will be rewarded with a government job in a fine office. Fall behind in your work, and it's the granite quarries for you. Or perhaps you'd rather sow seeds behind the rump of a foul-smelling ox?"

Jo had laughed out loud the first time she heard it, and Sinuhe's cane came down hard across her lap desk. "You think I am humorous?" he demanded. The rest of the class stared in horror.

"No, sir," she responded. *No siree, not a trace of a sense of humor.* She spent hours fantasizing about zapping Sinuhe into the twenty-first century and watching him annihilate ol' Foster. She wouldn't have to get even with Foster; she could let Sinuhe do it for her.

They studied math also and solved problems twenty-first-century math teachers would have loved. Jo calculated the number of men needed to transport an obelisk seventy yards long and gave the proportions of the ramp needed to raise it. Another time, she had to figure the volume of a burial chamber and calculate how many jars of wine could be stored in the anteroom. She was also required to memorize the geography of the Kemetan Empire and beyond. It was the toughest school she'd ever attended, and Jo was the best student she had ever been. Within a few days of beginning school, she understood that Sinuhe and the students, including Meritaken, admired her intelligence. For the first time in her life, it was okay to be smart.

Sinuhe prepared her well for life as a Kemetan princess. Not only did she learn to read and write the hieroglyphs, she also came to understand much of Egypt's history from reading the old scrolls. She read about the gods and goddesses, the battles for power, and the accomplishments of the pharaohs. She read history that would be erased long before she was born—primary source documents that would crumble and disappear and never be seen in the modern world.

The more she learned, the more she wanted to know. She still didn't understand why she'd been sent to Egypt, and she didn't know how Sinuhe and his class fit into the whole picture. But she did know that the more she could find out about Egypt, the safer she would be.

If nothing else at all, she'd return to the twenty-first century a more accomplished Egyptologist than any on earth. Perhaps that was all part of Foster's plan. Then again, maybe there was no plan at all.

Who knew?

Jo sat with her back against the banyan tree, doing her best to decipher an old scroll. She was ahead of the class again, working on her own, while Meritaken and the others recited for Sinuhe. The day was unusually warm, even in the shade of the tree, and Jo was having trouble concentrating. She was reading the story of Hatshepsut, one of the few female pharaohs and a battle-hardened warrior. The story was interesting, but two of the pharaoh's chimpanzees were playing in the top branches of the tree—it looked like they were playing a game of tag—and Jo could hardly keep from watching them.

Under Sinuhe's careful eye, the others dared not pay attention to the commotion above them, but Jo was far enough removed from the group to relax. Transfixed, she watched, a smile on her face.

That was the way Tutankhamun found her as he stormed across the courtyard. Jo looked down, suddenly conscious that the rest of the class had gone quiet, and saw him as he approached, a dark cloud rolling across an otherwise peaceful garden. He wore all his regal finery, obviously having come straight from the Hall of Audiences, and clenched a small scroll in his right hand.

Jo's classmates were immediately on their knees, foreheads to the ground, but Jo locked eyes with the pharaoh and never got around to bowing.

He knows.

"Your Highness." Sinuhe hadn't bowed either. "You have an urgent matter to discuss, I trust?"

Tutankhamun said nothing, but handed the scroll to Sinuhe. The old teacher read quickly and glanced at Jo. She sat motionless, the color draining from her face.

"I would counsel you not to act too quickly," said Sinuhe in a low voice. The pharaoh continued to stare at Jo, but Sinuhe continued. "We should talk. There are things you need to know." The older man took the younger by the elbow and led him away from the class. They continued a hushed discussion.

Jo watched, paralyzed.

Then, with once last glance in her direction, Tutankhamun strode away. Class resumed, and after a while, Jo went back to her scroll.

The young pharaoh worked alone in his office that night, a small army of guards outside his door. Late in the evening, he was interrupted by a knock. "Let him in!" he yelled to his guards, without getting up from his desk. The door opened, and Sinuhe entered. "What takes you so long, old man? I grow weary."

"And you call me *old man*?" Sinuhe laughed. He stepped around the desk, and the two men embraced quickly before sitting, one on either side of the desk.

"Don't blame your weariness on me," Sinuhe said, his voice more serious now. Tutankhamun did not reply. "How goes it with your co-viziers? They get along well these days?"

"Certainly, now that they have united against me."

"You cannot really think they are plotting against you?"

"No," sighed the young pharaoh. "Nothing as traitorous as that. But they agree on one thing: they both think I am too green to rule this kingdom."

"Then they have not tried to outwit you in a game of chess … or find you in the taverns of a foreign city when you did not want to be found." He smiled again. "Bring them to me, and I'll tell them that you were my second-best student ever."

"Second-best?"

"Yes, the one you would cast out has surpassed even you."

Tutankhamun paused. "Nekhare has told me that this Princess Johenaten is an amazing young woman. But he is in love, so I thought he was exaggerating."

"He's in love? Then I feel badly for him. She is not his destiny."

"Perhaps she lied, came here already having had some training—"

"No," replied Sinuhe, shaking his head.

"Who is she?" asked Tutankhamun.

"I don't know. I only know that her arrival here, at this time, is no coincidence. Keep her close," advised the old man. "She will become a weapon in your arsenal."

"Are you suggesting that I use her as a spy, marry her off to some Hittite king?"

"That is not what I had in mind."

The two old friends talked well into the night.

CHAPTER 8

Jo had expected to be called to the Hall of Audiences immediately. Instead, weeks dragged by, and her life became as predictable as the Kemetan sun. Each day the servants arrived, and they went through the same hour-long princess-making routine. There were no "days of the week" in the Kemetan calendar, no Sabbath on which to rest. However, government employees like Sinuhe had every tenth day off, so Jo and her classmates went to school for nine days at a time.

Jo and Meritaken spent afternoons floating in the pool, ruining the look they'd worked so hard to achieve in the morning. But no matter; the servants put them back together again before the evening meal. At other times, they lounged in the shade or played *senet* in one bedroom or the other.

Nekhare was another constant in Jo's life. Tutankhamun kept him busy, but he showed up to eat with them every other day or so and sometimes played *senet* with them in the evenings. Jo and Nekhare hadn't been alone together since they had paddled downriver, but still she sensed some sort of connection between them. When he made no attempt to see her alone, Jo figured he had his reasons. Perhaps it was because she was not of royal blood. Perhaps he was waiting, just like she was, to see whether someone would come to get her.

By Jo's calculations, it was near the holiday season back home when she left the palace for the first time. She'd been thinking a lot about Christmas lights and the smell of a real Christmas tree—a luxury her mom hadn't given up even after her dad moved out. Anyway, she was feeling homesick, so when Nekhare showed up at breakfast one day and announced that he had obtained permission for her to skip school and accompany him on some errands, Jo was only too ready to break the routine—and only too glad to spend some time alone with Nekhare.

"We can be on the lookout for the man with the beard," she said.

Nekhare laughed. "We can look, but I doubt we'll find him."

Tutankhamun had sent Nekhare to deliver messages to high priests at both the Luxor Temple and the Temple at Karnak, so the two of them left the palace and set out southwest, toward the Nile. Nekhare placed two small scrolls in a leather bag he carried around his waist and slung a small bow and a quiver of arrows across his back.

Their route took them through the heart of the city, the marketplace. Jo had never seen anything like it and could only compare it to a low-tech version of a South Florida flea market. The narrow roadway overflowed with people of all shapes, sizes, and colors, wearing a variety of clothing. Nekhare was right; it would be near to impossible to find the man from Foster's book in this setting.

On either side of the road was an explosion of wares for sale: piles of huge pottery jars and thickly woven rugs, bolts of exotic silk fabrics (imported from the East, Nekhare explained), and table after table of fruit, vegetables, and assorted baked goods, all displayed under the shade of huge awnings supported by crude poles driven into the sand.

From all directions came the sound of haggling—arguments between buyer and seller over price and quantity. Chickens squawked, and children cried. The marketplace was nothing like the peaceful environment to which Jo had grown accustomed. She was struck by the difference between the palace, which was beautiful and luxurious, and the living and working conditions of the merchant class.

The city was not dirty, but it was crowded. Buildings here served a dual purpose: the first floor of each was business space, and the upper floors and the rooftops provided living quarters for the owners. The buildings were built adjoining, and the streets swarmed with people going about their everyday business. There were no beautifully sculpted gardens, just dry sand everywhere. And here the sand was not continually watered, like it was in the palace gardens, to keep it from blowing about.

They caused quite a commotion as they strode down the street, the dark-eyed prince and the golden-haired girl. Shopkeepers and patrons alike stopped to watch the pair. Men smiled, and women whispered. "Who is the girl?" they asked each other, for even though she looked the part of a princess in her fine clothing and heavy jewelry, they knew they hadn't seen her before. Nekhare seemed not to notice those who slid out of his way as he moved down the street.

But Jo did.

She saw the looks on the faces of the people—something between respect and awe. Nekhare was well known here, or perhaps his gold armbands and heavy, gold-beaded collars gave him away. Or maybe it was just the way he carried himself. He walked with the authority and arrogance his birthright lent him. Beside him, Jo felt almost regal. *I could get used to this*, she thought.

She slowed a bit to look at some colorful silk fabric on display, and Nekhare obliged by slowing also.

"These people find you interesting," said Nekhare as he stood behind her.

"I thought that it was you they were staring at," she replied.

"They are trying to figure out who you are. I know how they feel. As a matter of fact, I'm thinking that they know almost as much about you as I do."

"There's just not that much to know," she replied.

The fabric merchant, a tiny man with a dark mustache and a few missing teeth, approached from the other side of the table. "You like?" he asked.

She nodded. There was some sort of nonverbal communication between him and Nekhare, and the silk disappeared from the table. Jo knew it would be delivered to the palace. They continued down the street, Nekhare walking half a step behind Jo.

"Sinuhe says that you are smart, the brightest student he's ever had," Nekhare said, after a few moments of silence. "He says that you remember everything you read and that you can solve problems twice as fast as anyone else."

"So?" she asked, feeling nervous.

"So I'm wondering how someone so smart knows so little. About yourself, I mean. Or perhaps there's something you are hiding?"

She stopped and turned to look up at him. "I'm not trying to hide anything, especially not from you. After all, you're the one who … rescued me." She gave him her best "helpless female" look, figuring that it had worked once and was worth another try. "I just don't understand everything that happened to me. All I know is that I'm here now, and I'm beginning to be glad that I am."

The activity of the marketplace continued in a blur as they stood, toe-to-toe.

Nekhare smiled. "I'm glad you're here, too," he said, "and I'm very glad that my sister isn't along today to annoy us."

Laughing, Jo started off down the street; this time it was Nekhare who struggled to keep up.

"Oh, whatever that is, it smells good," Jo said, looking for any topic other than herself to keep the conversation moving.

"Over here," Nekhare said, and he veered to the other side of the street. She followed him through a narrow doorway, and they entered a small, windowless room. The heat from the huge stone ovens that lined one wall was almost unbearable.

Behind the counter worked a girl about Jo's age. She wore a simple white tunic, and her long, dark hair was tied back with a torn strip of fabric. Her eyes were blackened with the usual *kohl*, but she wore no jewelry at all. She looked up as they entered, and Jo noticed a flicker of recognition in the girl's eyes.

"Where is your father?" asked Nekhare.

"Gone to get the wheat ground for tomorrow," the girl replied, her voice soft, her eyes downcast.

"And your mother?"

"Gone with him."

"All right then. We would like two of those honey cakes we smell baking. Do you think you can manage that?" Jo was surprised by the tone of Nekhare's voice, stern and condescending, not the Nekhare she knew.

"Yes, sir," the girl replied, her nervousness visible. She moved to the back of the narrow room and pulled a tray from a shelf high on the wall. The tray slid from her trembling hands and fell to the floor in a puff of dust.

"Well, we don't want those now," Nekhare said impatiently. "Do you have more?"

"Yes …"

"Then hurry up about it. We don't have all day."

Jo stared at Nekhare, taken back by his impatience with the girl. "You're frightening her," she said. "You know, you do that sometimes. You just about scared me to death the first time I saw you."

Nekhare turned, a smile sliding across his face. He stepped closer and used his forefinger under her chin to tilt her face upward. For an instant, Jo felt sure that they both imagined that they were once again standing knee-deep in the Nile, wondering what to think of each other.

"Well, I am very glad that I didn't scare you away," he said. Then he did something completely unexpected—he kissed her.

He turned back to the girl; Jo struggled to swallow the butterflies that were fluttering in her chest. "What is your name?" he asked, more gently.

"Senen, sir."

"Then, Senen, you have my sincerest apology. I have been properly reprimanded." He bowed to her. Looking astonished but no less nervous, the girl handed over the cakes. "Please make sure these are added to the palace account," Nekhare said as he motioned for Jo to step out ahead of him.

"Do you know that girl?" Jo asked, trying not to act as if she had just been kissed for the first time.

"Yes," he said. "Sometimes her father bakes for events; you know, when there is too much work for the palace cooks. I just didn't remember her name."

They left the bakery and proceeded southward. Soon the street widened, and they approached the Luxor Temple. In a city known for its hundreds of temples, Luxor was neither the largest nor the most ornate, but it was one of the oldest and therefore was held in high esteem. Like all the temples, it was painted white and decorated with color everywhere. Nekhare and Jo entered the temple between two huge pylons and proceeded down a long corridor to a maze of offices.

Stopping alongside a double door, Nekhare said, "Wait here while I deliver my message to the high priest." He motioned to a bench nearby. He knocked at the door and entered without waiting for anyone to answer.

He was not gone long, and they continued their journey, this time traveling north along the river on a glorious, wide road lined with sphinxes.

"This roadway was built by Pharaoh Amenhotep, Tutankhamun's grandfather, for the Festival of the Opet," Nekhare explained. "You'll take part in that festival just before the next inundation."

If I'm still here, Jo thought.

The Karnak Temple came into sight. Jo had read about the temple and seen photographs of it in twenty-first century books, but she was still unprepared for its grandeur. Situated on the bank of the Nile, it was larger and more ostentatious than either the temple at Luxor or the palace. It had been whitewashed and then decorated with colorful murals. Everywhere the powerful Kemetan sun reflected off gold trim.

They entered the temple through a mammoth stone arch carved with the image of Amun, the ram, and inlaid with gold and gemstones. They skirted the Holy Lake just inside the doors and then passed through yet another huge gate. They strolled through a large courtyard, their sandals slapping the stone floor, and Jo slowed to marvel at the dozens of sculpted columns that framed the huge, open space.

"Awesome," Jo said, her amazement profound enough to make her revert to twenty-first-century slang.

"Yes, the temple is awe-inspiring," Nekhare agreed. "It is ancient, of course, and has been embellished many times over the course of history. Amenhotep added the massive outer walls and is responsible for the temple as it stands today."

"The high priest here must be a powerful man."

Nekhare laughed. "Oh, yes—much to Tutankhamun's frustration." They entered a long hallway and the office section of the temple. Neither of them would be allowed to enter the sanctity of the inner temple, an honor reserved for the high priests, the *wab* priests who tended the shrines, and the pharaoh himself.

"Ah, Nekhare, welcome," said the high priest, Piay, who appeared from within the temple. "Who is this lovely girl you have with you?"

Nekhare smiled in Jo's direction. "Princess Johenaten of Akhetaten."

"Ah, yes. I should have known. I've heard much about the Golden Princess. Welcome to the Holy City."

"Thank you, sir." *He's heard about me?*

"I also hear things in Akhetaten are not going well," the priest said with a sly smile. "You must be relieved to be here in Waset, where Tutankhamun can look after you."

"And where I am free to worship Amun," Jo said with an ever-so-slight bow. *What a suck-up I am*, she thought.

"A diplomat!" the priest exclaimed. Behind him, Nekhare smiled broadly. "Perhaps you should consider changing your name, then. That nasty *aten* ending makes one wonder where your loyalties lie. *Johenamun* might be a more suitable name for you."

"I shall present that idea to the pharaoh," Jo replied, mindful of the power struggle and unwilling to let the high priest believe that anyone but Tutankhamun could make decisions regarding the royal family.

The priest started off down the long hall.

"I'll be a bit longer this time. Wait for me here," Nekhare said, pointing to another elaborately carved bench in the hallway. He disappeared around a corner with the high priest.

She waited, but the minutes stretched into what felt like half an hour or more, and still Nekhare did not return.

Jo decided to wander back out to the courtyard, certain Nekhare would look for her there. She started back out, but on the way she noticed a door that opened into a beautiful garden. She strolled the length of the garden, stopping to smell the flowers that grew there.

"He is but a sun-worshipper, just like his father." Jo recognized the voice of the high priest. She stopped just before an open window. "Kemet will never be what it once was until we have a pharaoh who is truly committed to the old ways—one who will pay proper homage to Amun."

"Tutankhamun believes that a return to tradition is the best way to strengthen Kemet—" Nekhare began.

"So he continues to tell me. But I don't believe that this is what he feels in his heart. Mark my words: he will return to Akhetaten … to his father's palace and his father's folly."

"But Ay and Horemheb …"

"Ay and Horemheb are losing their grip on Tutankhamun. He is maturing and determined to take the helm himself."

"Yes, this is true."

The priest dropped his voice to a whisper. "Consider my offer, young friend. I am a powerful man, more powerful than your young pharaoh can imagine. I can make those things I spoke of happen."

"I will remember what you have said," replied Nekhare as he stood. From Jo's position in the garden, she could hear the scrape of chairs on the marble floor and knew that the conversation was over. She hurried back toward the courtyard but met Nekhare in the corridor.

"Did you get lost?"

"No, I discovered a beautiful garden," she said, trying to sound casual, hoping Nekhare wouldn't notice the uneasiness in her voice.

What did the high priest offer Nekhare? she wondered. *And why didn't Nekhare tell him to get lost?*

"Are you in a hurry to return to the palace?" he asked. "The pharaoh does not expect me back right away." Nekhare smiled and took both her hands in his.

He was relaxed and upbeat, not at all like a man under pressure or struggling with his conscience. Jo realized that he probably dealt with men like the high priest regularly. She knew Nekhare would do the right thing.

"I certainly don't want to go back before classes are over for the day," she replied.

Nekhare laughed. "Then let's take a detour down to the river."

They left the temple the same way they had entered and then veered off the paved road and across the grassy field to the river. The Karnak temple had its own pier from which all manner of goods were shipped and received. Jo and Nekhare were just a couple of hundred yards downstream from the pier, so she could see the bustle of activity there. Boats of various sizes clogged the river; some were obviously cargo ships, and others—tiny boats made of reeds—were manned by pairs of men who pulled fish from the river with nets.

"Why don't you rest here for a while?" Nekhare suggested, motioning to a tree that had fallen, providing a natural seat just a few yards from the river. He took the bow from his shoulder and pulled an arrow from the quiver.

He aimed at a duck swimming near the bank. The arrow flew through the air and found its mark. Nekhare waded through the shallow water to pick up the dead bird.

"I'll take this back to the palace cook. We'll have it for dinner tonight."

Totally repulsed by the bloody, limp duck, but fascinated with the bow, she said, "Let me try that."

"You?"

"I can shoot a bow and arrow, probably better than you!"

Laughing, Nekhare handed her the bow and pulled another arrow from the quiver.

"Of course, you'll have to show me how first," she said, giggling.

"Nock the arrow here," he said, demonstrating where to slide the arrow onto the bow, "and turn the feathers away from the bow. That's it. Hold the bow with your left arm straight, and pull the bowstring all the way back to your eye."

She did as he instructed but was surprised by the increased weight of the bow with the arrow nocked and the bowstring pulled. Noticing her struggle, Nekhare stepped behind her and put his left hand over her left; with his right hand over hers, he helped her to pull the bowstring all the way back.

"Our target is that log sticking out of the water. Aim the arrow a few feet in front of it. Now, when you are ready to fire, just release all the fingers of your right hand at the same time. Ready? One ... two ... three."

The arrow landed about twenty feet away, its wobbly flight mirroring the way Jo's body felt with Nekhare standing so close.

"Okay, so I just need a little practice." Jo grinned.

Nekhare handed her another arrow, and they repeated the process, his body pressed to hers, their cheeks touching. This time, the arrow flew straighter and landed just a few feet short of the log.

"Ready to try it on your own?" he asked.

"Umm, I don't think so," she replied, not wanting to let go of the moment.

He pulled another arrow from the quiver and helped her nock it, all without stepping away. "Elbow a little higher," he said. "There you go."

Thwack. The arrow hit its target and remained embedded in the rotten log.

"Again," he said, and another arrow flew straight into the dead wood of the log.

"One more time, this one on your own."

Nekhare stepped away, leaving a very empty spot where he had once stood. He handed Jo yet another arrow. She nocked it, pulled the bowstring with all her might, and let the arrow fly. Much to her amazement, it landed just short of the mark.

"Not bad," he said, and he handed her another arrow. "Try again."

This time the arrow hit the log just inches from the first. "You're not going to try to tell me that you've never shot an arrow before, are you?" he asked.

"I *swear.* I'm as surprised as you are." Archery was one thing she had never even considered trying. Jo smiled. In truth, nothing surprised her anymore. "Nekhare, will you bring me here again so I can practice?"

"Of course. Or we can use the practice range at the north end of the palace. You can shoot at targets instead of logs—or ducks." He retrieved the duck and what arrows he could, and the two of them strolled back to the palace, newly aware of each other. The butterflies fluttered in Jo's chest again.

CHAPTER 9

Winter deepened, and Jo was no closer to finding her way home or even understanding why she had been sent to Egypt. In the beginning, she had just assumed that one day someone would come for her, that eventually she'd understand all that had happened.

She'd imagined returning home to a hero's welcome, that her mom and maybe even her dad would be relieved and thrilled to have her home again. She'd be the first person *ever* to travel through time and return home to tell about it. *People* would run a story about her, and all across the U.S.A., newspaper headlines would read FLORIDA GIRL MEETS KING TUT. She'd be on all the morning news shows.

And Foster would pay big time for everything she had done.

But as the months passed, tiny snippets of doubt crept into her head. She pushed them back, tried to ignore them. Then, every once in a while, she'd take one out, let it sit in her consciousness for a while, try it on for size. *Stay here forever? It might not be so awful.*

Of course, Nekhare was the major reason for her change in attitude. Nothing changes a girl's dreams and plans faster than attention from a guy, especially if that girl is naïve and lonely and has no real plans in the first place. Make that guy a prince—cousin to the pharaoh, no less—and the future looks even brighter. Who cares if the prince can sometimes be a little moody?

Jo didn't. At least, not much.

They had been together until late in the evening the night before, hiding from the moonlight in one of the pharaoh's gardens and using a very uncomfortable, tiny bench for things Jo was quite sure the gardeners had never intended. Things had spun almost out of control, but she had said no, and Nekhare had respected that, although Jo thought he was a bit ticked off. He walked her back to her room, but she could tell he was pouting, even if she hadn't been able to see his face in the dimly lit hallway.

Later, after the servants had bathed her and prepared her bed, she lay awake wondering why she had stopped him. *He can have any girl he wants, and he wants you, idiot.*

The next morning he was not at breakfast. "Have you seen Nekhare?" Jo asked Meritaken, who had arrived on the rooftop ahead of her.

"You've seen him more recently than I have, I'm sure," Meritaken replied. Jo noted the similarity of her pout to her brother's. "I thought the three of us were going to play *senet* last night."

"Nekhare … had work to do," Jo said, "and he asked me to help. You know, he's still working on those temple inscriptions—"

"You are a terrible liar," Meritaken said, smiling, to Jo's relief, "but I'll tell you where he is if you promise not to leave me alone in my room tonight."

"I promise."

"He is preparing to leave for Medinet Habu with the king."

"Medinet Habu!" Jo recognized this as the site of Tutankhamun's mortuary temple, the spot where she had first arrived in this time and place. "He didn't tell me. I've got to go with them," she said.

"You can't go—you just promised!" wailed Meritaken. Jo hardly heard; she was already out the door.

She found Nekhare in his room, preparing for the journey.

"Meritaken told me that you are going out to the temple with the pharaoh. Why didn't you tell me?"

"Mainly because he just now decided. I sent a message to Meritaken, but I wanted to see you to tell you myself. We're going to be gone a couple of days."

"I've got to go with you!"

Nekhare shook his head. "Tutankhamun will never agree to that. He wants to take as few people out there as possible. Ankesenamun is not even going. Why would he take you?"

"But this might be my last chance to find my way home—or at least find some clue about how I got here. Will you at least ask him? What harm can it do to ask?" Thinking fast, she said, "I know. I'll tell him I lost a piece of jewelry out there and I need to find it. An amulet my mother gave me. Before she died."

"I don't understand why it's so important for you to go back out to the temple. What is it you are expecting to find out there? Is it worth telling Pharaoh another lie?"

She paused. "I'm not sure what I am looking for. I only know that I can't just ignore an opportunity to look around."

"If this is about last night—"

"It's not," she said quickly, blushing. "Look, I wanted to tell you—"

"Then you don't have to worry. You don't have to run away."

"This has nothing to do with you and me. It's just that this might be my last chance to find out what happened—who brought me here and why."

Nekhare was pouting again.

"The temple may hold some sort of clue," she continued, speaking more to herself than Nekhare. "Maybe there's a portal of some kind—"

"A what?"

"Oh, never mind. Look, I've got to try. If Tutankhamun takes me out there and I don't find anything, well—"

"You'll forget about going home?" He wrapped his arms around her, and she laid her head on his shoulder.

"Yes."

"All right," Nekhare said quietly. "I will take you to Tutankhamun. But I'm still not sure this is a good idea."

The pharaoh's guards admitted them into Tutankhamun's apartment, where they found him in his office. He stood behind a delicately carved desk with his back to the door, studying a long scroll on which were drawn the architectural plans for his temple. Upon hearing their arrival, he turned to face them.

He was dressed without all the fancy pharaoh gear, but hanging from his waist was a bull's tail, the symbol of pharaonic power. At a time when most well-to-do Kemetan men shaved their heads and wore wigs, Tutankhamun and Nekhare had taken to wearing their hair long and, occasionally, like today, tied back with a leather cord. The king's eyes were heavily lined with *kohl*. He was so young—Jo knew he was about Nekhare's age—but something about his demeanor made her knees knock and her palms sweat. Maybe it was the way he had of looking at people with those dark eyes—like he could see right to the very core of a person and read all the secrets locked up inside.

His face was knotted in a frown.

It was, of course, the first time Jo had seen Tutankhamun since the day he had interrupted Sinuhe's class, but if he was thinking of that day, he gave no indication of it.

Get a grip, she warned herself.

"May we enter?" Nekhare asked.

"What is it?" Tutankhamun set the scroll on the desk, motioning for them to come in.

Even though Jo had become accustomed to the luxury of the palace, she was stunned by the splendor of the pharaoh's office. All the furniture seemed made of gold, and every square inch of wall and ceiling space had been filled with colorful, intricate murals. The highly polished floor was constructed of alternating black and white tiles. The entire room glittered.

"I already approved your request to change your name," the pharaoh said to Jo as she approached his desk.

Nekhare didn't give Jo the opportunity to respond. "Your Highness, Princess Johenamun requests permission to accompany the royal party on the trip to Medinet Habu."

"Why would you want to go out there?" Tutankhamun asked, clearly surprised.

"I know you will pass through el Sedu," she explained, finding her voice, "and I lost an amulet when I was last there."

"What were you doing in el Sedu?" he asked. "The village is south of the palace—not en route from Akhetaten."

She hadn't thought of that. "I ... I'm not sure. I was taken there for some reason. I was ... ill. I don't remember much."

"I see."

"The amulet is very precious to me; my mother gave it to me just before she died. I would like the chance to search the hut I slept in—"

"I will have one of my men look for it," Tutankhamun said gruffly. He seemed to have made up his mind. "There is no need for you to go. We will be away for several days, and we are not taking servants. You will not be comfortable."

Jo was not about to give up so easily, despite her fear of the pharaoh. "Pardon my boldness, Your Highness, but I am the only one who can retrace my steps. I will have plenty of time to search, whereas your men will be anxious to fulfill more important duties. Please let me go."

Tutankhamun didn't answer. *He's thinking about it*, she thought.

Jo continued, "Certainly you can understand that the amulet is important—"

"You would be the only woman on the trip," the pharaoh interrupted.

"I know, and I will stay out of the way, I promise. The men will hardly know I am there."

"There will be no servants."

"I'll do without."

"Pack only what you can carry. A blanket and a change of clothing, perhaps. We will depart shortly." Having made up his mind, the pharaoh turned his attention back to the scroll.

They left through a gate in the north end of the palace, and although several of the members of the party stared at Jo, no one said anything or asked why she was traveling with the pharaoh. She wore a loose dress with a wide skirt, more appropriate for travel than her usual narrow dress, and she carried a draw-string bag with a clean change of clothing.

Under heavy guard, they proceeded across a flat field toward the river. Using this route, they were able to avoid traveling through Waset and attracting the attention of the citizens.

General Nankti accompanied them that day. He commanded the *medjai* and was the person most responsible for the pharaoh's safety. Younger than the other generals and fiercely loyal to Tutankhamun, he was the perfect man for the job.

Before leaving the palace, Jo had borrowed an amulet from Meritaken, quizzing her to be sure that it was one that Tutankhamun would not recognize. She wrapped the amulet in a piece of linen and slipped it into the bag with her clean tunic.

At the river's edge, the party boarded a large boat rigged with sails and equipped with oars. With wind and muscle power, they made quick progress up the Nile. The day was postcard-perfect. The light breeze that filled the sails also provided welcome relief from the heat. Nekhare and Jo sat together in the stern of the boat, watching the landscape slide past.

Jo had arrived in Kemet during the inundation, the annual flooding of the Nile, but that season had passed to emergence, when the river was at its lowest. Now it was just a narrow ribbon of water moving lazily through the lush valley. On either side, farmers dug deep furrows in the still-moist ground, their plows each pulled by a pair of oxen. The women walked behind the plows, scattering seeds from wicker baskets.

"What is that?" Jo asked Nekhare. She pointed to a tall, wooden contraption at the river's edge.

"A *shadoof*," he replied. "It's part of the irrigation system." Even as he spoke, a group of men put the device to work hauling bucket after bucket up from the Nile and dumping the water into long wooden gutters. Further upriver, crocodiles sunned themselves on the river's banks, and a family of hippos bathed in a river bend.

Soon they arrived at the familiar campsite, the place where Nekhare and Jo had first stumbled onto each other. The little group of huts was a poor substitute for the palace, but the plan was to use el Sedu as a base for a few days' work at the temple, thus eliminating the need to travel back and forth across the river each night.

As the men unloaded supplies, Jo located the hut she had hid in and prepared for the acting job of her life. She would have to convince the pharaoh that she had found the amulet and then persuade him to include her in the party going out to the temple. Otherwise, he would leave her at el Sedu while the rest of them headed into the desert. Gathering her courage, she ran from the hut, squealing with feigned delight.

"Look, I found it already! It was lying right in the sand."

Tutankhamun, Nekhare, and General Nankti sat together, heads bowed over a scroll.

"How lucky for you," the pharaoh said. Jo thought she detected a hint of sarcasm, but she couldn't stop the show once it had started.

"So I guess I don't have anything else to do. I might as well go out to the temple with you."

Tutankhamun looked up and smiled. "You'll ride a horse?" he asked.

"She can ride with me," Nekhare offered.

"A horse?" Jo asked, finding it difficult to hide her excitement, as it had been at least a year since she had been on horseback.

"Yes, I keep a stable just downriver from here. The stablehands will arrive shortly with horses, and we will ride out to the temple," Tutankhamun explained.

Soon enough, Jo spotted a line of horses approaching, and without further preparation, Tutankhamun called for the departure of the entire party.

"You can ride behind me," said Nekhare. "I'll put you up first."

He offered his knee as a stool, and Jo mounted the horse, settling herself on the narrow blanket that served as a saddle, glad that she had chosen a less confining dress.

Nekhare gathered the reins in his left hand on the horse's neck and prepared to mount, but just as he stepped onto the stool that had been provided, a piece of white cloth blew loose from someone's gear and startled the huge animal. Before Nekhare could calm him, the spooked horse shied and then reared, his front hooves pawing at the air.

The slender reins were yanked from Nekhare's hands; Jo barely managed to stay astride.

Just as the horse settled and she began to think she was out of danger, the wind picked the linen up again, tossing it high into the air, where it floated down … down … down.

Jo could feel the animal tense under her, and she knew he was about to explode. She stroked his withers in an attempt to settle him. "Easy, boy … easy," she whispered.

Another gust of wind sent the cloth sailing straight at them. This time, the horse bolted. Instinctively, Jo wrapped her legs around the powerful animal, leaned forward, and threw her arms around his neck. The horse picked up speed and galloped away from the river into the desert, sending sand in every direction.

Jo thought of nothing other than getting the horse under control. She reached forward as far as she could, her cheek against the stallion's straining neck, and caught one of the reins that flew in the wind. She pulled it toward her, clasping it in her left hand, and wrapped her fingers into the horse's mane. With her right hand, she reached for the other rein, still flapping in the wind.

The sand blurred beneath the horse's hooves as Jo used every muscle in her body to keep from tumbling off.

Finally, she secured the other rein, and using all of the strength she possessed, she pulled the horse to a skidding halt. He reared, but Jo managed to stay seated. She pulled the horse around, took a minute to settle him, and released him into a trot back toward the startled party of men.

Several of them, including the pharaoh, had started off in pursuit of her wild ride, but upon seeing Jo rein the animal in, they pulled their own mounts to a stop. They now sat as if rooted, their mouths hanging open, stunned by the display they had witnessed.

Jo pulled the horse up in front of Nekhare. Tutankhamun trotted his horse over to them.

"I'll have the groom bring you another horse, Nekhare," said the pharaoh. "I think Princess Johenamun can ride this one to the temple."

He shot her a curious glance and rode off.

The ride out to the temple was exhilarating, and Jo rode with a sense of satisfaction, knowing she had shocked the entire group and earned a measure of their respect. Far too soon, she dismounted and handed the reins to one of the men.

She felt like she had ridden onto a movie set. Thousands of shirtless men, their bodies glistening with sweat in the unforgiving heat, pulled huge blocks of stone across the desert on wooden sleds. The men formed long lines along thick ropes in two separate groups. Several dozen more kept the wooden tracks—they looked almost like railroad tracks—well lubricated with animal fat. More men swarmed the pile of stones that she now recognized as a temple. A third group of laborers pulled a stone up a long, muddy ramp that led to the top of the temple.

"So that's how they did it," she said to herself. The question was centuries old: *How did the ancient Egyptians move blocks of stone weighing several tons each?*

"What?" asked Nekhare. Jo hadn't heard him approach from behind.

"Nothing. I thought that construction had slowed, that the farmers were all back in the fields."

Nekhare nodded. "That is true, but this is a high-priority project, so Tutankhamun has all those who are available working at this site."

He doesn't know how high a priority it is, Jo thought.

"Most of these men are soldiers waiting to march to war," Nekhare continued. "By the way, you neglected to mention to me that you knew how to ride. Or was that your first time?"

"No." She forced a laugh. "I used to ride a lot. That's not so unusual for girls where I come from. I just … didn't think to mention it."

"I see." Nekhare paused and moved a few steps closer to the temple, hands clasped behind his back. She braced herself, expecting a barrage of questions. None came.

"Tutankhamun is unhappy with the progress out here," he said, visibly distracted. "I think he suspects the foreman of sabotaging the job."

"Why would he do that?"

"Pharaohs are expected to make massive temples arise from the sand. Anything less indicates disfavor by the gods, a disturbance in *Ma'at*. The kingdom is watching, waiting, to see whether Tutankhamun can get this temple built. There are those who would like to see him fail."

"You mean all that stuff about Akhenaten and the cult of the Aten—"

"Yes. Remember, many see Tutankhamun as an extension of his father. They still don't trust him, which is one reason why he has chosen to build here, in Medinet Habu, near the tomb of his great-grandfather, Amenhotep. It is a symbol of his desire to return to the old ways and the Kemet that was before his father's rule."

"And is that what he *really* wants, to return to the old ways?"

Nekhare seemed surprised by her question. He smiled. "I guess you'd have to ask him."

I will, she thought, *if he lives long enough.*

Nekhare was called away to record conversations, and for a while Jo trailed behind Tut and his entourage as they inspected first a faulty support column and then a number of stones that had been set unevenly into the foundation. At each stop, the foreman explained the problem, and then the king and his advisers discussed how to remedy it. Jo watched Tutankhamun from a short distance and listened in on the conversation, fascinated by the speed with which the pharaoh assessed problems and made decisions.

The men moved to the back of the site, and Jo decided not to follow; she wanted to wander and inspect the temple on her own. She climbed the stairway and entered the building, finding before her a large chamber with massive pillars on either side.

Am I in the right place? I remember running up a hallway. I must have come out a different door.

She circled the entire temple, but there was only one entrance. She entered again and walked the perimeter of the room. There were several doors that opened into other chambers, but she couldn't find the hallway that led to the tiny chamber where she had first landed.

Weird ...

Outside again, she made her way around the column she had hidden behind, again out of sight of all those who might watch her. She ran her hands along the stone wall of the temple, convinced that if she could only find the right spot, the seemingly impenetrable wall would open up and reveal a door. She could run through it without hesitation, just like in the movies, if she so desired.

Then she saw it—not a portal but instead the tip of something sticking out of the sand.

A book? She dug at it with her fingers until at last she was able to pull it free. *Well, I'll be damned ... Foster's book! How did this get here? It must have traveled along with me when I came. But how? I heard it fall into the tub.*

She sat down, put the heavy book in her lap, and began to flip the pages. They were wrinkled, and every bit of ink had run, making the letters and words indecipherable.

Where is the old man?

She held the book upside down and shook it, half expecting the bearded man to fall from its pages.

Nothing happened. She shook the book harder.

She set it down in the sand, opened to the page about the pyramids at Giza, picked up a handful of sand, and threw it at the open pages, the way the bearded man had thrown sand out of the book at her.

Nothing happened.

I just don't get it. I know my time travel has something to do with this book and the old man. But how does it work?

Her frustration grew. She picked up the book and threw it against the temple wall; it landed facedown in the sand. *Damn!* She sat, once again hidden behind the column, and tried to control the tears that ran down her cheeks. She didn't know how much time had passed when she heard Nekhare calling for her. She buried the book in the sand, wiped away her tears, and went to join him.

CHAPTER 10

At el Sedu the men built a bonfire that provided light well into the evening, and many of the party sat near the fire, exchanging stories and drinking wine and beer from clay jars.

Nekhare and Jo sat close together, apart from the group, after the evening meal. "You are tired this evening," Nekhare said. "Quiet."

She nodded.

"Come here." Nekhare took her by the shoulders and turned her so that she could lie down on her back, with her head resting on his thigh. He brushed away a strand of hair from across her face. She studied the night sky, as dark as velvet and sprinkled with bright stars.

"And you are upset about not finding … whatever it was that you were looking for."

Jo thought for a moment. "I'm not sure what I expected to find out there, but I'd hoped to find some clue, something to indicate why or how I was sent here."

"I'm sorry."

"For what?"

"I've not been able to help you. I've sent out queries, but always, I've been careful. The *medjai* report to me daily with details about strangers who are visiting our kingdom. Visitors from Greece, the Far East … wherever. But everyone has a legitimate reason for being here. No one is looking for a girl."

"I know. I know. I don't blame you for anything. The people who brought me here have forgotten me, for sure." She was thinking about Foster and the old man, still wondering about their role in her adventure, wondering whether she would ever find out why she had been sent to ancient Egypt. *Maybe I'll never know.*

"Think about this: perhaps you are better off here, in Kemet. If your family has not bothered to look for you—"

"I don't have much family," she interrupted. "Just my mother."

Nekhare picked up a piece of her hair, much lightened now by exposure to the Kemetan sun. He wrapped it around his finger. "Someday you'll tell me everything."

"Yes," she answered, thinking the opposite—and then wondering about it. Would she ever be able to tell Nekhare *everything*?

He continued to play with her hair; the fire crackled, and laughter erupted from the men. After a while she said, "None of that matters anyway. I think … I think I was sent here to stay."

"Would that be such an awful thing?"

She smiled up at him. "No, it wouldn't," she said.

She wanted to explain about the way she had felt at home—lonely and out of place—but the right words wouldn't come. No matter what had happened … what was happening … between Nekhare and her, there was still no way to explain who she was or how she had arrived in Kemet, at least not yet.

"I am not yet ready for sleep. Shall I tell you a story?" he asked.

Storytelling, Jo had learned, was an important pastime in Kemet, and on this night, she just wanted Nekhare to keep talking. She wanted to hear the sound of his voice and know that she was not alone.

"Okay."

"Do you know the story of Osiris and Isis?" he asked.

"I read about them in school, I think. Or copied the story from one of Sinuhe's scrolls." They both laughed. "Tell me your version?"

Osiris and Isis were husband and wife, and Osiris brought civilization to Kemet. Osiris had a jealous, evil brother named Seth. Seth and his followers obtained his brother's exact measurements and built a beautiful and desirable wooden chest, into which only his brother could fit. He invited his brother to a party and offered the chest as a gift to whoever could fit into it, but of course, the only person who could was Osiris. As soon as Osiris squeezed into the chest, Seth nailed it shut and poured molten lead into the cracks so Osiris would have no air to breathe. Osiris died, but in his death he became ruler of the West, the afterworld. Seth threw the coffin into the Nile, and it floated out to sea, eventually landing in Byblos.

When Isis discovered what had happened to her husband, she set out to recover his body. Eventually she found the coffin and prepared the body for burial, but Seth discovered it and hacked his brother's body into fourteen pieces, scattering them about Kemet. Isis found every piece, reassembled her dead husband, and brought him back to life with some of her own magic.

Shortly after, Osiris and Isis gave birth to their son, Horus. Horus became Pharaoh, and he fought a battle with Seth to avenge his father. He defeated his uncle, thus returning harmony to all of Kemet.

"And so it is now the pharaoh's duty to restore harmony, to maintain *Ma'at*, at all times," Jo chimed in, repeating what she had learned in Sinuhe's class.

"No easy task in these treacherous times." Jo was so engrossed in Nekhare and his story that she didn't hear Tutankhamun approach until he spoke. She sat up quickly; both of them struggled to their feet.

"Sit," the pharaoh said, waving away formality. They did as he commanded, and he sat across from them.

Jo's nervousness grew.

"That was an impressive display of horsemanship out there today," Tutankhamun said to her. "Tell me how a young girl like yourself learns to handle horses as well as you do."

"I … learned to ride horses … in my homeland," she said.

"Your homeland," echoed the king matter-of-factly. He stared at her, and again she had the feeling he was x-raying her. "And just where would that be? Your homeland, I mean."

She gulped. She glanced at Nekhare, who sat as if he'd been turned to stone. Tutankhamun continued to stare, his dark eyes boring through her.

Careful …

"You are not from the palace at Akhetaten, as you would like for me to believe. No princess of my father's palace would have been trained to handle a horse like that. This alone would be enough to lead me to believe that you are no member of my family, even if that information hadn't already arrived by messenger many weeks ago."

Busted. I knew it. As much as she fought against it, a tear worked its way from the corner of her eye.

"Surely you must have known that I would attempt to confirm your story. It was a simple matter to send a message to Akhetaten. Long ago, a courier delivered a reply: there has never been a Princess Johenaten in Akhetaten. In fact, my dear uncle never even had a second wife. And you," he turned his glare on Nekhare, "have abused my trust in you."

"No! It was not his fault!" Jo exclaimed. "I tricked him. It is my lie, not his."

Tutankhamun paused. "Your loyalty is admirable, but Nekhare is too smart to be easily fooled," he replied. "And if he's not as smart as I thought he was, he should not be working for the palace as a royal scribe. So, I ask again: who are you, and where do you come from? Are you a spy, perhaps, for some Hittite king?"

"No! I didn't even know what a Hittite king was until a few weeks ago! I'm just … a girl. My name is Jo," she replied quietly, "and I come from a land far away. It's called America." She felt Nekhare tense beside her.

"America? I have never heard of such a place."

"I know. That is why I have lied to you all. There are things I don't know how to explain, but you have to believe me," she pleaded. "I meant no harm."

The pharaoh continued to appraise her; Nekhare said nothing.

"I could have helped. Why not come to me and tell me the truth?" asked Tutankhamen, finally.

Nekhare spoke up then. "We wanted to, but before we could get a private audience with you, Horemheb discovered Jo—"

"And you lied to him."

"Yes."

"Then *that* is how it is. Once you had made up your story for Horemheb, you did not feel safe in confiding in me. You decided that I was powerless—not able to handle my own general."

"I planned to tell you, but the time never seemed right. And we have been so busy—"

"You lied again to get me to bring you to the temple," Tutankhamun said to Jo, cutting Nekhare short. "What is it you expected to find out here? What is it that you want?"

"Want? Nothing. I have already been given everything I need. I thought I might return home someday, that I might find some clues out at the temple as to how I came to Kemet, because that is where my … captors … left me."

"And?"

"There were no clues, and whatever happened in the past … well, it just doesn't matter. I know now that this is where I am meant to stay, that this is where I *want* to stay." She looked at Nekhare and then back at Tutankhamun, and she knew it was true.

The pharaoh let the pause grow long. Finally he said, "What we have said here tonight must remain between the three of us. Is that clear?" Tutankhamun glared at them through narrowed eyes.

They nodded.

"And this I say to both of you: do not so much as attempt to hide anything from me ever again. Horemheb is not Pharaoh; I am. There is enough subterfuge in this kingdom without the two of you conspiring against me. We must stick together, the three of us and Ankesenamun. If I can count on your loyalty, then you can count on mine."

Jo was speechless for only about the second time in her life.

"*Is that clear?*"

"Yes, Your Highness," Nekhare and Jo responded in unison.

"One more thing." The king directed his attention back to Jo. "My old friend, Sinuhe, is impressed with the speed with which you have learned the hieroglyphs. He calls you 'quite remarkable.' I have decided that you will serve as a royal scribe. Report to me on the first morning after we return to the palace." Tutankhamun rose and strode away, leaving Jo staring in astonishment and feeling like she had just escaped the executioner.

"*America?*" Nekhare asked when he had recovered. She nodded. He was angry.

"I'm not trying to keep secrets from you," she fibbed. "It's just that little bits and pieces of information come floating back to me sometimes. You know everything that there is to know about me: I'm smart. I can ride a horse and shoot an arrow reasonably straight. I was stolen from my home and brought to Kemet, but I don't know how or why. I was born in America in the state … kingdom … of Florida. Not that any of that matters." She sighed. This was a strategy that had worked for her in the past: pretend to be traumatized to the point of selective memory loss.

Nekhare continued to pout.

"My mother's name is Jennifer, and my father's is William."

"You said there was just you and your mother."

"I haven't seen my father in a very long time."

"He went to war?"

"Yes. War with my mother."

She wiggled up close to where Nekhare sat, cross-legged, in the cool grass, put her cheek on his shoulder, and wrapped her arms around his waist. "Maybe someday I will tell you everything—all that I can remember, at least. But for right now, isn't it enough that we are here together?" She looked up at him and smiled. "Some greater force—say it was the gods, if you like—brought us together. No matter how improbable the circumstances may be, the simple truth is that we are here together now, and I love the way I feel when your arms are wrapped around me."

Nekhare smiled back, his anger visibly dissipated. "And somehow we have managed to obtain the blessings of Pharaoh Tutankhamun, despite the fact that we committed crimes for which others have been severely punished. I wonder what the pharaoh is doing."

"What do you mean?"

"Well, just that we got off very lightly, don't you think? But you are right—let's not worry about any of that right now. The night grows cool. Let's go find a place to sleep that is closer to the fire."

Tutankhamun tossed and turned on his cot.

Perhaps it was the lack of amenities that kept him awake, for he had refused to bring along the cadre of servants required to construct a kingly bedroom. His father, on the other hand, would have demanded the construction of an entire suite, complete with carpet and oversized bed, just for one night's stay. Akhenaten would have had his bed checked for scorpions and his food tasted for poison.

But Tutankhamun was not like his father. That was a point the young pharaoh wanted to make exceedingly clear, so he slept on the narrow cot while a minimum of guards watched his door. He brought no servants, carried his own equipment, and withstood the sun just like his men did, without the benefit of shade-bearing slaves. He would not turn into the weak, insipid man his father had been. He would be like his grandfather, the great warrior Amenhotep—proud, strong, and independent.

And Tutankhamun feared neither the scorpions nor the snakes because he did not fear death.

The afterlife would be a far better place, free from the machinations of mortal life on earth. The gods would cast him into eternity when the time was right. Until then he would bear the burden they had placed upon his shoulders. He would rule Kemet and lead her to her rightful glory.

The night grew long, and still the young pharaoh could not sleep. Had he been at home, he might have braved a swim in one of the pools or perhaps worked the night away in his office. Why waste time tossing and turning in bed when there were contracts to be reviewed and verses to be written? But he was not at home; he was condemned, instead, to a restless night. He could try to sneak past the guards—he'd become very adept at that—perhaps hike to the cliffs at Meretsega to watch the sunrise, but Tutankhamun suspected that Nankti had a careful eye on the door.

And truthfully, it was not the lack of a better bed that kept the young pharaoh awake. No, it was the girl who kept him tossing and turning, the fair-haired girl who had been living in his palace for half a year. She had *lied* to him, and so had Nekhare. The idea was almost incomprehensible. He should have had them both executed.

So much for childhood friends; Nekhare had yet to prove his loyalty. Yes, he was good at writing verse and figuring sums, and he'd proven himself a skilled warrior on the practice field. But whose side would he be on when *everything* was on the line? *His own, no doubt.*

Still, Tutankhamun couldn't help feeling intrigued by the girl. She wasn't who she had claimed to be, but she could read and write, she could handle a horse, and according to Nekhare, she was a deadeye shot with a bow and arrow. And she was beautiful, exotic even. Had he noticed that before?

More intriguing still was Sinuhe's insane idea that the two of them, Pharaoh Tutankhamun and Princess Johenamun, were destined to accomplish great things together, that their fate was somehow entwined.

Sinuhe was the wisest man in all of Kemet.

And sometimes he was nothing but a crazy old fool.

The next morning dawned bright and clear, and the pharaoh and his party returned to the temple.

Jo took with her the blanket she had brought to sleep under, and she made a great show of spreading it in the sand near the stairway into the temple. There she sat for most of the day, moving to stay in the partial shade, glad to have a jug of water this time. Not one of Tutankhamun's party missed seeing her there, so they didn't think it odd when she packed her blanket and carried it back to the campsite at el Sedu.

Inside the blanket was Foster's book. She had managed to hide it at a point during the day when no one was paying her any attention. She wasn't sure why she wanted it—after all, it was useless—but she took it with her anyway.

Later in the evening, after a light dinner of bread and cheese, Jo and Nekhare sat together once again, as the others in the party gathered around the campfire.

"Nekhare, do you have any idea what Tutankhamun has planned for me when we get back to the palace?"

"No. He hasn't said anything other than the fact that you will be a scribe. Of course, there are thousands of jobs for scribes. We'll just have to wait and see."

"I was thinking I'd like to take my towel back to the palace when we go."

"Your what?"

"My towel. You know, that thing I was wearing when you first saw me. Do you think you could find it?" she asked.

"Yes," replied Nekhare. "But you must keep it out of sight."

"Of course."

He asked, "Why do you want it anyway?"

"I don't know … just a keepsake, I guess. A memory from my other life."

She returned to the palace with Foster's book and her sand-covered pink towel stuffed into her drawstring bag.

CHAPTER 11

Jo sat upright in bed. The morning sun radiated through the narrow windows and filled the room with yellow warmth, but her body went as cold as the glare in Horemheb's eyes. Something was nagging at her, felt really wrong, but what?

She rolled over in her bed, pulled the coverlet over her head, and tried to shake off the feeling. The pharaoh knew her secret, at least some of it. He had granted her permission to stay in the palace. More than that, he had as much as given her his seal of approval. She was in love; all was right with the world, right?

Then she remembered. *King Tut is going to die.* Ever since she had arrived in Egypt, she'd been so concerned with her own welfare that she had almost forgotten about his early demise. She was living through well-researched history. This was Tutankhamun's real life.

Soon he would die a real death.

What would happen if—when—Pharaoh Tutankhamun died? She was living in the palace as Princess Johenamun because he had permitted it, ordered it. Would the next pharaoh be as generous? Probably not.

And there was something else that Jo discovered on the trip to Medinet Habu. Tutankhamun was a real person, not just the Boy King. She had sailed up the Nile with him, ridden across the desert with him, and watched him in command at Medinet Habu. She'd lied to him, twice, and he had forgiven her.

She wanted him to stay alive. *He's good man. He doesn't deserve to die.*

Jo knew she was the only person in that day and time—except for the person or persons plotting his murder, if there was to be a murder—who knew he was about to die. Therefore, she was the only person who could do something about it.

But what should she do? What could she do? Tell him the whole truth? No, he'd have her thrown in the Kemetan equivalent of an insane asylum. A better approach might be to wait, watch, and listen, gain the pharaoh's trust. Then perhaps she could make her confession, help him see the danger he was in. She didn't have much time to dwell on the idea, though.

Just as they did every day, the servants arrived to help Jo through her morning routine. At breakfast she gulped down a thick chunk of coarse bread, a few dried figs, and a flask of goat's milk before hurrying off to find Nekhare.

"Has Tutankhamun been ill?" she asked when she bumped into Nekhare in the corridor.

"Ill? You saw him out at the temple. Did he look sick to you? No, Tutankhamun is quite well—at least, recently," replied Nekhare.

"What do you mean *at least, recently?*"

"Well, as a boy he was frail. You know, sick all the time. But he got over that as he grew older. Now he's in perfect health."

Lowering her voice, she asked the big question, "Nekhare, is there anyone who would want him dead?"

"Dead? Of course. You know that many would like to see him dead, or dethroned, at least. Any number of Hittite kings. Many kingdoms would benefit from a less-powerful Kemet. Any time a pharaoh dies, Kemet becomes vulnerable—especially during the mourning period and before a new pharaoh is crowned."

"I mean, anyone immediate? You know, a Kemetan? Someone with access to the king?"

"What's this all about?" Nekhare's eyes narrowed, and he stepped closer to Jo. "Do you know something that I should know? Where have all these questions come from? What have you heard?"

I was born in the twentieth century, and I just happen to know that Tutankhamun dies before his twentieth birthday. "Nothing. Forget I said anything."

"You know what Tutankhamun said about hiding anything from him. We've pushed him past normal limits. You must be careful."

"I know, I know." She sighed. "Forget I mentioned it. It was just a bad dream."

"Pharaoh is in the Hall of Audiences, and he's expecting you. You'd better go to him now."

"You're not coming with me?" Jo suddenly felt sick with panic.

"No. He has sent me on an errand. You must go alone, but why worry? He already knows the truth and has apparently decided to let us off the hook. What could possibly go wrong now?"

If you only knew, she thought as she hurried toward the Hall of Audiences. *If you only knew!*

Jo had learned about protocol and expected to wait her turn in line to see the pharaoh, but upon seeing her enter the huge throne room, Tutankhamun motioned her to the front of the line.

Immersed in her thoughts, still trying to sort out her emotions, she walked right into a wine merchant who had been pleading his case to Ankesenamun. The clay jar he carried with him hit the stone floor and shattered into a hundred tiny pieces. Red wine splattered across the tile floor.

"I'm so sorry!" Jo apologized, infinitely embarrassed. Much to her surprise, the pharaoh himself stepped down from the dais and began to help pick up the shards of pottery. It was an excuse, she realized, to speak to Jo without being heard by anyone else.

"You are much less clumsy on horseback than you are on your own two feet," said Tutankhamun in an amused whisper.

She continued to pick up the pieces without looking up.

"In fact, I've been thinking, perhaps I should have enlisted you in the cavalry instead of as a scribe. Nekhare tells me that you are a dead aim with a bow and arrow."

"You're teasing?" she responded, looking up finally, her face just inches from his.

"Yes. At least I think I am."

Just a joke between me and the king of Egypt. A servant arrived to clean up the mess; the pharaoh stood, and turned to the queen.

"Ankesenamun, Princess Johenamun is to replace Nekhbet as your personal scribe."

Ankesenamun did not look surprised.

He continued, turning to Jo. "Your personal belongings will be moved to the room adjacent to the queen's bedchamber. Make yourself accessible to her at all times. You are to help her with her personal correspondence and keep a daily log of household items delivered and used."

He paused.

"Yes, Your Highness," Jo replied.

"The queen is pregnant, as you probably know. She will need assistance preparing for the upcoming festivals. Assume whatever responsibilities you can in order to lighten her burden."

"Of course, Your Highness." Jo glanced at the queen, who sat motionless on her throne. *This won't be easy*, Jo thought.

Tutankhamun continued. "Nekhare will provide you with any supplies you need, and he will be on hand to answer any questions you might have. I understand that your schooling is not complete, but the Great Royal Wife's personal scribe has taken ill. Your gender and your lineage make you perfect for this assignment, especially since Meritaken appears to have no interest in learning the necessary hieroglyphs."

So he has not told Ankesenamun that I lied.

"Any questions?" he asked.

"No, Your Highness. And … thank you." *This is perfect*, Jo thought, as she hurried out of the room. *What better way to keep an eye on the king?*

Even though she had been in Kemet for only a few months, Jo had amassed an amazing collection of personal possessions. By order of the pharaoh himself, she had received the clothing, makeup, and jewelry befitting a princess. At any time, her tiniest whim had been satisfied by a simple request. A few more pillows for her bed? They'd been delivered immediately. A new chest to hold her growing stash of makeup and perfume? The palace carpenters had arrived to measure her room.

Needless to say, her move to new chambers required several trips by servants, directed by an always stodgy Sitamun, to transport all her personal effects. All the while, Meritaken complained about being left alone again.

"I'll be just down the hall," Jo said. "And across the garden … and down another hall." They both laughed. "Besides, you have Mahu to keep you busy." Meritaken had recently begun dating the son of the late mayor of Waset.

After everything else had been moved, Jo remembered Foster's book and her pink towel, both of which she had tucked into a basket under her bed. Returning to her old room alone, she pulled the book out and ran her fingers over the colorful cover. She opened the book to the chapter on the Great Pyramid. As she had noticed before, the pages were ruined, incomprehensible, and she couldn't help wishing that the book had not been destroyed. It might have given her something to do on quiet nights. She squinted at the muddled pages and managed to make out a few lines:

The Death of Tutankhamun:
Was It Murder?

Theories about the death of the Boy King abound. While some historians point to his frequent ill health and maintain that

and then a few more lines:

Tutankhamun died of natural causes, others are not so quick to dismiss the possibility of foul play.

Suddenly she realized that the words on the page were becoming clearer and clearer:

At the time of the Boy King's reign, Egypt was relatively unstable. For many centuries, the Egyptians had worshiped a variety of gods and had paid homage to those gods through an elaborate temple system. Priests in control of the various temples were powerful men.

Akhenaten, Tutankhamun's father, became convinced that there was only one true god, Aten. He shut down all temples that honored other gods and, in so doing, caused a huge disruption in the political system.

When Akhenaten died and the nine-year-old Tutankhamun succeeded him to the throne, Egypt was in chaos. The Boy King's advisers restored the temples and attempted to return Egypt to its former glory. As Tutankhamun grew older, chances are he would have wanted more control of Egypt, something Ay (the king's vizier) and Horemheb (the general of the armies) may not have wanted.

Tutankhamun was succeeded by Ay and then by Horemheb. It is this fact in itself that leads many to believe that the Boy King might have been murdered by either of the men.

Ay? Horemheb?
Jo could not believe her eyes. It was as if some invisible person had taken a pen to the book and was writing just for her. She continued to stare, hoping

the mysterious writer would continue, but there was no more. She flipped the pages; the rest of the book remained illegible.

The book was astounding enough on its own, and then there was the revelation that the king's most trusted men might be out to murder him. From what Jo had seen and heard up to that point, she was ready to put her money on Horemheb.

But Horemheb was in Nubia, helping the viceroy, Huy, put down a rebellion there. Jo wondered whether that meant that Tutankhamun was safe for a while. At least she'd have a chance to focus on Ay, see what she could learn about the vizier in charge of Upper Kemet.

Footsteps echoed in the hallway; the servant girls were approaching, so Jo slammed the book shut and shoved it back into the basket.

"I'll take that for you," said Sashri, reaching for the basket.

"No, it's all right," Jo said quickly. "I'll carry this one."

Just as Jo finished unpacking her things and arranging her new room, she was summoned into the queen's chambers. Their rooms were side by side and connected by a door, so Jo realized right away that she would be "on call" to the queen all hours of the day and night.

When she entered the queen's room for the first time, Ankesenamun lay draped across a chaise. Two servants stood behind, fanning the queen with huge ostrich feathers

Jo stood before her new mistress and waited, but the queen didn't say a word. "I'm ... sorry ... Your Highness. I do not understand the protocol for this. Being here, before you, in your chambers, I mean. Should I kneel?"

"Pharaoh has explained that your brain is much better than your manners. Let's hope that's true." She continued to stare at Jo with those dark eyes. Jo decided to kneel.

"No," the queen said. "Stand up."

Jo obeyed.

"You *claim* to be an Amarna princess, but here in my chambers, you are my scribe." The queen stood then, crossed her arms, and circled around Jo as if inspecting her.

"I understand, Your Highness." Jo didn't dare turn to look at her. Ankesenamun was proving to be every bit as difficult as Jo had suspected she might be.

"You must never sit unless I ask you to do so."

"Yes, Your Highness," Jo said, resisting the urge to roll her eyes.

"The servants will wake you at sunrise and prepare your bath. You may take a quick morning meal, but after that, you will report directly to me. On most mornings, we will begin our day in the Hall of Audiences, where you will record all conversation between me and those who come to speak with me. In the afternoons, you will write my personal messages." She paused.

"Yes, Your Highness," Jo said again. The Hall of Audiences was right where Jo wanted to be, and writing messages didn't seem like a difficult task. *In fact,* Jo thought, *Ankesenamun's correspondence should be interesting.*

She circled to stand in front of Jo. "Should you not perform your duties acceptably, you will be dismissed. You will *not* be sent back to your carefree life with Meritaken." She paused again. "Your loyalty is now to *me.*"

That will be the hardest part of this job.

The queen stepped closer. It was quite a dramatic show, one Jo was sure Ankesenamun had carefully orchestrated. No doubt intimidation had worked for her in the past.

"Nothing you hear or see in these chambers leaves these chambers. Any questions?"

"No, Your Highness." *Not yet.*

"Good. My correspondence needs catching up. Let's see if you're as good as Nekhare and Tutankhamun think you are." She paused. "You may sit over there." She pointed to a large desk in one corner of the room. The desk faced out into the room, positioned so that when Jo sat behind it, she had a view of the entire room, the balcony, and the blue sky beyond.

Jo found a basket of blank scrolls on the floor next to her seat, and several long feather pens lay across the desk.

Ankesenamun dismissed the servants. "Let's get to work," she said.

For the next hour, Ankesenamun paced back and forth in front of the desk, dictating letters that Jo transcribed verbatim. Occasionally, she paused in search of the correct word or phrase, and Jo waited patiently.

Ankesenamun's mail was not interesting at all, at least not on this day, so Jo's mind wandered. She thought about her trip to Medinet Habu, Foster's unusual book, and her conversation with the pharaoh. She thought about Nekhare and the possibility of spending the rest of her life with him. Most of all, she thought about the impending death of the pharaoh.

It had all been completely irrelevant to Jo while she sat, bored to tears, in social studies class. Who cared how old the Boy King was when he died? She certainly hadn't. She had been only mildly curious about his fate since arriving in Kemet. But now she could hear Foster's question repeating in her head, over and over again, like one of her mother's old, scratched records with the needle stuck.

Did he die of natural causes, or was he murdered?

CHAPTER 12

Jo stepped onto the balcony and into the first rays of the morning light. It was her favorite time of day, before the palace was fully awake, before the garden beneath her balcony was overrun with gardeners and water bearers. At this very moment, Tutankhamun would be in the family shrine, paying formal homage to the sun and administering the daily rites; that was part of his duty as pharaoh. In an hour or so, the queen would also arise and say the ritual prayers, these to Hathor, goddess of pregnancy and childbirth.

Over the last few months, since she had become the queen's personal scribe, Jo had adopted her own form of homage to the sun. She began every day on her balcony, devoting a full fifteen minutes to watching the sun rise and listing out loud all those things for which she was most grateful.

Yes, *grateful* was the best word to describe how she felt about her new life in Kemet. At first she had been stunned, then angry, and then accepting, but now she was simply happy—for the first time in her life.

Her list of things she was thankful for had grown long, but on this day she concluded with, "I am grateful for the miracle of the sunrise every morning and for the orchids that bloom outside my window."

As a scribe, Jo had indeed been as good as promised, and the queen's office had never been so efficient or so well organized. Ankesenamun delegated more and more responsibilities to her. In fact, it was Jo and not the queen who now worked closely with Sitamun to manage the household. Jo didn't mind; in fact, with every new responsibility, and with every new day, she felt more vital and more alive.

And as Jo's star had risen, so had Nekhare's. There had been informal conversation, Jo knew, about appointing him heir to the pharaoh. Who would become heir was a dilemma that continued to plague Tutankhamun, as he had no living siblings. He and Ankesenamun had suffered two stillbirths, and the queen's health during this pregnancy had not been optimal. The palace—the entire kingdom—nervously awaited the birth of her baby. If the king had no children, Nekhare was the pharaoh's closest living male relative and the one most likely to inherit the throne.

I might be queen one day, Jo thought. And then she shrugged off the idea. No, if Nekhare became pharaoh, he would undoubtedly marry Ankesenamun to solidify his right to the crown—not that two wives was at all unusual in Kemet.

But no matter. Jo's desire, first and foremost, was to see Pharaoh Tutankhamun live a long, full life and continue to rule Kemet. He was a good man, and he deserved that much. Kemet deserved that much. Even though she had come to this land with a vague knowledge of his early demise, Jo could not see any signs of his death in his future. He was healthy, strong, and well protected at all times. Horemheb was still in Nubia, and Ay seemed far too grandfatherly ever to harm Tutankhamun.

Jo was beginning to wonder whether her time travel hadn't somehow changed the course of history. Perhaps her appearance in Kemet had guaranteed Tutankhamun's safety. Stranger things had happened.

She heard a quiet knock, and her servants entered. Jo selected a few grapes from the tray that they provided. She would be bathed, groomed, and meticulously dressed before Ankesenamun even got out of bed.

Soon Jo was on her way to the kitchen, toward the rear of the palace, where she would consult with the head cook to plan the meals for the day. She needed to oversee an inventory of the clay bowls used to serve meals and be prepared to place an order with the potter later in the afternoon.

Early in the evening, Nekhare and Jo walked out to the archery range. She'd been practicing with a larger bow, the type used in battle. It was made from laminated strips of wood, and it could send an arrow twice as far as the bows she had first used. The composite bow required a great deal of strength to operate, so Nekhare devised a set of exercises to build her arm strength. He arranged for instructors from the pharaoh's chariot corps to teach her proper stance, bowstring tension, and how to judge the angle of flight. Her progress had been remarkable.

Women of the royal family didn't normally learn to shoot. As a matter of fact, no one could remember the last time one had, so Jo's abilities were garnering much attention. Quite routinely, the pharaoh's best archers came out to challenge her, and quite routinely, she beat them.

Tutankhamun had even watched her take target practice.

Around the palace, people were connecting her name with the word *warrior*.

"I want to learn to shoot from a chariot," Jo had said, so Nekhare had ordered up a chariot. It had arrived one night in a cloud of dust. The charioteers demonstrated the procedure; one man drove while the other shot, held in place by a leather strap.

First she learned to drive, a relatively simple task because she knew horses so well. She was not at all afraid of the pharaoh's huge stallions, and the horses sensed that. Then Nekhare drove while Jo, securely fastened in, attempted her first few shots from a moving vehicle.

It wasn't long before she was regularly hitting the targets.

This particular evening, the air hung heavy with a sweet scent that Jo couldn't readily identify. Before she had a chance to ask about the aroma and its source, the chariots arrived. The charioteers were practicing a sophisticated military maneuver involving multiple chariots and several targets when Tutankhamun appeared on the scene. He brought the entire group to a halt just by raising his hand.

"Nekhare, is this not, perhaps, too dangerous a maneuver for Princess Johenamun?" the pharaoh asked.

Nekhare laughed. "Dangerous only for the targets, Your Highness, or anything else that gets in her way."

Tutankhamun nodded, and the drill resumed. A few minutes later, the pharaoh stopped them again.

"I would like to trade places with that bowman," he said, pointing to one of his men. The man jumped from the chariot, and the pharaoh belted himself into position.

"A challenge," he yelled to Jo. "Best shot, two out of three."

The drivers slapped the reins against their horses' rumps, and the chariots circled the field. Two more chariots circled from the opposite direction. All four drivers loosed their arrows at the same time. One of the pharaoh's men checked the targets.

"Closest to the mark," yelled the man, "is Pharaoh Tutankhamun's arrow!"

Jo rolled her eyes. Nekhare sent the horse into a gallop again.

"Closest to the mark," began the soldier, "ah … I'm afraid she's beat you this time, Your Highness."

Tutankhamun smiled. "This will decide it, then."

The horses were off, making their wide sweep of the field. Jo nocked her arrow as they approached the target, determined to beat Tutankhamun at the game, but before she could loose the arrow, she found herself spinning, tumbling out of control.

She woke up with several of the pharaoh's men standing over her. Before too long, Nekhare and Tutankhamun were kneeling beside her.

"Don't get up," ordered the pharaoh.

"I … I … I think I'm fine," Jo said.

"Send for the doctors," Tutankhamun said quietly to one of the men.

"No, really, I'm not hurt," Jo said. She tried to sit up, but the pharaoh held her shoulder to the ground.

"You will lie here until the doctors arrive," said Tutankhamun firmly.

Jo looked up at the dozen or so men who were gathered around them, and she understood his tone. The pharaoh had given her an order, and his men were watching.

"Yes, Your Highness," she replied.

Tutankhamun strode away, but he had only gone a short distance when he turned and said, "By the way, I win."

"This time!" she yelled after him. She saw Tutankhamun smiling as he left the field.

A whole team of doctors arrived and confirmed what Jo already knew: she had a few bumps and bruises but no breaks.

"The strap broke," said Nekhare.

"No kidding. By the way, what is that odor I've been smelling all night?"

He drew a deep breath. "Ah, yes. That would be the perfumed oil factory. There," he said, pointing northward, "a short ride up the river. The wind must be blowing just right tonight."

"I want my mother's sarcophagus moved from Amarna," Tutankhamun said.

The evening had grown long, and all the major players were still gathered in the pharaoh's chambers: Tutankhamun, Ay, Pentju the vizier of Lower Egypt, Nekhare, and several other military types whose names all sounded alike to Jo—older men who looked as if they'd seen one too many battles. The meeting had begun upon their return from the archery range, and Jo attended in place of the queen who was feeling too worn out.

"We've discussed this before," replied Ay. "You know that I agree with you in essence. But it would be unwise to move Kiya's body to the Valley of the Kings at this time. Better to leave her in Amarna until we have completely distanced ourselves from the Aten."

Jo could see another power struggle brewing, one that could take them well into the night.

"No. The city crumbles, and with it, my mother's tomb," insisted Tutankhamun.

Ay said, "Your mother will always be thought of as Akhenaten's wife. The people would think it heresy to move her—"

"I understand that. My father was not popular, and the people of the Upper Kingdom do not want to be reminded of him or his wives; I have heard that before. But my mother had nothing to do with the Cult of the Aten. I want her buried near where I will spend eternity. I have that right. *She* has that right. After all, she is the mother of a pharaoh."

"We understand," Ay tried again, "but—"

"It is so ordered," the king declared. "Nekhare, send a message to Maya right away. Is he still in Memphis?"

"Yes, I believe so. His last letter, delivered yesterday, was carried from there."

"Perfect. Send these instructions to him: on his journey upriver, he will stop at Amarna and retrieve my mother's sarcophagus from her tomb."

"Yes, Your Highness."

"Might I at least recommend discretion?" This from Pentju.

"What do you mean?" asked Tutankhamun.

"Have Maya remove her cartouche from the sarcophagus and any other burial materials before they leave Amarna. No one need know whose body is being moved. Maya can be trusted; you counted on that when you appointed him Overseer of Royal Building. And even if some people put two and two together, the removal of your mother's name from her funeral possessions may lessen the offense."

"It seems like a good compromise," Tutankhamun said.

Jo kept thinking about Foster's book and what it said about Horemheb and Ay. Would they grow tired of taking orders from a teenager, even a royal one?

Jo returned to the queen's chambers and found her surrounded by servants, priests, and midwives. They had removed her wig, scrubbed her unmercifully, and dressed her for bed. Then the priests, shaved bald for cleanliness and dressed in long white robes, took over, muttering incantations designed to appease the goddesses of pregnancy and childbirth, Isis and Hathor. They lit dozens of pots of incense, stinking up the room and making the queen cough. Just an average evening for the queen, Jo realized.

Jo read the look on Ankesenamun's face; she just wanted them all to go away.

"Leave," Jo commanded all those in the room.

They turned to look at Jo, and then they continued their attentions to the queen.

"No, I mean it. I said *leave*."

They looked to Ankesenamun, and she waved them off. When they had gone, the queen laid back on her pillows, her long black hair in startling contrast to the sun-bleached linens.

"What was the meeting about?" she asked. She had long ago given up trying to intimidate Jo; instead, the two of them had become cautious allies.

"More discussion of Kiya's tomb."

"Oh, that again. I'm glad I didn't go. Did Tutankhamun get his way?"

"Yes," Jo replied. "The old guys finally caved."

The queen smiled. "I am glad for him, then."

"Your Highness," Jo said, "you need your rest. What you don't need is to worry about such matters. You also don't need those priests hovering over you and keeping you awake."

"The goddesses need proper appeasement, Johenamun, so that my baby will be born healthy."

"The goddesses have nothing to do with it."

Ankesenamun gasped.

"Did the priests perform these rituals with your other two pregnancies?"

"Of course," the queen replied. There was a long silence. "Are you saying that there is no hope? No way to ensure that my baby is healthy? And how do you claim to know anything about having babies at all? You have certainly never been pregnant."

"That's true," Jo said. "But my mother ... back in my homeland ... she is a nurse, and I have often heard her talk about caring for pregnant women."

The queen motioned for Jo to sit on the edge of her bed. "And if your mother were here, Johenamun, what would she advise?"

"She'd tell you to get plenty of exercise and lots of rest. She'd tell you to eat well—more than you do—and never to drink beer or wine. Milk or water only."

The queen smiled, too tired for comment. Jo blew out the candles that had been placed around her chamber, and returned to the bedside.

"Your Highness?"

"Yes?" Her reply was sleepy, her eyes heavy.

"Tell me about Ay?"

"What about him?"

"Is he loyal to Tutankhamun?"

Jo's question surprised the queen; her eyes popped open. "Of course."

"How can you be so sure?"

"Because that's just who he is. His family—the Akhmim—they were Akhenaten's most loyal supporters."

"That doesn't necessarily mean—"

"He has taken the oath. He would die before he would see any harm come to his king."

"And what about Horemheb? Does Ay get along with him?"

The queen laughed. "Ay detests Horemheb. Remember on that first day, when Horemheb called you a lowborn imposter'? Well, I laughed because that's what Ay always calls Horemheb. He is nothing but a soldier who got lucky, who woke up one day and found he'd become general."

"But Horemheb has the support of the armies?"

"Yes, so we must always be cautious ..." She was drifting off to sleep, so Jo made sure to ask one more question.

"Ankesenamun, did Horemheb take that same oath?"

She nodded.

Jo moved a few pillows from the bed and put out the candle by the bedside.

CHAPTER 13

Jo woke to the usual tap, tap, tap on her door and rose just as the servants entered with her bathwater. They had already completed her bath and were almost done with her hair when Nekhare made an unusual early-morning appearance. Startled, she waved off the last of the servants. Nekhare crossed the room and stood near the door of the balcony.

"Ankesenamun has asked me to tell you that she will not go to the Hall of Audiences this morning. You are free to conduct whatever business you deem necessary."

"Is she all right?" asked Jo. "The baby?"

"She's fine. Don't worry. It's just that Tutankhamun is ... will not be working this morning, so she has decided to rest." Nekhare fidgeted with his wristbands.

"What's going on?" Jo asked, realizing how unusual it was for the pharaoh not to report to the Hall first thing in the morning.

"Tutankhamun is not in his bedchamber."

"What?" Jo asked, panicking.

"He's nowhere to be found."

"You don't know where he is?"

"I don't know, exactly. I told Nankti and Ay that he is not feeling well, but the truth is, he is not in his chambers. I had to do some fast talking to keep Nankti out of there. Ay wanted to call in the doctors—"

"Aren't you worried about him?" Jo interrupted.

"No, I suspect he's gone off to clear his head a bit. He does that once in a while. If he's not back before nightfall ... well, then we'll worry."

"How did he get out without the palace guards noticing him?"

"He has his ways. I'm off to cancel his appointments. I'll see you later."

All kinds of horrible scenarios ran through Jo's head, the most obvious being that Tutankhamun had been kidnapped or murdered—or both. What should she do? Find Nankti and Ay and tell them the truth, that the pharaoh was missing? No, she couldn't do that unless she was willing to make Nekhare very, very angry. And if Tutankhamun was really just off "clearing his head," then he would be upset with her as well.

Should I go next door, ask Ankesenamun what she thinks? No, probably not a good idea to upset the queen, considering her condition.

All she could do was wait and worry, and pray that Pharaoh Tutankhamun returned to the palace safely. In the meantime, she would have to find a way to stay busy, something to occupy her mind.

After a quick breakfast, Jo had a groom saddle one of the horses. Tutankhamun had given her permission to use his stable of horses as if they were her own and to leave the palace grounds whenever she wanted. This, Jo knew, was a great compliment—Tutankhamun's way of saying that he trusted her and believed in her ability to take care of herself. Staying out of the city for the most part, she spent hours galloping through the desert on the outskirts of town, feeling freer than she ever had in her life.

Riding was tough in Kemetan clothing: the tunics were too tight, and the more formal dresses had too much material that ended up wound all around her. So she had drawn some sketches for the palace dressmakers, and they had whipped up some baggy pants and sleeveless tops. Jo's new riding wardrobe was scandalous by Kemetan standards, but it worked for her.

On that particular morning, she rode north along the Nile, until she came upon a hubbub of activity that could only be, by the smell, Pharaoh's scented oil production. Curious, Jo urged her horse closer.

The workers, men dressed in the usual loincloths, stopped what they were doing. Some stared, and others made as if to kneel; they could tell that Jo was part of the royal family, after all, she was riding a horse whose gear bore the pharaoh's cartouche. But clearly they were confused by Jo's unconventional and unannounced appearance.

She waited for someone to speak.

No one did.

Finally, she asked, "Who is in charge here?"

An older man came forward. "I am."

"Please send your men back to work," Jo said as she slid down from the horse. "Will you show me around?"

"Of course." He issued a sharp command, and the men snapped back into action.

"What is your name?"

"I am Wanankh," he replied. "Maker of the Royal Bath Oils. Permission to ask a question?"

"Certainly."

"We have just been inspected by the pharaoh's men. Why does he send yet another to check on our work?"

"Tutankhamun didn't send me. I was just … curious."

He stared at her, clearly puzzled.

"I was just out for a ride, and I saw your operation," Jo said, suddenly feeling a little bit foolish. She lowered her voice and spoke directly to Wanankh. "I don't remember seeing oil production in Akhetaten—"

"Ah, you are Princess Johenamun." He nodded, as if that cleared up all confusion.

Jo blushed, wondering what he had heard about her. "I'm sorry. I didn't introduce myself. And I see that I am interrupting your work. Maybe I should leave—"

"Please," said Wanankh. The last thing he needed was for the princess to go back to the palace and report that he had been anything less than accommodating. "I will show you everything."

As it turned out, she could have done without seeing how the oils were extracted from dead hippopotami, but the rest of the process was interesting. The workers boiled the oil in huge kettles and added various quantities of blossoms and spices. Once the fragrant odors seeped into the oil, it was cooled and forced through linen bags to clean it.

"This is Tutankhamun's favorite scent," Wanankh said. "It's made with iris roots, flowers of the henna bush, and cinnamon." He wafted a bottle under her nose. Jo smiled politely but was thinking of something else.

"You know, if you could get some lye, you'd have a soap-making plant here," she said. Jo had studied soap making for a project on colonial America at her old school.

"Lye? Soap? I don't understand."

"Soap is a substance used … elsewhere … to clean the body. It's made with oil, fragrances, and lye. Lye can be made from the ashes of wood. I can show you how."

"But I don't understand."

"Trust me; you're going to be popular with Tutankhamun—even more so with the Great Royal Wife."

She spent the rest of the morning carefully detailing soap-making to an increasingly interested Wanankh. By the time she left, she had his promise to send her an experimental batch.

She returned to the palace to find that Tutankhamun had reappeared. Jo met him in the hall outside Ankesenamun's room, but she knew it would be inappropriate for her to ask where he had been.

"Ankesenamun has been asking for you," he said, without any explanation of his own whereabouts.

"She said she didn't need me today," Jo explained. "I went out for a ride."

"Apparently she has changed her mind." Much to Jo's surprise, Pharaoh Tutankhamun rolled his eyes. "You had better get in there."

Jo pushed open the door. The queen was draped across her chaise, complaining of the heat, while a bevy of servants tried to cool her with huge ostrich feathers. Two young girls rubbed the queen's swollen feet with oils, and another pair stood nearby with platters of fruit and cheese.

"There you are," the queen said as Jo entered. "See if you can organize this chaos." She swept her hand in front of her to indicate that she was not happy with the services being provided. "And then sit with me awhile. Tell me where you have been this morning. Off riding again, I see."

Jo smiled and went back to work.

The wind came up later that night, and Nekhare sat at his desk, fingertips pressed together, a long scroll before him. The message demanded an immediate reply, but how to answer? He knew he was among the most privileged, that he'd already obtained almost all a man could ever want, and that in so many ways the gods had been good to him.

Soon he would ask for permission to marry Princess Johenamun, and he was sure that the pharaoh would grant his wish. This would be a disappointment to the dark-haired beauty he'd spent most of the previous night with, but that girl would just have to get used to the idea of being one of many, one of the harem that he would collect over the years. It was, after all, what powerful men did. But Jo was the girl he most needed, the one who could be of value to him in his quest for power. She was the diamond in his pile of rubies. Even the pharaoh was talking of her amazing resemblance to the warrior-queens of the past. Yes, he would marry Johenamun, and they would have many children, grow old together, and continue to enjoy all the luxuries of the palace. There had even been talk of making him heir to the throne, at least temporarily, until Tutankhamun could produce a son.

Of course, Nekhare had no desire to inherit the crown from Tutankhamun, because he did not want Tutankhamun to die. Nekhare loved his king.

But then again, he had always wanted to be king.

On the other side of the palace, the wind howled through the narrow windows in Jo's room and woke her from a fitful sleep.

She hadn't meant to fall asleep at all, but now she continued the work she'd been doing when she had dozed off. She propped herself on her bed with a scroll and quill. She had begun keeping a journal, which she kept hidden in the basket under her bed with Foster's book. In it she recorded the events of each day and any tidbits of information that might help her solve the murder of the king before it actually happened.

If it happened.

She made a list of possible suspects.

The candle at her bedside had not burned low, leading Jo to believe that the hour was still young. Suddenly, it sputtered and went out.

She found the candle, groping in the dark, and relit it from the torches in the hallway. "Is there a problem?" asked the guard on duty outside her door.

"No, I've got it under control."

She went back to her journal, but the candle continued to flicker, casting strange shadows on the walls. She couldn't dismiss the feeling of uneasiness that had come over her. Was it just the wind? The shadows on the wall?

What had she been dreaming about, anyway?

She closed her eyes and tried to recall her dream. *The king is dead.* She could still see his cold, ashen face. *Nubia.* She'd dreamed that Tutankhamun had died on the battlefield in Nubia. Perhaps it was some kind of premonition; stranger things had happened.

In truth, Horemheb was still there, and Tutankhamun was planning to sail south to meet him. It would be his first military campaign.

I've got to talk to Nekhare. I'll confess everything if I have to, but we have to figure a way to keep Tutankhamun from going to Nubia.

Cracking the bedchamber door, she peeked out. The guard had moved down the hallway; the servants had not yet extinguished the torches. Encouraged, she made her way down the stairs, across the garden, and down the long hall toward Nekhare's quarters.

His candle still burns. He is awake. The door hung open, but as Jo approached, she realized that Nekhare was not alone.

"Take this message straight away to Piay, high priest at Karnak. He is expecting you."

"Yes, sir," replied a voice—a young boy.

"And make sure you are not seen or heard. I swear; if you are seen by anyone, you will not live to see the light of day. Is that clear?"

"Yes, sir."

"Be off now. Report back to me at once upon your return to the palace. Shut the door on your way out."

"Yes, sir."

Jo ducked into a darkened alcove as the young boy slipped from the room. *What the hell was that all about?*

Confused and frightened, she hurried from Nekhare's door, unsure of where she was going, just going. She flew through the garden, her bare feet pounding along the sandy path. She threw open the wooden door at the entrance to the royal wing and scurried inside.

Pulling the doors shut, she turned and ran smack into Tutankhamun, who caught her by both shoulders to keep himself from being plowed over.

"What are you doing out at this hour in this weather?" Jo saw him take in her disheveled appearance.

"I … couldn't sleep. The wind woke me, frightened me. I thought I'd see if anyone else was awake."

"Any luck?"

"Just you," she lied.

Tutankhamun laughed. "Just me. I'll try not to be offended."

Jo blushed.

"Why don't you come in and sit a while? We haven't had many opportunities to talk."

The last thing Jo wanted to do at this moment was have any conversation with the king. She wanted to get back to her own room to sort out everything she'd overheard while eavesdropping at Nekhare's door, but no one ignored an invitation from the pharaoh.

He led her down the hallway into the office that adjoined his chambers and motioned for her to take a seat in front of his desk.

On this evening, he wore a white tunic and a panther skin draped over his shoulders to protect him from the chill. Jo shivered, and he took another animal skin from the chair in the corner of the room and wrapped it around her.

"Does the wind not blow on winter nights in America?"

She just sat there, staring back at him, stunned by the intimacy of his gesture.

"The wind. You said you were frightened by the wind."

"Oh, right. We have horrible storms, actually. I was just … spooked."

"Spooked? Afraid, you mean? You? I won't let word get around. It wouldn't be good for that warrior-princess image you're cultivating."

"Your Highness?" She wasn't sure whether he was teasing, complimenting, or scolding.

"People are talking about the Golden Princess, who rides like the wind and shoots as well as the God-Kings." Tutankhamun stretched his long legs in front of him, rested his elbows on the arms of his chair, and continued to study Jo in a way that made her unable to think straight.

"Please forgive me, Your Highness, if I am behaving in a manner not appropriate for a member of the royal family."

Tutankhamun laughed. "Do as you like, Jo."

His use of her real name caught her by surprise.

"That is the benefit of being *Princess* Johenamun, is it not?"

"Yes, Your Highness." Jo still wasn't sure where the conversation was headed. "I'm afraid I never thanked you," she chose her words carefully, "for letting me stay."

He didn't reply but instead waited for her to continue.

"And I'm sorry for lying to you. And for dragging Nekhare and Meritaken into the whole thing. Please understand, I never meant any harm. I was desperate."

"No harm has been done," he replied quietly.

"May I ask a question?"

He nodded.

"Why did you let me stay? You let me *become* Princess Johenamun.

"Yes." He paused. "I'm not sure why. I saw something in your eyes on that very first day. That desperation you spoke of. And then, very soon after that, I realized that we were much alike, you and I."

"Us? Alike?"

"Very much so."

"I don't understand, you are—"

He cut her off. "We are both imposters. You pretend to be Princess Johenamun, and I pretend ..." He searched for the right words.

"To be content here in the Holy City?'

"Yes," he said quietly.

"While your heart remains in Akhetaten?"

"Sometimes, on nights like this," he let his head roll against the back of his chair, "I wish I could return to more carefree days."

Jo knew that he was sharing his innermost thoughts; she wasn't sure why. She found herself wishing she could be totally honest with him, tell him all about her crazy time travel. After all, he would no doubt benefit from information she could give him.

Instead she said, "We have something else in common."

"We are both good with a bow and arrow?"

She smiled. "Yes, that also. But we were both raised to believe in only one god."

He sat bolt upright in his chair. "In your kingdom they pay homage to the Aten?"

"In America people are free to worship as they please, but in my family we honor only one god who created the heavens and the earth and then created man in his own image."

"Those ideas are not so different from my father's. He wrote:

> *O great Father,*
> *Wondrous Aten,*
> *Creator of all life,*
> *He who made the earth,*
> *Who created all men.*
> *You rise each day in the East*
> *And fill our land with light.*
> *You guide us with your glorious rays,*
> *And when you rest in the West*

Only then do we, your children,
Rest.

She began to recite with him,

Our Great Pharaoh,
Son of the Aten,
In this earthly abode does rule,
And all over this great land
We sing praises to our father,
Wondrous Aten.

Tutankhamun stared at her in amazement.

"I remember that prayer from Sinuhe's class."

"Sinuhe taught that to you?"

"He gave it to me one day when I finished early. I have a ... an ability to remember things I only see once," Jo said, avoiding the term *photographic memory.*

"Jo, my father had that prayer engraved on an obelisk at the entrance to Akhetaten."

"So ... if I was truly an Amarna princess, I'd be familiar with the prayer. Sinuhe expected me to tell him that I already knew it."

"Yes. He must have been testing you."

"Then I failed."

"I suppose that's why he wasn't surprised when I showed him the message from Amarna."

"The day you came out to class."

"Yes. You were sitting under the banyan tree, watching the monkeys and definitely not doing any schoolwork."

"I thought ... I thought you might have me thrown out of the palace, or worse."

"I might have, if not for Sinuhe."

"I don't understand."

"Neither do I, except to say that Sinuhe is a cagey old man. He talked me into keeping you around." Tutankhamun smiled.

"He was your tutor?" Jo asked.

"Yes. And Nekhare's. There are many things he never told my father. Childish pranks, mostly."

"Your Highness," Jo chose her words carefully, "why not go back to Amarna and leave the day-to-day administration of the kingdom to Ay and the others? Spend the rest of your life hunting and fishing and doing all those things you enjoy so much? Would that be such a terrible thing?"

"It's not that simple. I believe in the power of the Aten, but I am also drawn to the old ways, to the traditions that made Kemet the greatest kingdom on earth. My father ... well, my father was an ineffective pharaoh. I must repair the damage he did to this great kingdom."

"Perhaps someone else ..." Jo began, ever mindful of the danger that she knew lay before him.

"It is my destiny. Of course, I didn't know that, at first. I was a sickly child and spent most of my time recuperating from one illness or another. When I wasn't sick, I went hunting or played silly warrior games. Nobody, including my father, ever thought I would one day be pharaoh. It was my brother who would be king. He was groomed for that position. When my father died, Smenkare took the throne. And then he, too, died. I never desired to be pharaoh, Johenamun, but that was the path chosen for me."

"I understand. It's just that I worry about you. We were all worried about you today."

He laughed again. "You might have been, but Nekhare knew where I was."

"He did?" *So there are some things he doesn't trust me with*, she thought.

"Of course. I was out at Meretsega. Nekhare knows that is where I go when I need a little ... distance. But don't tell anyone else, especially Ay or Nankti."

"Of course I won't tell. But where is Meretsega?"

"It's the cliff high above the Valley of the Kings. I arrived there just as the sun was coming up. It's so beautiful there in the early-morning hours. I almost forget about all the madness here at the palace."

"You went there by yourself? Without the palace guards?" Jo felt a little panic rising in her throat once again. "That's just not safe!"

This time, he laughed loudly. "You sound like Ay or Nankti."

"Well, they're right. You could have drowned crossing the river or fallen from the cliff. What is so special about this place that you would risk your life?"

"I'll take you there, and you will see," he said. "Soon. But perhaps we should call it a night for now."

He rose and led her to her room. Jo watched him walk down the shadowy hallway toward his own apartment.

She crawled into bed. Her conversation with Tutankhamun hadn't made her feel any less nervous about his fate. Here was a man who had the capacity to worry and fret about nearly everybody else, but he seemed to have zero concern for his own safety. And what was Nekhare up to? As hard as Jo tried, she could not come up with a plausible reason for Nekhare to be sending secret messages to the high priest at Karnak in the middle of the night. She knew that the high priest was an enemy of the pharaoh's. And what was it she had overheard him saying in the temple? *Consider my offer, young friend.*

Jo unrolled her journal and added Nekhare's name to her short list of people who might be planning to murder the king.

CHAPTER 14

A week or so later, Jo woke in the middle of the night to find Tutankhamun standing over her. She was startled out of her sleep and, needless to say, surprised by his appearance in her room.

"Quiet!" he said. "Get dressed for horseback."

She hurried into her dressing room and pulled on her riding gear.

The palace hallways were eerily empty as Tutankhamun and Jo passed through them. He led her away using the same route they had followed on the trip to Medinet Habu. The two of them paddled across the river, now receded to a little more than a stream, and walked upriver until they reached the stables. He hardly spoke, but the silence between them was easy.

They found two horses cross-tied and waiting for them, even though there was not a stable boy in sight. The ride across the narrow band of desert didn't take long, and soon they were dismounting at the base of a cliff.

The climb might have been difficult if Tut had not known his way. He went ahead, choosing the path and offering Jo a hand up over the steeper climbs. They reached the top just as the sun began to stretch its long, golden fingers across the great kingdom that was Kemet. Behind them lay the Valley of the Kings, a maze of secret passageways and burial chambers where Tutankhamun's grandfather, Amenhotep, was entombed along with the other great pharaohs of his dynasty. Before them stretched the sand dunes, the flood plain, and then finally, the shimmering river.

He took Jo by the hand and led her to the very edge. "My kingdom," he said. "Is it not beautiful?"

"Yes," she whispered. It was beautiful, breathtaking even.

"Three million people, Jo, and they are my responsibility." He dropped her hand and climbed onto a boulder that sat atop the cliff.

Suddenly the sun's rays converged upon him and bathed him in light even as the rest of the world remained in that place before the dawn. It was as if the sun, upon finding Tutankhamun on the cliff, focused all its energy on the young pharaoh. His body radiated a brilliant golden glow.

Jo watched, spellbound, while the golden light that emanated from his body faded and turned into a barely purple haze.

He stood perfectly still for a few moments, his eyes closed, and then turned to face the Valley of the Kings. Raising his arms, palms up, he said, "I am honored, Grandfathers, to be anointed with your wisdom. I will not disappoint you."

Jo was stunned and speechless—for only about the *third* time in her life.

And then the moment was gone. Tutankhamun jumped from the boulder and stood beside Jo again.

"My grandfathers—buried in the tombs behind us—worked to build Kemet into the most powerful kingdom on earth. They waged wars and built temples; they preserved the divine order. They were wise and well prepared for their kingship. I am neither of those things."

"You are a great king—" Jo began, but Tutankhamun cut her off with a wave of his hand.

"There," he said, "to your left."

Her breath caught in her throat. Not more than three feet away, a huge snake lay coiled on a rock, its head lifted, jaws open as if to strike.

"Stay still," he said. He squeezed her right hand, and then, to the snake, he said, "Have we disturbed your sleep, my friend? Then so be it. I am Pharaoh—Lord of the Two Lands—and I go where I want."

A full minute passed; the two of them continued to challenge each other in silence. Jo thought she might pass out.

The snake hissed, its ugly head wavering still closer. Tutankhamun never took his stare from the snake's cold, black eyes. Finally, it slithered away.

Jo's knees gave out, and she would have fallen if Tutankhamun hadn't caught her. He held her, and they stood there on the cliff, not talking, while the sun continued its climb into the eastern sky. His body radiated warmth, and Jo could feel a strange energy soak into her skin.

"Let's go," he said.

"Already?" Despite the snake, Jo wasn't ready to leave.

"We'd better get back before the whole palace is in an uproar."

They climbed back down the same way they had come. He gave her a leg up, and she climbed onto her horse.

"I'll race you!" he said, after he mounted, a boyish grin on his face.

The two of them sped across the desert, their horses neck and neck. They arrived at the stable at virtually the same time, and Tutankhamun declared the race a draw, "… unlike our archery contest, which I clearly won."

"The strap broke," Jo said, exasperated.

"A warrior takes better care of his—or *her*—gear than that," Tutankhamun teased.

"I want a rematch."

"Done. Just let me know when I should show up."

"I will." Jo turned to hide her smile, amazed at this man—this *pharaoh*—who could, at times, be such a teenager.

Jo didn't worry about leaving the horses in a sweat. A stable boy or two would appear on the scene to care for them as soon as they left. They didn't speak again until they were back in the boat. The morning sun glittered off the river and sent splinters of light everywhere.

Tutankhamun sat in the front of the canoelike boat. Halfway across the Nile, he stopped paddling and let the boat drift with the current. "I spoke with Sinuhe. Our secret is safe with him. He believes you are destined for greatness, and so do I."

Startled, Jo asked, "Me? I'm just an ordinary girl!"

He laughed and used the tip of his paddle to flick a fair amount of water at her. She gasped and tried to pay him back, rocking the boat dangerously.

"Right. So you keep telling me." He thought for a few minutes. "But seriously, the God-Kings do not present themselves to just anyone. Their appearance at Meretsega is proof. You were delivered to Kemet by the gods to do great things."

"That was another test?" she asked.

"Sort of," he replied. "I wanted you to see Meretsega, but I also wondered how the gods would react to your presence on the cliff."

Maybe he's right, she thought to herself. *Maybe I am part of some grand scheme. What if it wasn't Foster, after all?* Jo knew that everything—the time travel, her natural ability with the language, her newfound skill with a bow and arrow, all of it—was just too much to be coincidental.

They paddled across the Nile and returned to the palace.

They arrived back in time for Tutankhamun to meet with his first appointments, and Jo managed to convince Nekhare that her absence from her room—he had been looking for her—was due to the fact that she had climbed out of bed with the sunrise and decided to take an early-morning ride.

She didn't know why she didn't tell him about her trip to Meretsega with Tutankhamun. She had a feeling that he wouldn't like the idea of her taking off in the middle of the night with the pharaoh. Jo's relationship with Nekhare had become a little strained over the past week, no doubt due to her increasing suspicion of him, and she didn't want to say anything to make matters worse. She also suspected that the pharaoh wouldn't mention their trip to Nekhare. A conspiracy was growing between Tutankhamun and Jo, a comfortable trust that she was beginning to enjoy.

During the afternoon council, Tutankhamun detailed his plans for traveling to Nubia, and even though Jo had become part of the pharaoh's inner circle, she was in no position to advise him not to go. The whole idea sent her into a state of anxiety, for she knew that this trip would be very risky—an opportunity for him to die on the battlefield or be murdered in his tent. Still, she had no idea what to do. The longer she remained in Kemet, the more she became convinced that she could never tell anyone that she had information about events of the future.

She said nothing, and instead she went to her room that night agonizing over the danger that Tutankhamun would be placing himself in. Nekhare would travel to Nubia with him, and Horemheb would be there also. She still wasn't sure how she felt about the old general. Did an oath of allegiance guarantee that he wouldn't try to kill the pharaoh? And what about Nekhare and his midnight messages to Piay?

She lit a candle and took Foster's book from under the bed. "I know there are answers in here, but how do I find them?" she asked out loud.

She opened to the same page, the one where the article about the king's death had appeared, but nothing had changed. The article was still there, but the rest of the book was still unreadable.

She turned the page and ran her hand across the paper. "Tutankhamun travels to Nubia soon," she said. "Horemheb will go with him. Amun, if I pay you proper homage, will you keep Tutankhamun safe?"

And then it happened again, gradually at first, so that she wasn't even sure it was actually happening. The words appeared on the page as if someone were writing them at that very moment.

TUTANKHAMUN TRAVELS TO NUBIA

There is much evidence to suggest that Tutankhamun made at least one trip to Nubia. While his experience in battle situations was certainly limited, inscriptions on his tomb indicate that he traveled to Nubia in the ninth or tenth year of his reign. Pictures show Nubian kings bowing before him and offering tribute in the form of gold and animal skins. Other paintings indicate that he returned home to a hero's welcome. More than likely, the general of his armies, Horemheb, traveled ahead of the king in order to put down a rebellion and ensure the safety of the young pharaoh.

So, he returns from Nubia, at least. That buys me a little more time to figure out what's going on. She searched every page of the book for more but found nothing. She shoved it back into its hiding place under the bed, blew out the candle, and went to sleep.

CHAPTER 15

With just a few days left before Tutankhamun and Nekhare were to depart, the palace hummed with activity. Out in the field on the north side of the palace, hundreds of metalsmiths and weapon-makers rushed to restock the army's munitions, in case the pharaoh and his men met with unexpected resistance. Army officials arrived daily in twos and threes, many of them captains and generals who would accompany Tutankhamun on this important first military campaign. They all had to be fed and housed in the palace. In the evenings, after the drills were over for the day, they could be heard singing and boasting about past exploits, their voices carried across the palace by the evening breeze.

The Hall of Audiences was a blur. Ankesenamun had excused herself from this morning ritual until after the birth of her baby, opting instead to stay in her room or in the shade of the gardens. She was uncomfortable, and Jo was only too happy to fill in for the queen. Tutankhamun spent an hour or so each day receiving visitors; after that, he and Nekhare were off to the training field to supervise preparations for their trip.

They were holding audience one morning when a message arrived for the pharaoh: a fire had accidentally touched off in the large tent that functioned as a tack room—a storage facility for the army's saddles and chariot gear. The pharaoh and Nekhare were needed at once.

"But you are scheduled to meet with the high priest," said Teynek, the doorman. "He's already in the anteroom, waiting."

Tutankhamun looked directly at Jo. "You'll have to receive him."

"Me? Where's Ay? I'm not sure I can do this."

"He's conducting a meeting with the mayors." The king shrugged. "The rest of us have had no luck with the high priest. Perhaps you can pacify him a bit. No doubt he's here to complain about some perceived injustice. If he's still here when I get back, I'll see him. Teynek, take Piay to the garden and make sure he is served the palace's best wine. Johenamun will meet him there."

Stunned, Jo watched as the two men left the room.

Figuring she had no choice, she exited the Hall of Audiences through a side door that led to a private garden, one where Tutankhamun met privately with the most privileged of guests.

The high priest, shaved bald and dressed in flowing white robes, stood as Jo entered the garden. "Where is Tutankhamun?" he asked.

"He's been called away to tend to an emergency. He's asked me to speak with you."

The high priest laughed. "Either you have come up fast, or I have sunk very low."

Jo struggled for the right words; she knew that if she offended the high priest in any way, Tutankhamun would be left to pick up the pieces.

"These are difficult times, sir, and we beg your forgiveness. Pharaoh Tutankhamun would not ordinarily send one such as I, and he has asked me to tell you that he will return as quickly as possible from the field. He understands that you are a very busy man, and he did not want to send you away, nor did he want to keep you waiting. Either way, your time is wasted."

Piay heaved his considerable bulk onto the wooden bench, and Jo sat beside him. A servant entered the garden carrying a silver tray, which he set on the low table in front of Jo and Piay. Jo leaned forward and poured two glasses of wine.

"Princess Johenaten—"

"Johenamun."

"Yes, of course." Piay smiled. "Princess Johenamun, you are a diplomat. I said so the first time we met, did I not?"

Jo nodded.

"And now I've been hearing all kinds of interesting things about you. Quite a remarkable young lady, aren't you?"

Jo had no idea where Piay was going with this conversation. "All in service to His Highness, sir."

"Yes, yes. His Highness, Pharaoh Tutankhamun. He inspires such loyalty in his young *courtiers*." Piay reached for his wine glass.

Jo ignored the insult. "He deserves our loyalty."

The high priest hesitated before sipping his wine and setting the glass back on the table. "Admirable, my dear, admirable. But what do you know of it, really? You come from Amarna, the pharaoh throws a few baubles your way, and you do what you are told."

Jo forced a smile and tried to remain calm. "Your Excellency, you are absolutely correct. There is much I do not understand. I would be honored, sir, if we had the opportunity to talk again. You could school me in the intricacies of temple politics." *I'd rather have every one of my eyelashes pulled out.* "But this I do know: Tutankhamun reveres the Karnak Temple—"

"I've heard all this before."

"Well, apparently you're not listening."

The high priest stood. "I do not need any more propaganda from any of Tutankhamun's family or servants or whatever you are. Tell the *pharaoh*—"

"Wait, sir." Jo stood and laid her hand on his forearm. He looked at her, aghast, and she realized she had broken protocol. She pulled her hand away. "You are right, of course." Jo lowered her voice and glanced around the garden. It was empty but for two peacocks near the reflection pool. "Can we speak honestly?"

Piay sat.

"Of course Tutankhamun feels some … affection for the Aten. How could he not? It is difficult to walk away from what you were brought up to believe. But the restoration of Kemet to her former glory is always foremost in his mind. Pharaoh Tutankhamun may be young, but he is smart enough to know that he needs your help. You are a powerful man, Your Excellency. We need your help."

"I knew the Aten ruled his heart," Piay said, with satisfaction. "Ay and Horemheb should have left Tutankhamun in Amarna; they should never have moved the boy here."

"His grandfather was responsible for the restoration of Karnak. He built the great pylons at the gate."

"His grandfather is long dead," snapped the priest.

"This family supports Karnak and reveres Amun. Tutankhamun will restore Karnak to its rightful place in Kemetan society. He will repair what Akhenaten—"

"Akhenaten—"

"Was an aberration. A freak."

Piay laughed. "A what?"

"A freak, a wacko. You know, crazy." Jo couldn't help but smile.

"Yes, yes. A *freak*." Piay was amused by the twenty-first-century slang.

"But Tutankhamun is not—"

"No, not a *freak*." He laughed again and took a long sip of his wine. "Tell Tutankhamun that I will stay out of his way until he gets this nasty little rebellion in Nubia under control. Then we will talk."

He stood. "I'll show myself out; my attendants are waiting at the gate."

Jo stood and followed the high priest out of the garden. "Sir, you wanted to ask—"

"It can wait."

Jo returned to the Hall of Audiences, and not long after, Tutankhamun and Nekhare returned also.

"Piay?" Tutankhamun asked, a doubtful look in his eyes.

"He says he'll speak with you when you return from Nubia. The fire?"

"Destroyed about a quarter of our gear. Our departure may be delayed a few days."

The departure of the Southern Army was, in fact, delayed, and during this time Tutankhamun and Ankesenamun decided to attend the funeral celebration for the mayor of Waset. It was unusual for the king and queen to attend a social event, but the mayor had been a political ally, and Tutankhamun decided to pay his respects. The banquet was to be held on the first anniversary of the mayor's death, as tradition dictated, and would be a lavish affair.

On the day of the party, Ankesenamun slept most of the afternoon, and then she and Jo and Meritaken bathed in the first batch of Wanankh's soap. It was crude, like brown gelatin, but the lather was a big hit. Jo made a mental note to direct Wanankh to add salt to the final product. She'd forgotten to tell him that salt would make the soap whiter and firmer.

For the occasion, she chose the dress that had been made from the silk Nekhare had purchased for her at the market, and around her waist she wore a thick belt of solid gold links. Gold hoop earrings dangled from her ears, and she completed the look with the gold snake armbands Nekhare had given her on her first day in the palace.

As usual, the servants applied layers of makeup. They would wear wigs to the party, but there were no blonde wigs in Kemet, so, for this night, Jo became as dark-haired as Ankesenamun and Meritaken. The servants wove the wigs into intricate braids and then placed perfumed wax cones on top—they were tied on with strings that were knotted under the chin. The wax would melt during the hot Kemetan night and provide additional fragrance.

"You are gorgeous," the queen said to Jo, as she checked out her appearance in Ankesenamun's full-length mirror.

Yes, not bad, Jo thought. Since her arrival in Kemet, she had grown another inch, and her body had become a bit shapelier. "So are you and Meritaken," Jo said.

"Oh, please," scoffed the queen. "I'm as fat as a hippo. A pregnant hippo. I'm so jealous of you tonight. And by the way, this is your night—yours and Nekhare's. Go as his escort, not as my personal assistant."

"Thank you, Your Highness. I am looking forward to the evening," Jo replied.

They were escorted to the mayor's huge estate by a dozen of the pharaoh's bodyguards and were led straightaway into a large banquet room. Servants hung leis of lotus blossoms, symbols of rejuvenation, around their necks and seated them around a low table.

The party was already in full swing, and the room was hot, the air heavy with fragrance. Wine flowed everywhere, and guests sampled tastes from clay bowls filled with every kind of food found in Kemet—fish, fowl, vegetables, fruits, breads. The air became thick enough to slice, crowded with an exotic blend of scents—food, wine, body odor, and the heavy perfume left behind as the wax cones melted in the intense heat. As the room grew warmer, servants arrived to fan the royal family with perfumed-soaked ostrich plumes.

Ankesenamun and Tutankhamun ate nothing and drank only what had first been tasted by the Royal Food Taster, but as the night wore on, Nekhare drank enough to get a little buzz. Jo could tell because his face grew flushed and he laughed too much. Just as she was beginning to think she might ask Nekhare to take her back to the palace, the entertainment arrived.

Young girls referred to as "priestesses" entered the room, some of them playing flutes, and others strumming stringed instruments that looked something like harps. Dancers wore nothing but narrow belts around their waists. They circled the room, leaping and twirling to the music. Guests clapped with the beat and hooted when the young girls performed a particularly provocative dance. They moved through the crowd, stopping every now and then to dance for selected individuals.

Please keep them away from us, Jo found herself thinking. But as soon as the thought crossed her mind, a particularly lithe young thing zeroed in on Nekhare. She spun in circles before him, her back arched, and her long hair, weighted with beads, skimming the floor. She stopped and draped a long scarf around his neck. She used the scarf to pull him closer and closer before finally releasing him, with a smile and a wink.

Jo knew she was expected to pretend the whole thing didn't bother her.

Nekhare watched the girl dance off.

Just then Jo heard a little gasp from the queen, who sat to her right.

"Are you feeling all right?" she asked Ankesenamun. "You look flushed."

The queen looked as though she might faint. Jo signaled Tutankhamun—he was talking with a distinguished-looking older man—and he turned his attention to Ankesenamun.

"Shall I take you back to the palace?" he asked his queen.

"It's too stuffy in here," Ankesenamun replied.

Jo moved aside to let Tutankhamun continue his conversation with the queen, and noticed that Nekhare had disappeared. She scanned the room and spied him just as he exited through a rear door.

The king was busy moving Ankesenamun to a cooler spot. A bevy of servants surrounded them, so no one noticed when Jo left.

She exited the same door Nekhare had used and found herself in a wide corridor. She followed the hallway until she came to a small garden. She still could not see Nekhare, but she could hear someone talking in hushed tones. She tiptoed closer to the voices, careful to stay in the shadows.

"I told you that I will not talk with you here." This was Nekhare's unmistakable voice.

And, from another man, "Relax, my young friend. No one suspects you of anything."

"Still, it is not safe, not with so many partygoers wandering the gardens."

"And what could possibly be wrong with a meeting between Tutankhamun's trusted adviser and the most powerful of all priests?"

It's the high priest of Karnak, Jo realized. *Why is Nekhare meeting with him here?*

Suddenly she felt a pair of strong hands grab her from behind. She gasped.

"Look what I found lurking in the corridor," snarled the brute as he dragged Jo toward Nekhare and the high priest.

"I wasn't *lurking.* I was looking for Nekhare. Nekhare, I want to go home."

The high priest caught Nekhare by the arm as he rose to go. "Nothing will stop me from reaching my goals … not you, not anything. Minor inconveniences—he looked pointedly at Jo—can be eliminated."

It was Nekhare's turn to threaten. "She's part of this, or you can count me out."

"She's completely loyal to Tutankhamun."

"If you want me, then you will ensure that Princess Johenamun remains alive." Nekhare took Jo by the arm and led her from the garden, casually, as if he were not even the least bit concerned by all that had just taken place.

They didn't return to the party.

Instead, Nekhare led her out of the mayor's house. Soon they were fleeing together across the city—Nekhare walking, almost running, in long strides, Jo running along behind him. She arrived breathless at the palace. Nekhare hadn't spoken during their flight across the city, but clearly he was angry.

He dragged her into her room and slammed the door behind them. "Whatever did you think you were doing, following me into the garden?"

"*Me?* What am *I* doing? A better question might be what are *you* doing? Conspiring with Tutankhamun's enemies?"

"You don't know anything about it."

"Don't I? I think I heard enough to figure—"

"No, you don't know anything."

"I know that the high priest wants Tutankhamun dethroned—or better yet, dead; that much is obvious. That man is evil. And I've overheard you conspiring with him not once, but twice. I saw you sending a messenger to him in the middle of the night, too. It's *you*, isn't it? You're the one ..."

"I'm the one *what*?"

"Trying to murder Tutankhamun!"

She saw his eyes grow dark, but she never saw the blow coming.

The next thing she knew, she was on her knees holding her cheek, which stung as if she'd been hit with a hot iron.

Nekhare pulled her to her feet by her elbows and pinned her up against the bedroom door. "How dare you doubt my loyalty to Tutankhamun!"

She just stared back, unable to speak, unable to believe that he had just slapped her with the same force with which he might hit a man. She refused to cry.

"And you've been spying on me?" His face was very close to hers now, and she could see the fury in his eyes.

"No," she choked out. "Not spying—"

"What do you call it then? I can't believe you would think that of me—that I would even *think* of murdering Tutankhamun."

She tried to push him away, but he grabbed both her wrists and pinned them against the door, over her head.

"Let ... me ... go!" Jo demanded.

Sounds from the next room indicated that the queen had returned home.

"I'm trying to *save* Tutankhamun," he said in a whisper. "What you say is true, Piay does want him … eliminated. Everyone knows that, including the pharaoh. But I have managed to convince the high priest that I am in league with him. I am hoping to flush out his plans and then turn him over to Nankti."

"Let me go," Jo said again, "before I scream my head off."

"You wouldn't—"

"Get out of my room, now!" she demanded, loudly.

"Jo—"

"I swear, I'll scream …"

He let go of her wrists, and she scrambled away from the door. He left but not before looking back.

"Jo, I'm sorry …"

"Just leave," she said.

After the door had closed behind him, she fell onto her bed and sobbed into the pillow. *Perhaps he's telling the truth*, she thought. But it didn't matter. He'd hit her, and she knew she'd never forgive him.

An hour or so later, Jo called for a bath. The servants pretended not to notice Jo's tearstained cheeks and the welt that was forming beneath her eye.

CHAPTER 16

Jo spent the next two days ignoring Nekhare, pretending that she didn't care if she never saw him again and feeling more confused than she had ever been in her life. Kemet had been all about Nekhare, but that was over. Now there was a huge void there. Even worse, it was now clear to Jo that Piay was still conspiring against the pharaoh. Her conversation with him in the garden had done nothing to bring him around to Tutankhamun's side. What was she to believe about Nekhare?

And should she spill her guts to the pharaoh? Tell him all that she had heard? Or in doing so, would she just complicate his life? Perhaps Nekhare was telling the truth, and perhaps he and Nankti had it all under control.

Despite her confusion, Jo went about her business the best she could and explained her black eye as an accident. She didn't think that either Tutankhamun or Ankesenamun believed her, but they were gracious enough to not press the issue, although Jo thought she saw concern on both their faces.

On the eve of the king's departure for Nubia, she cried herself to sleep for the third night in a row. Then, very late, she was awakened by a knock on her door.

"It's me," Nekhare said.

He entered without waiting for her to answer and strode to her bedside. Jo sat up, not knowing what to expect; he sat on the edge of the bed. "I cannot leave in the morning without first securing your forgiveness."

"Nekhare, I can't be with someone who—" she began.

"I know, I know. I swear I will never hit you again. I don't know what came over me. I just couldn't believe you could think such a thing … that I would do *anything* to hurt my king."

"It sounded like—"

"I know what it must have sounded like. But you have to believe me. I know what I am doing, Jo, but I can't go to Nubia until I know that you believe me and that you forgive me for … hitting you like that."

"Nekhare, I don't know …"

"Listen to me." He moved closer and grabbed both her hands. "Tutankhamun and I grew up together in the palace at Akhetaten; we are brothers, not by blood, but in spirit. We have been together always, and he knows me better than anyone else, except perhaps Meritaken. But I will tell you what I have never told anyone, not even Meritaken: I have always been jealous of Tutankhamun, and I think I would have made a better pharaoh. I am bigger and stronger, and I am less … kind."

"His gentleness is part of what makes him great—" Jo began.

"No. His *gentleness*, his inability to be ruthless, is what makes him weak. But that does not matter. As much as I've always wanted to be pharaoh, it is not my destiny. It is not what Amun has chosen for me. I long ago accepted my position, and I will be forever loyal to Tutankhamun."

"Yes … yes. Of course …" she said.

"But that does not mean I cannot achieve greatness. I will be powerful one day, and other great men will bow before me."

He began running his lips over her neck and her throat, planting tiny kisses everywhere. She had missed him so much.

"And you will be right by my side." He kissed the very spot where he had struck her. "Please, Jo. I must have you."

Her resistance faltered. *Okay, so he hit me once*, she thought. *That doesn't mean I can't be with him.*

"I love you, Jo. Please tell me that you forgive me."

"I forgive you," she whispered.

When the next morning dawned, Nekhare and Tutankhamun left for Nubia. It would be several weeks before they would return—probably just in time for the birth of Ankesenamun's baby—and Jo knew she'd spend those weeks missing Nekhare and worrying about the king, despite the reassurances she had gained from Foster's book.

Jo and the queen said their goodbyes to their men in the garden outside their chambers. The queen was unable to walk as far as the river, and it was Jo's duty to stay behind with her.

Tutankhamun was reserved, as usual, but before he left, he motioned for Jo to come near. "I am grateful to leave the Great Royal Wife in your hands while I am gone. Ankesenamun reports that you are invaluable to her, and with the baby coming ... her well-being is my greatest concern."

"Of course, Your Highness. The midwives are with her always."

"And the priests. But she is most relaxed when she is with you. You have some effect on her that she cannot explain."

"I am glad to be of service, Your Highness."

"Over breakfast, she told me of some of your interesting ideas with regard to her pregnancy," Jo picked up the change in tone of Tutankhamun's voice.

"Yes, Your Highness."

"*She* believes in you completely." The meaning of his comment hung over her for a while. "Do you think that you know more about unborn babies than the best midwives in all of Kemet? Need I point out the consequences if some mishap should befall the queen or our unborn baby?"

"No, Your Highness." It had never occurred to Jo that she could be held responsible for any problems that arose with Ankesenamun's pregnancy.

"Jo, you must understand that should something happen to the queen or the baby ... well, some in Kemet would blame you. Be judicious with the advice you give, and be careful about who hears you give it. I'm not sure that I would be in control of your fate if something should happen. The future of all of Kemet rests in Ankesenamun's belly. At this point, I would very much dislike having to order your execution."

She gulped.

"Still, I am off to Nubia, and I am glad that you will be here with the queen. I will be back in Waset well before she delivers."

"You are not in any danger, Your Highness?"

"No. We don't expect any problems. Just a simple collection of tribute, and we travel only as far south as the second cataract. My presence there is only symbolic ... for now."

With Tutankhamun and Nekhare both away and Ankesenamun very pregnant and sleeping a lot, life at the palace became as slow and lazy as the Nile. Ay and Pentju handled the affairs of state, leaving the queen and Jo free to plan their days as they saw fit. They slept late almost every day, spent a few hours dealing with household details—how many jars of wine to order or what to serve the courtiers for dinner—and spent the rest of the daytime hours in the shade of the palace gardens. In those days, Jo and Ankesenamun were more like sisters than anything else.

Jo had finally grown accustomed to wearing next to nothing, and she'd long ago learned to enjoy swimming in the nude. She and the queen whiled away the afternoons floating in the pool just outside their quarters; usually Meritaken joined them. When Her Highness approached her final month of pregnancy, Jo advised her to stop swimming—something Jo remembered from listening to her mother—so she sat nearby while Meritaken and Jo played like children in the water. All the while, an army of servants stood close by, ready to shade them, fan them, or scurry to satisfy their tiniest whim.

Of course, Jo was anxious to have Nekhare and Tutankhamun back safe and sound, and she was nervous about Ankesenamun's upcoming delivery.

Then she awoke one night to find Ankesenamun standing over her. "It's too early," the queen sobbed.

Jo bolted upright in bed. "I swear, I won't let anything happen to you or your baby," she promised.

But she had no clue what to do next.

The midwives and the priests were summoned from their sleep and began their routine, burning incense and chanting, invoking the fertility goddesses Hathor and Isis to protect the mother-to-be and the baby. They applied a plaster of sea salt and emmer wheat to the queen's belly.

Jo stayed by Ankesenamun's side through the entire night and into the next day.

The afternoon grew long, and finally the midwives pronounced the queen ready to deliver. They moved her to the *meskhenet,* the birthing chair. An hour later, Ankesenamun delivered a healthy, perfect baby girl. Jo cried huge tears of joy and relief.

"The nursemaid is here," declared the head midwife.

"No, the queen will nurse the baby herself," Jo said, and then she remembered what Tutankhamun had said. "I mean … my mother … You could try nursing the baby yourself, Your Highness. Many people in my kingdom believe it's best for the baby."

The midwives were ushered from the room.

"Help me?" asked Ankesenamun.

"Just hold her like this," Jo said, and she positioned the baby like she had seen her mother do for new mothers several times. The baby latched on as though she'd been nursing for weeks.

Ankesenamun looked up at Jo and smiled. "She's perfect, isn't she?

Jo nodded.

"I wouldn't have her if not for you."

"No, Your Highness. You did it all yourself. All I did was hold your hand."

"No, there is something special, almost mystical, about you. I can't quite figure it out."

"There are a lot of things you don't know about me," Jo said. She didn't know what possessed her to say it; chalk it up to the emotion of childbirth.

Tutankhamun heard about the birth of his daughter long before he arrived at the palace, for all across the kingdom of Kemet it was trumpeted that the Great Royal Wife had given birth.

Because the baby was female, the question of whether or not there was now an heir to the throne was still to be debated. But the queen had delivered a healthy baby, and that meant that the gods had been rightly appeased. Clearly the young king and his wife had brought Kemet still closer to divine peace, and *Ma'at* was once again assured.

One afternoon a couple of weeks after the birth of the baby, messengers informed the palace that Tutankhamun's ships had docked in Waset. Jo made it to the pier just in time to watch the crew unload the tribute from the hold of the ship: hundreds of animal skins, dozens of ivory tusks, innumerable jars of wine, and chest after chest of gold in all forms—all of it paid to Tut by the Nubians, who had been defeated once again.

When it had all been loaded into horse-drawn carts, the pharaoh mounted a horse that had been delivered to him and paraded the tribute to the palace. Horemheb rode along beside him, and Jo thought that he looked more like a proud father than a potential assassin. Nekhare and Jo walked behind, their arms wrapped around each other's waists. They watched as thousands of the people of Waset lined the streets to celebrate the return of the victorious pharaoh.

It was a glorious moment and the first time that Jo had seen Tutankhamun out in public. She'd long ago learned to admire him; he was, after all, so young and so in-control. But now she found herself overwhelmed with a strange sense of pride—and something else that she couldn't define.

Ankesenamun waited for her husband in her chambers. Jo expected that the new parents would want some time alone together with the baby, but she was soon summoned to the room. When she arrived, she saw that Tutankhamun cradled his new daughter in his arms.

"Have you named this child yet?" Tutankhamun asked his wife.

"No. I waited for you," replied Ankesenamun.

"I would like to call her Kiya," said the pharaoh.

"Of course. It's only right that she should be named for your mother," said the queen.

Tutankhamun turned to Jo. "I am grateful for all you have done to ensure the health of my daughter. Please prepare the official documents and announce the child's name."

"Thank you, Your Highness."

CHAPTER 17

The palace did not have time to enjoy the king's successes for long, for from the north came word that the borders were under attack by the Hittites.

For as long as there had been a kingdom along the Nile, the Kemetans had been locked in conflict with those who lived to the north and to the south. In fact, since the very beginning of time, when the Nile was born in the highlands of Kemet and snaked her way across the desert to the sea, those who lived along her banks had waged war against each other. Eventually, the great pharaoh Menes united the kingdom. He became the first Lord of the Two Lands, and Kemet became the most powerful kingdom on earth. And in order to maintain her powerful position, Kemet needed resources.

But Kemet had no resources—just the fertile river valley and the waters of the Nile. So, what Kemet didn't have, she took from others.

For many centuries, millennia even, the greatest, most powerful pharaohs conquered the lands to the north and to the south. They forced those king-doms to pay tribute in gold, ebony, ivory, animal skins. Whatever the pharaohs wanted, they took, and they used the riches they acquired to build huge monu-ments to honor the gods.

Amenhotep, Tutankhamun's grandfather, drove the northern tribes back east, along the Horus Road that cut across Sinai into Canaan. His armies reached the Euphrates River, bringing the coastline of Canaan and the ports of Tyre and Sidon under Kemetan rule. The princes of Syria and Palestine to the north all bowed to him and sent their daughters to be part of Amenhotep's harem. Egypt rose to the full height of her glory.

When Amenhotep died, his son Akhenaten ascended the throne. The new pharaoh, a peace-loving man, refused to send out the armies to sustain Egypt's dominance over her neighbors. Instead he retreated to the desert and built a new capital city, Akhetaten.

The kingdom's enemies sensed weakness, and they began to encroach upon the northern borders. While Akhenaten built his palace, they pushed Egyptians out of Syria. Kemet was headed for political disaster until, as luck would have it, Akhenaten died, and then Smenkare died, leaving as heir the nine-year-old boy Tutankhamun. The prince was too young to rule Kemet; Ay and Horemheb made all decisions in Tutankhamun's name.

But Tutankhamun was no longer content to have others make his decisions.

"The time has come." It was Horemheb who called for immediate action. The major players had gathered in the throne room.

"The Hittites have united under the banner of Suppliminus," the general continued. "The Mitanni Empire continues to beg for our help. The Hittites have already taken our most northerly outposts—a few minor camps with little significance. But they test us, Your Highness. If we do not react, they will push further. They will sweep southward and attempt to seize the Horus Road. More Kemetan lives will be lost."

"The Northern Army is ready?" This from Ay.

"More than ready," Horemheb declared. "They are anxious to show our enemies to the north what befalls those who doubt the power of Kemet."

The room was quiet. All eyes were on the pharaoh. He stood.

"Then so it shall be. Prepare the Southern Army to march."

"The infantry and the cavalry are ready to depart at a moment's notice," said Horemheb. "In the morning, if you so order, Your Highness."

The fact that Horemheb had anticipated getting his way was not lost on Jo or anyone else in the room, including Tutankhamun.

"So be it," said the king. "How long before the fleet must depart?"

"Not until after the Festival of the Opet, Your Highness."

"Good. I will stay to lead my people through that celebration, and then we will follow the infantry northward."

"*We?*" asked Ay. "You intend to go into Syria yourself?"

Ankesenamun and Jo held their breath.

"It is time."

"This will be no simple collection of tribute," Horemheb said. "The Hittites are bloodthirsty warriors."

"I am aware of that," replied Tutankhamun. "I have prepared for this, and I will not disgrace the memory of my grandfathers by hiding here in the Holy City. I will lead the army into Syria, General Horemheb, and I will return victorious."

"Yes, Your Highness."

The old general bowed before the young king, but not before Jo thought she saw him hide a smirk.

All too soon, the Festival of the Opet was upon them. The preparations were complete, and the royal family was dressed in their finest.

The festival began at Karnak. The shrine of Amun was placed in a ceremonial boat, in which the entire royal family also rode, and the priests carried it to the Nile. Thousands of loaves of bread and hundreds of jars of beer had been distributed to the people. Along the way, down the golden street that led from the temple to the river, the citizens of Waset lined the roads to catch a glimpse of the royal family.

They were towed across the Nile and carried to the necropolis, on the western shore. Upon their arrival in the Valley of the Dead, Nekhare and Jo opted to walk behind the palanquins that carried the king and Ankesenamun through the narrow river valley and into the desert.

The city's wealthier citizens, all those rich enough to have tombs in the necropolis, followed the royal family across the river. There, at the tombs of their ancestors, they laid out food, wine, and other items needed in the afterlife. They shopped among the stalls of the artisans and craftsmen for any necessary funerary equipment. The celebrants feasted and drank until they were inebriated and entered the twilight state between life and death that brought them closer to their loved ones.

Nekhare and Jo strolled hand in hand past the elaborate entrances to the tombs, watching the revelry of the partygoers. He was quiet, sullen almost, but Jo attributed this to his imminent departure for Syria.

"I have something to show you," he said mysteriously. They walked down dusty paths toward the steep cliffs that rose from the desert. Here the tombs were built into the side of the rocky cliffs.

"Is this where Tutankhamun's tomb is?" Jo asked.

"No. His is further out still, in the Valley of the Kings." He led her through an entrance and down a narrow flight of stairs. "This is a series of interconnected tombs that are being built for high-level officials," he explained.

They traveled further into the cliff through a maze of dark hallways lit with torches. Although the entire area was still under construction, workers had already begun the elaborate scenes and hieroglyphs that would adorn every inch of wall space.

"Nekhare, I'd never find my way out of here on my own," Jo said.

"Sure you would. See, the main passageway is marked with gold sphinxes, miniatures of those that line the road between Karnak and Luxor." He stopped long enough to point to a few of them. The sphinxes were painted into the murals and would have been hard to notice if Nekhare hadn't showed them to her. "But here, we have arrived at our destination."

"Where are we?" Jo asked. They entered yet another tomb, but the entrance had no markings, so Jo did not know who it belonged to. They had entered through the rear hallway that connected this tomb to the others, but she could see that this tomb also had a doorway to the outside. A long flight of stairs led to a hint of light at the top.

"This is the tomb I am preparing for my own burial," Nekhare replied. "Tutankhamun has been gracious enough to assign me this spot, as both my parents are entombed at Amarna."

Jo noticed that the artists had already begun painting the murals that would tell the story of Nekhare's life. One wall depicted him as a young boy, hunting with a bow and arrow alongside a young Tutankhamun. He strolled over to a tall clay jar and pulled out a scroll. "Here are some of the inscriptions I have already written."

"Nekhare!" shouted someone from the top of the stairs.

"Yes?"

"Tutankhamun requests your presence."

Nekhare turned to Jo. "I thought Tutankhamun and Ankesenamun left for the palace already. I wonder what is going on. Are you all right here alone?"

"Of course," Jo said.

Nekhare handed her the scroll and bounded up the stairs.

Being careful not to disturb the work being done there, Jo continued to survey the tomb. She stuck her head into the adjoining chamber but could see nothing in the darkness. A little shiver ran up her spine. *Eternity*, she thought, *in this deep, dark hole.*

She returned to the main room and began reading the inscriptions, her back to the stairway. She was glad to hear Nekhare's footsteps on the stone stairs.

Only it wasn't Nekhare. It was an older man with a long gray beard.

"It is time to go home," he said as Jo turned to face him.

Jo didn't reply but continued to stare.

"We have been searching for you for a long time, Jo."

"Princess Johenamun."

"Yes, well ... *Princess*, then. Surely you are glad to see me? Come, I will take you home now."

"I *am* home."

The man in the picture! From Foster's book! Nekhare, where are you? She stared over the old man's shoulder, praying for the sound of more footsteps on the stairs.

"Now, now, Jo, dear. I can understand that you've ... how shall I say it? Stumbled into a good life here, but—"

"I said, it's *Princess Johenamun*. And don't talk to me as if I were a child. I know what I want, and I am not going *anywhere* with you."

Her mind raced. How would she escape him? Somehow she knew she had to stay far away from him, not let him touch her.

"I cannot and will not leave Egypt without you, *Jo*. I will take you by force if I must. Don't you want to see your mother again? She wants you home."

Jo nodded, biding her time, trying to figure how to escape. *If I can just hold him off until I can figure out ...*

He took a step closer.

"You saw my mother?" she asked. "She really wants me to come home?" Jo babbled, saying anything to keep him from coming closer. The strategy worked; he stopped advancing.

"I really do miss my mother," she said. *But that doesn't mean I want to go home.*

She kept talking. "I think you're right. I should go home." Wild hippos couldn't have dragged her from Kemet. She'd finally found a place where she belonged.

"Absolutely. The portal isn't open just yet, but come with me, and we will be ready when it is."

All she could think about was not letting him touch her. "If we go up the stairs, we may run headlong into Nekhare ... my boyfriend. He won't let me go easily."

The old man nodded. "I saw him leave a few minutes ago and thought you might be here alone."

"There is another way out," she said, thinking quickly. "We can go through the tunnel."

He looked at her skeptically.

"I know the way, and the exit is hidden. No one will see us," she lied.

"All right then," he said. "Lead the way."

Walking as slowly as she dared, Jo started off down the passageway, following the path marked by the sphinxes. Her brain went into overdrive, trying to figure out how to ditch the old guy. She knew she didn't have much time. Soon they would enter the section of the tombs that was older, more complete, and she knew they were likely to run into partygoers. She could think of only one thing to do; she let the scroll she was still carrying slip out of her hands, and she kept on walking.

Such a stupid trick—but it worked.

"You dropped this," the old man said. "Is it something you would like to take with you?"

He bent to pick it up. Jo shoved him as hard as she could; he toppled over, and Jo ran faster than she had ever run before.

"Jo, wait!" he called after her, but she never looked back. She heard his footsteps behind her, and then there were none. A couple of quick turns, and she'd lost him. Slowing, she nodded politely to those who stopped to stare at her, and then she began to wonder what had happened to Nekhare. She exited the tombs up a long stairway and ran across the short stretch of sand to the river's edge, her bulky ceremonial dress billowing behind her. One of the pharaoh's oarsmen rowed her to the other shore.

Nekhare found her much later, huddled in the chair in one corner of her room. She hadn't moved from there since her flight from the tomb. Nekhare entered her room, obviously angry with her for ditching him, but it didn't take him long to figure out that something was very wrong. He crossed the room and pulled her out of the chair. She wrapped her arms around his neck and clung to him. That was when she started to cry.

He just held her until she sobbed it all out, and then he asked, "What?"

"He's here. In the tomb," she said, still sniffing.

"Who's here?"

"The old man with the beard. The one who brought me to Kemet. He tried to take me with him."

"What?"

"He tried to take me back with him. Nekhare, you can't let him take me."

"I knew something was not right. Pharaoh had gone back to the palace after all. Someone was trying to get me out of the way."

"Please, I don't want to leave Kemet!"

"Of course not. You're not going anywhere—ever. But there's no need to run, either. I'll go back and—"

"No!"

"Don't you see? It would be much wiser for me to go back and deal with him now. I am not afraid, Jo. You shouldn't be either. We have the power of Pharaoh—"

"No. He has … some kind of … magic. Don't go near him. Just hide me, hide me forever. Can you do that?"

"No one will ever take you, Jo. I promise." She clung to him and stifled another sob into his shoulder. "At one time you sought him out."

"Yes, but this is my home now. Tutankhamun—"

"We will enlist his aid this time. You are safe in Kemet. I will alert the guards to our situation and inform Tutankhamun that you have officially requested sanctuary." He pulled away and looked Jo directly in the eyes. "You have nothing to fear."

She nodded.

"Jo …"

"Yes?"

"I requested Tutankhamun's permission for us to marry."

He caught Jo completely by surprise—but not because she hadn't been thinking about it too. What surprised her about Nekhare's proposal was that he hadn't discussed it with her first. In truth, she'd been thinking about what it might be like to marry Nekhare almost since the moment she arrived in Egypt. Suddenly—or maybe it wasn't so sudden—she'd begun to doubt whether that was what she really wanted.

Not that she wanted to go home. No, the bearded man's appearance in the tomb had only reminded her how she didn't want to return to her former lonely life. *You are destined for greatness*, Tutankhamun had said. Jo wanted to believe it, and she thought her greatness would only come here and now, in ancient Egypt.

"He said no." Nekhare's voice interrupted her thoughts.

"What?"

"He denied us permission."

"I … I … don't understand."

"He said that you are destined for great things and are not free to be married to me. What did he mean by that?"

"I have no idea," Jo said. But she was thinking, again, of the conversation she'd had with Tutankhamun in the boat on the way back from Meretsega.

Nekhare held her by both shoulders and looked into her eyes. "Surely you know what he is talking about."

"No, I don't. Why didn't you ask him?"

Nekhare's eyes started to darken; Jo had seen that happen before. "Jo, what have you been up to—"

"Nothing. I've been up to nothing," she said.

She could think only of keeping Nekhare from losing control. "Look, you know that I love you and want nothing else other than to be married to you," she lied. "I'll go to him—we'll go together—and ask again. Surely he will see it our way. He can't deny two people who are so obviously in love." She wrapped her arms around his neck and pressed her body to his. She felt his anger dissipate.

"Perhaps you are right," he said. "I'll be late, but I'll see you later, and we can decide upon a plan."

Jo nodded, and Nekhare left, pulling the door closed behind him.

Confused and anxious, Jo retrieved Foster's book from under the bed. She turned to the last entry that had appeared—been written for her—and stroked the pages.

Nothing happened.

She flipped the pages back and forth and ran her hands over them again.

The book had run out of words.

"A lot of good this does me," she said to herself. She shoved it back under her bed.

CHAPTER 18

The afternoon faded away, and still Nekhare didn't return. Jo decided to check on the queen but found her chambers empty. Just as she turned to leave the room, a messenger appeared at the doorway.

"I have a message for the queen," he said. It was one of the younger messengers Jo had seen frequently over the last few months.

"Fine. I'll take it."

He hesitated. "I was told to give it only to the queen."

"Don't be silly. Give it to me," Jo insisted. He looked around the room.

"Where is the queen?"

"What business is it of yours?" Jo asked. She couldn't believe the audacity of his question. "I am her personal scribe, and I will take the message *now.*" She snatched the scroll from his hand, and he backed out the doorway.

Jo opened the scroll, thinking she'd get a head start on the next day's correspondence.

> *Your Highness, Queen Ankesenamun, our plan has been set in motion. Do not go near the pharaoh's bedroom tonight.*

Jo stared at the scroll; the signature was unfamiliar to her. Plan? What plan? Who could possibly be warning the queen to stay away from Tutankhamun tonight? Why?

Because something is going to happen to the pharaoh tonight! And Ankesenamun knows all about it …

Jo shoved the scroll into her belt, stunned by what she had read, and wandered into the garden outside the royal chambers. She sat by the pool and tried to convince herself that there were many ways to interpret the missive she had just read. She took it from her belt and read it again.

There's just no way, Jo thought. *Ankesenamun would be the last person …* But there it was, evidence of the queen's conspiracy against her own husband.

Was nothing as it appeared in Kemet? Jo laughed at her own question. *What do I do now?* She heard footsteps behind her and turned, expecting Nekhare or the queen.

But it was Tutankhamun who entered the garden. Jo hurried to get up.

"Sit, Johenamun," directed the pharaoh, and Jo did as he commanded.

Tutankhamun approached the spot where she sat, and much to Jo's surprise, sat down on the damp, cool grass beside her. So close in fact, that their knees touched and Jo could smell the fragrance of his bath oils. He was wearing only his kilt—no armbands or wristbands or heavy beaded collars. Without all his finery, he was not so much the powerful pharaoh as he was the vulnerable young man.

Several minutes passed before he spoke. "You are deep in thought tonight."

"Yes, Your Highness."

"Nekhare told me of the man who searches for you, and he also reports that you have chosen to stay here in Kemet. You seek asylum from those who would take you from us?"

"Yes."

"Asylum is granted, of course. Measures have already been taken to ensure your safety."

"Thank you, Your Highness."

"I would not have you leave Kemet. Not now, not ever," he said. "But I wonder, do you miss the people you left behind?"

"Not really," Jo answered. "There is only my mother. I missed her a lot at first, but now I have ... all of you. This is where I belong."

"Yes. I know that you have an important role to play in Kemet. Your destiny is entwined with mine—with this kingdom's."

If my destiny is entwined with yours, she wondered, *then what happens when you die?*

"Your Highness," she ventured. "I'm not sure of my own destiny, but I fear for your safety. I think someone may be trying to kill you."

Tutankhamun laughed. "I'm sure there is. There are those who are loyal to me, and I'm sure there are just as many who are plotting, dreaming about the day I die. So many with agendas of their own. I am young and unwise, but I see treason in the eyes of so many of my people. I hear it in the whispers of the wind at night."

"I think I should tell you—"

"No. Don't tell me anything that could compromise your position, your own safety. Let Nankti tend to the business of keeping me safe."

"You trust the general?" Jo asked, her voice no more than a whisper now.

"I trust no one. A policy that you might want to adopt, by the way."

"Me?"

He leaned closer. "*Trust no one, Jo.*" He became quiet then, and the two of them sat there, shoulder to shoulder, taking in the night air. "But, yes. I trust Nankti as much as I trust anyone."

"Your Highness, why must you go to Syria? Why not send Horemheb with the armies and remain here in safety?"

"If I am to lead my people, I must appear strong and ready to defend my kingdom. This is my first such opportunity—a chance to present myself as a man of power. I have been trained in the art of warfare, and in truth, I am safer on the battlefield than I am here in the palace, where my enemies do not reveal themselves. I would rather die looking my enemy in the eye than with his sword in my back."

"Are you afraid?"

"Always, but to be Pharaoh is to live with fear. I am accustomed to it. Remember, death is only the door to another world." He paused, "When I return, *if* I return, things will most assuredly change. Kemet will be strong and prosperous again." He looked more carefully at Jo. "Nekhare asked for my permission for the two of you to be married."

"Yes, and you denied us."

"Do you know why?" he asked.

"No."

"I am aware that you and Nekhare think you are ... in love. But it is not your destiny to be his wife. You are destined to be queen."

"I don't understand."

"Sinuhe was the first to suggest it, but now I know it is true. Amun sent you to *me*. You will be my queen."

Stunned, Jo could do nothing but stare back.

"You will help me lead this kingdom to its rightful glory."

"You are asking me to marry you?"

He laughed. "No, I am not *asking*."

"There is so much you don't know, so much I can never tell you."

"I do not care who you are or where you came from. Amun could have snatched you from the gates of the Netherworld, for all I care. I just know that it is no coincidence that you arrived in Kemet when you did."

"But Nekhare ..."

"He will do as he is told. That is his duty."

"You would marry a girl who is in love with another man?" Jo asked.

Truth be told, Jo wasn't sure she was in love with Nekhare, at least not anymore. Perhaps she'd stopped caring about him on the night he hit her; perhaps it had just taken her this long to figure that out. Nonetheless, Tutankhamun didn't know anything about that, and she was amazed at the pharaoh's willingness to step between her and his supposed friend and ally.

He leaned closer and whispered, "Love is the luxury of the poor and the powerless. You and I care not of love, Jo. Before all else, we care about duty, about *Ma'at*. If love follows, then we will be truly blessed."

She didn't know how to respond.

"I offer you this: think about what I have said. If you decide that your love for Nekhare is deeper than your loyalty to your pharaoh and your love for your kingdom, then I will grant the two of you permission to marry. I will respect your decision. But, remember this: *you are destined for greatness.* I believe that *Ma'at* and the future of this kingdom lie with you."

With that, he was gone, leaving behind just the tinkling of the garden chimes. Jo knew what she had to do. She set off to find Nankti.

Late that night, two soldiers left the encampment on the north side of the palace and made their way to the royal family's apartments. They slipped through the shadows virtually unnoticed and arrived at the door of Tutankhamun's wing, where they found fewer guards than normal, just as they had been promised.

They hid in the shadows and went over the plan again. Then one of the men stepped into the dim light. He carried a clay jug and played his part—that of a drunken soldier—very well. One of the pharaoh's guards went to investigate. The guard was then knocked unconscious by the accomplice who stepped out of the shadows.

A few minutes later, another of the pharaoh's guards went to check on the first. He too was dispensed with. That left only one man at the door. The two soldiers were able to overtake him with relative ease; they hauled the guard into the bushes, where they bound and gagged him. One man kept watch, while the other crept into Tutankhamun's bedroom. He carried with him a long sword.

This is almost too easy, he thought to himself. In a few minutes, he'd be a wealthy man, on his way to Greece. There would be no more sleeping in the sand, no more army rations. In Greece, there would be wine, women, and everything else he could possibly want.

The young pharaoh was sound asleep and facing away from the door as the soldier drew nearer the bed. The soldier smiled to himself and raised his sword over his head. He brought it down hard. He waited for the warm, sticky blood that would most certainly spurt from the dying man. He expected to hear his raspy last gasp.

But something was wrong; the sword had gone in too easily.

Pillows, he thought to himself. *There's nothing in this bed but pillows. I've been betrayed!*

He turned to run and slammed right into Nankti, who had moved from the shadows in the corner to stand right behind the soldier.

"Fool," muttered Nankti, as he drove his knife into the soldier's gut.

The day following the festival was declared a day of rest. The navy stood poised and ready for departure, while normal operations at the palace were put on hold.

The evening before, Jo had delivered the note to Nankti, and he had read it while she watched.

"Go to your room," Nankti had said quietly, "and stay there. Do not come out until sunrise."

"But Tutankhamun—"

"Go now," he said, and Jo had no choice.

She had gone to her room, and she had lain in her bed all night, listening but hearing nothing. Finally, in the wee hours, she had fallen asleep. In the morning, the servants arrived as usual. Jo studied them carefully. If anything had happened in the palace overnight, the servants would know; they'd be talking about it.

Nothing.

Jo had decided to take her breakfast in the great room. There she found Meritaken and several of the courtiers. All of them laughed and chatted over breakfast. Jo figured she'd been terribly wrong, and she was embarrassed about bothering Nankti with the note. Either way, she had said nothing about any of it.

As was her duty, Jo reported to Ankesenamun.

She found the queen with the baby in the garden outside her chambers, the very same garden where Tutankhamun had proposed to her the night before—if *proposed* was an accurate description. In the morning sun, Jo thought Ankesenamun looked more beautiful than ever, and she couldn't imagine, even for a moment, that the queen could conspire against her husband. Surely the note and everything that Jo had suspected had been all wrong.

"Tutankhamun has informed me that you will be his wife," said Ankesenamun.

Jo blushed.

"You have no reason to feel ashamed."

Jo blushed even deeper.

"You have done nothing wrong," continued Ankesenamun.

"But he is your husband, and I am your friend," replied Jo.

"Yes, you and I are friends." She smiled. "So I can tell you that I was hoping this day would never come."

Jo nodded.

"I even tried to convince him to arrange your marriage to Nekhare."

"You did?"

"Yes. I saw Pharaoh's growing fascination with you."

That makes one of us.

"I know he admires your strength. He and I both believe that Amun sent you here to aid him in some way."

"Yes, so he said."

The queen continued. "Tutankhamun and I were married when he was only nine years old. Together we were taken from our home in Amarna and brought here to Waset—a strange city and a strange new life. All that we had known before—our families, even our God—was gone. All that we had was each other, and we have grown to truly love each other. But all along I knew that someday he might seek out another wife. Such is the way with the pharaohs. It is his *duty*, especially since I have been unable to give him a son."

"You still have time—"

"I will soon be beyond the child-bearing years. I am ten years older than Tutankhamun. He needs you. You were sent to us by Amun, and you will bear many sons. You are the perfect choice. The kingdom knows you as *Princess*

Johenamun, so the marriage will be natural in their eyes. We know, however, that you are not truly of the royal family."

"How did you know?" Jo asked.

"I have my sources. Nothing goes on in this palace that I don't know something about. Anyway, you bring new blood, something the royal family desperately needs. Many more healthy babies will be born. Truly there are worse fates than being joined by marriage to the Lord of the Two Lands."

"But Ankesenamun, what if I can't produce sons for Tutankhamun?"

"Then you will do what I did," she replied. Jo stared back, unsure of what she meant. "You will find a way."

Jo was speechless. "Are you telling me that Kiya is not Tutankhamun's baby?"

"No, I am not telling you that, but you can assume what you will. I had to produce a child."

"But if anyone ever finds out …"

"No one will ever find out."

"How can you be sure? Ankesenamun, what if Pharaoh—"

"He won't. Kiya's father cares only for his kingdom. He will never tell Tutankhamun, and neither will I. And you won't, either."

"Ankesenamun, this is difficult. You are my friend," Jo repeated.

"Yes, I am. And you are mine. If Tutankhamun must take another wife, then I am grateful that she will be my friend, rather than my enemy. Together we will help to make this kingdom great again. Many challenges confront our king, and he will need both of us by his side." Ankesenamun took both of Jo's hands in hers. "Accept your role graciously."

They sat together in silence.

At last, the queen spoke. "He is Pharaoh, and he will have what he wants."

Jo looked up at her then, startled by the determined edge her voice had taken on. "What will I tell Nekhare?"

"Tell him that this is your destiny. It is what the gods have chosen for you. Tutankhamun is a kind and gentle man. He will treat you better than Nekhare has."

CHAPTER 19

On a grassy plain north of the palace, several hundred of the pharaoh's men prepared for departure. Tutankhamun sat on a throne that had been carried to the field and placed upon a raised platform. He wore the full battle regalia of the kings of Kemet, complete with mail, the bull's tail hanging from his belt.

The elite chariot corps, the unit that the pharaoh himself would eventually be part of, had left for Memphis two weeks earlier; the infantry, earlier still. A group of soldiers known as the retainers remained in Waset. These men had been hand-selected to march into battle with the pharaoh. They would sail downriver to Memphis with the king and were prepared to fight on land or at sea. Among them were the generals Nankti and Horemheb.

The departure of the troops had been carefully timed. Eventually ten thousand soldiers from the Upper Division would meet ten thousand from the Lower Division just outside Memphis, in the delta region. Together, under the king's banner, they would march north toward Syria.

Officers shouted orders at the sweating men as Tutankhamun surveyed the troops. Nekhare supervised army scribes who kept detailed records of supplies and weapons as they were handed out to the men. Meritaken and Ankesenamun stood to Tutankhamun's left, the baby Kiya asleep in her mother's arms.

Jo watched this scene as she approached on a white stallion she had borrowed from the pharaoh's stables. She'd spent the night preparing and planning, and then dressed herself in her riding gear and a short-sleeved coat of bronze mail that she'd stolen from the garrison. She braided her hair in one long braid and placed a visored helmet on her head. The only makeup she wore was the *kohl* around her eyes.

She saw Tutankhamun stand and point his sword at the sun. The crowd fell silent.

"Go forth and destroy all those who would threaten this great kingdom. Bring glory to Kemet and to Amun! March into battle without fear, for we shall return victorious with the heads of our enemies atop our spears!"

A cheer went up from the assembled crowd, and when the troops finally quieted, they heard the thunder of hooves. Jo urged the huge stallion into a gallop, his silver mane and tail sparkling in the sun, and directed him toward the crowd. She pulled the horse to a skidding stop in front of the platform. Sand flew everywhere.

The entire assembly stood in stunned silence.

"Princess Johenamun! An interesting send-off," said Tutankhamun.

Out of the corner of her eye, Jo saw Nekhare approach the platform.

She drew a deep breath. "I have not come to say good-bye. I am going with you."

"Absolutely not," replied Tutankhamun. He turned to leave.

"Wait." She spurred the horse to block his descent from the platform. "It makes perfect sense."

"It makes no sense at all. We are not off on a little adventure. We go to *war*. I will not subject you to such danger."

"And I'm not in danger here? Your Highness, my greatest fear is being here in Waset, at the palace, without you and without Nekhare."

"I assure you, the palace guards will protect you from the one you fear."

Jo moved the horse closer still, ignoring Nekhare, who now stood near the platform. "You know I can be of assistance to you. You need people who are loyal, who can ride and are true with an arrow."

"I need you here to assist the queen."

"She does not need me here; we both know that. You said it yourself: I'm better on horseback than on my own two feet. Ay remains here to assist the queen. Take me with you."

Tutankhamun did not reply.

"Surely you are not considering her request," interjected Nekhare. "She will only be in our way."

Stung by Nekhare's hurtful remark, Jo continued, "I know it's not the usual thing to do, but what about me has ever been usual? And it's not without precedent. There was Hatshepsut, after all. She fought in many battles—"

"I know, I know. Don't quote Kemetan history to *me*."

He was irritated with her. She tried a different approach. "Amun sent me to you, but not because I'm good at running the royal household or managing the accounts. He sent me to you because I can ride, I can shoot, and because he knew that I would grow to love … this kingdom … enough to march around the entire world, if need be."

The assembled crowd was so quiet they could have heard the passing of a crocodile in the Nile half a mile away. The horse pawed at the ground.

"You said that I am destined for greatness," Jo continued. "I say that this is my destiny: to march to Syria with you."

"And what if it is your *destiny* to die in the desert at Kadesh or Megiddo? Are you prepared for that, Princess Johenamun?" Tutankhamun moved down the stairs and stood eye-to-eye with Jo as she sat upon her horse.

During the course of the night, she had considered that possibility. "I am," she replied, sounding more confident than she was feeling.

He didn't respond but continued to stare at her.

Jo turned her horse and faced the assembled crowd. "Like these brave men, I too would be honored to die in defense of my king and my kingdom."

A resounding cheer went up from the pharaoh's troops.

"Come here," the pharaoh said.

She jumped from her horse and climbed the stairs.

He spoke for all to hear, "If you are to travel to Syria with me, then you will go as my wife. We have only to declare it to be so."

"Then I declare it to be so," Jo said.

CHAPTER 20

They sailed downriver in three of Tutankhamun's huge barges. Each of the ships had tall masts, but they were also equipped with stations for thirty rowers, should they need to travel faster than wind or current could take them. Tutankhamun and Jo traveled on *The Wild Bull* and Nekhare on *The Power of Amun*. Jo never asked who had made the decision for Nekhare and her to travel on different boats, but she knew she was glad not to have to see him regularly. With Nekhare comfortably distant, it was easier to pretend he wasn't hurt and to push guilt aside.

She had done what she had to do. If Nekhare was feeling betrayed—and Jo was quite sure that he was—he'd just have to get over it. Love, as Tutankhamun had pointed out, was for those with smaller roles to play. Sometime in the middle of the night, while the palace lay in shadows, she had seen clearly for the first time.

I was sent to save the king.

She did know that all events had led to this, her journey with Tutankhamun to Syria. Perhaps it was Foster who had originally sent her to Kemet, but Jo knew it was bigger than that. More likely it was a greater power, perhaps the gods that Tut was so devoted to. It didn't matter. Either way, she accepted, even relished her role. Her wedding might have been impromptu and somewhat less than ceremonious, but she was no less committed to her husband and her kingdom.

She was queen of the greatest kingdom on earth.

It would take some getting used to.

In the early evening, they disembarked, and the soldiers used their shields, tips buried in the sand, to form a temporary wall around Tutankhamun's tent. The men went about the business of making camp—cooking, repairing equipment, cleaning weapons.

Of course, Jo's addition to the trip had been last-minute, so at first, the soldiers were unsure of where she was supposed to sleep. It was customary for

Pharaoh and his queen—not just this royal couple but all of them—to keep separate bedrooms, but they hadn't made any preparations for Jo. Tutankhamun solved the dilemma by offering to share his bed. She accepted his offer, since the alternative was to sleep in the sand with the scorpions.

On that first night, without servants to prepare her evening bath, she bathed herself with water lugged in by a couple of soldiers and combed out her own hair, which had grown long and was streaked lighter from the sun. Tut had offered to send back to the palace for a couple of her servants, but Jo declined. Like most Kemetans, she was in the habit of sleeping in the nude. After much deliberation, she ended up crawling into bed in her makeshift trousers and top. Tutankhamun came in after she'd already fallen asleep, but she awoke later in the night to find him curled against her, his breath warm on the back of her head.

It wasn't until breakfast the second day that Jo heard about the foiled assassination plot. She and Tutankhamun were still in their tent, sitting on low stools, their breakfast on a table before them, when Nankti, Horemheb, and two of the captains entered. They spent a few minutes debriefing while Jo listened in, and then Nankti said to Tutankhamun, "You must tell her."

Tutankhamun didn't respond right away. Horemheb stood, arms folded, near the exit.

"She needs to know."

"Where's Nekhare?" Tut asked, finally.

"Supervising the inventory," Horemheb replied.

"Your Highness—" began Nankti.

"Yes, yes. I know," said the pharaoh. He turned to his bride. "The note that you intercepted, we think it was from Suppliminus. It seems he thought he could save himself a lot of trouble if he had me murdered before I left the palace. He hired a small group of mercenaries to infiltrate my men."

Jo could only stare.

"Two nights ago, there was an assassination attempt. If you hadn't handed that note to Nankti, well ..."

"An assassination attempt? No one said anything," Jo said finally.

"It was imperative that no one know. *Ma'at* must not be disturbed. Only the six of us in this tent know anything about this. Not Nekhare, not Ay. Nankti cleaned up the mess, and—"

"Ankesenamun?"

The tent grew very quiet.

"We don't really know—"

"Your Highness," interrupted Nankti, "what is it going to take for you to see—"

Tutankhamun cut him off with a wave of his hand. "We don't know anything for sure. Ankesenamun …" he looked at Nankti, "… deserves the chance to tell her side of the story. That much at least. Until then, we will assume that she had no part in this conspiracy."

Nankti shook his head. Horemheb visibly relaxed.

Tut turned back to Jo. "You saved my life. I am grateful."

"*We* are grateful," said Nankti. He knelt before Jo and touched his forehead to the sand, a gesture of respect always reserved for pharaoh and his queen. "Your Highness." The two captains followed suit.

Horemheb remained standing by the doorway.

Jo spent the first few weeks of her married life—her honeymoon, so to speak—listening to the sounds of the camp at night, the footsteps of the guards who continually circled her tent, and the whispers of those who were entrusted with her safety. Inside the tent, hushed conversations were ongoing. Jo told Tutankhamun everything she suspected about Nekhare, about the conversations she'd overheard, about his late-night confession that he wanted to be king, and about his adamant denial of plotting murder.

"Then most likely he was telling you the truth," replied Tutankhamun. "He might very well have been plotting to bring Piay down. We have talked about it many times. When this is all over, I'll talk with him about it again."

"And until then?" Jo asked. "What about the remote possibility that he might be trying to kill you?"

Tut laughed. "He certainly isn't stupid enough to try anything while I am surrounded by hundreds of my best men."

He isn't stupid, Jo thought, *but he craves power.*

They talked about Ankesenamun also, and Tutankhamun struggled with the idea that Ankesenamun had plotted against him. What could possibly be her motive? The death of the pharaoh would only bring chaos and uncertainty. It would be a dangerous time for all, including the queen and her baby. And how did Suppliminus fit into the picture?

Of course, Jo had the one piece of information that Tutankhamun did not have: Kiya was not his child. He'd find that out, eventually, but Jo was sure she didn't want to be the one to tell him. She spent a lot of time thinking about the last conversation she'd had with Ankesenamun. Perhaps the queen was hoping to marry the baby's father. Then again, perhaps she had been set up. It was all so very confusing, and in the back of her head, always, was the information she had read in Foster's book.

"Horemheb?" Jo asked.

Tut laughed. "He doesn't like taking orders from me, that's for sure."

"And he *really* won't like taking orders from me," Jo added.

"But he has taken the oath. Horemheb is nothing if not an honor-bound military man. He will not harm me, nor will he conspire to."

"But ..."

"You will have to trust me about this," he said.

"You said I should trust no one."

He grew very serious. "It's a dangerous place we are in, and I'm not talking about the battle we may end up fighting against the Hittites." Jo nodded. "You saved my life because you were alert and suspicious. That's a good lesson for both of us."

They sat on his big bed, a *senet* board between them. He leaned across the board and kissed her before continuing—though Jo wished that he would kiss her again. "Just for tonight, let's trust each other. Let's pretend we are the only two people alive."

She gazed into the eyes of her pharaoh, her husband, and the truth hit her. She hadn't married him out of duty or because of some sense of destiny; she had married him for love. In that moment, it occurred to her that she even knew when she had fallen in love with him: it was the morning before they had all traveled out to Medinet Habu, the morning she and Nekhare had asked his permission for her to go along.

On that morning, her knees shook, her heart did backflips, and she had thought that she was afraid of the great and powerful Pharaoh Tutankhamun. Funny how she had confused the two—fear and attraction—but then maybe Nekhare, and Jo's belief that she was in love with him, had something to do with that.

"Yes," Jo responded, finally. "I'd be happy if we were the only two people on the face of the earth." *So much less to deal with.* And then she leaned forward, and *she* kissed *him*.

Word of their marriage scurried along ahead of them, and people lined the riverbanks in hopes of catching a glimpse of the pharaoh and his golden-haired bride. Everywhere there was a sense of joy and pride and high expectations. Tutankhamun's men called Jo *Your Highness*. Even Horemheb was forced to acknowledge her new role.

About halfway through their journey, Tutankhamun pointed Jo to the west and whispered in her ear, "There, on the horizon. Akhetaten." He paused. "The northern wind throws sand at her, and she crumbles in the sun."

Jo could see the outline of the distant city. The pharaoh stood behind Jo and wrapped his arms around her waist; she rested her head against his shoulder. Jo smiled at the intimacy of the moment and wished with all her heart that they could stay right where they were—in that moment in time—and forget about all that was behind them and ahead of them. As the two of them watched, his boyhood home slid out of sight.

In her haste, Jo had left her journal and Foster's book tucked safely under her bed in Waset, but upon request, an army scribe had provided her with a slender scroll of papyrus and a fine quill. With so much time on her hands, she kept her journal religiously and recorded everything that happened and everything she saw as they sailed downriver.

She made sketches of the landscape and some of the temples and other buildings they passed, not really understanding why she felt compelled to do so; Nekhare's team of scribes would record the entire journey, and more than likely her own work would never be needed. Perhaps it was her short training to be a scribe that compelled her, or perhaps it was that *intellectual curiosity* Foster had talked about so long ago. Jo knew that many of the temples she sketched would disappear before archaeologists and scientists would have the opportunity to study them.

And what about her own life? Would she show up in the footnotes of history texts—second wife to the famous Pharaoh Tutankhamun? Perhaps that was up to Nekhare; after all, he was in charge of the official record.

Her dedication to her journal did not go unnoticed. One night, just a few days from Memphis, Tutankhamun asked, "Will you read to me from your scroll?"

Jo read a few pages she'd written as she observed some farmers laboring in the fields.

"You have a way with words," he said. "I'm glad you are writing ... all of this. Nekhare will write his account, of course, but I think that your point of view might be more optimistic."

"Perhaps," Jo said. It wasn't hard for her to imagine what Nekhare's mood might be like since her hasty marriage, but she also knew he'd do his duty, no matter how betrayed he was feeling. She and Tutankhamun sat crossed-legged, facing each other, on the big bed that had been assembled for them. The only sounds were the hushed conversations of the guards.

"You do not regret ..." he searched for words, "any of what has come to pass?"

"No. Never. Your Highness, there is much I still don't understand, but of this I am sure: this is the way it is supposed to be. You and me, together."

He nodded.

Jo rolled the scroll back to a poem she had begun a few days earlier and read:

> *She arrived from a land too distant*
> *to be imagined,*
> *a fair-haired girl, confused and lonely,*
> *blinded and not yet able to find*
> *the path that lay before her.*
> *He too was born of another time,*
> *When gentle grace was the way of the land.*
> *They thrust upon him the role of God-King,*
> *and he accepted his destiny.*
> *He saw in her a Golden Queen,*
> *and on a brilliantly blue day*
> *they joined hands.*
> *He showed her how duty*
> *can turn to love;*

*she reminded him that
trust can sometimes be found
where it is least expected.*

"It's not yet complete," she said.

"It's beautiful. No wonder Sinuhe demoted me to Second-Best Student Ever," he said, smiling. "You've told our story better than I could have."

The river widened and became more of a marsh as they approached Memphis, the northern capital, where they would stay for a few days while they restocked supplies and met up with the Northern Army.

Although Waset was the religious capital of the kingdom, Memphis was the administrative capital. It was a huge city, but it lacked the beauty of Waset and its magnificent temples. Tutankhamun kept a palace there—larger than the one in Waset—even though he rarely stayed in it. Jo received her own apartment, and a legion of servants waited on her, hand and foot.

They held court in the Royal Audience Hall, and Memphis socialites, dignitaries, and courtiers paraded before Jo. All of them had some excuse to capitalize on the rare chance to catch a glimpse of the pharaoh. Jo knew that many of them wanted to check out the new wife as well. While in Memphis, she ordered the servants to take extra care with her hair and makeup. She sat by her husband's side and smiled benevolently at even the most difficult visitors. She considered her words carefully and gave opinions only on those matters she fully understood.

Tutankhamun spent the afternoons inspecting the troops and refining travel and battle plans. As queen, Jo made dozens of decisions about furniture and pottery and food to be served at royal dinners. Bored with that role, she begged Tutankhamun to take her with him to his meetings.

"Danger comes soon enough," he replied.

"So I need to understand what you are planning," she insisted.

"You will be briefed soon. Until then, enjoy the comforts of the palace. Who knows how long it will be before we are able to enjoy such luxuries again?"

On the third night of their stay in Memphis, Tutankhamun had been out on the practice fields all day, and it was late when the door opened and he strolled in. The servants who had been attending to Jo's bath disappeared like a desert mirage.

"You are upset," she said. She could tell by the frown on his face and by his body language; he seemed like a tiger ready to pounce.

"Messengers report that the infantry has already encountered some minor resistance. We didn't expect that so early—in the Sinai."

"I see. But we have been … victorious?"

"Of course." He smiled. "It's not so much to worry about, really. The infantry is still on schedule to meet us at the designated spot." He continued, "You are well taken care of?"

"Of course."

"We will depart the day after tomorrow, and I worry about you."

"Me? Why?"

"You do not understand what lies ahead." He stepped close and freed Jo's hair from its braid. Jo held her ground and looked up into his dark eyes, eyes she once feared. "I'm afraid you might try something foolish or dangerous. Promise me that you won't."

"I won't," she said.

He pulled her close and ran his hand down the length of her hair. "You won't do anything foolish, or you won't promise me?"

"I won't promise you," she replied.

He smiled. "I can think of no other who would dare defy me, at least to my face."

"I'll do anything else you ask," Jo said, "but I can't promise that I'll watch you die. If it comes to that, I'll be right by your side."

"Perhaps I should leave you in Memphis."

She laughed. "You can try."

When she awoke, Tutankhamun was gone, but she received a message from him later that morning asking her to come out to the practice field to review the troops. The procedure was ceremonial, especially considering that the infantry had already left ahead of them, but Jo appreciated the fact that she was included.

Dressed once again in her "warrior princess" clothing, she waited for her escort. She'd worked on her wardrobe since arriving in Memphis and had convinced the royal seamstresses to make her several tank tops with matching trousers—baggy, gauzy things that wouldn't inhibit her movement. Over the tank top, she wore her chain-mail jacket.

Nankti arrived to lead her from the apartment. "We will review the chariot troops from the Ptah division, the one that is headquartered here in Memphis. Tutankhamun waits for you on the field."

He led her through the palace and into the courtyard, where the palace guards waited with horses. He offered her a leg up and then, much to her surprise, a fine spear with a golden tip. They galloped off toward the field with the palace guards struggling to keep pace.

"Tutankhamun is over there, under the banner," Nankti pointed out as they reined the horses in. They trotted over to meet him, and the ceremony began.

Tutankhamun and Jo rode first, with Nankti and the other generals following. As they passed the soldiers, each one in turn fell to his knees and touched his forehead to the ground. When the soldiers returned to their feet, Jo heard a murmur among them.

Tutankhamun laughed. "You seem to have taken my men by surprise," he said. "I hope they recover before encountering any enemy forces."

"I'm … s … s …sorry," Jo stuttered. "Perhaps I shouldn't have worn this …"

"Your manner of dress is perfect," he replied.

When they reached the end of the line, they swung the horses around, and Tutankhamun held his spear high over his head. "To the Glory of Amun!" he shouted.

He dug his heels into his horse, and the huge stallion leaped into a gallop. Jo had only to release the pressure on the reins for her horse to follow. The two of them raced a huge circle around the whole battalion, while the sand flew and the men cheered.

Later that night, after her bath, Jo lay in bed listening to the muffled sounds of the palace at rest. She was waiting, hoping the pharaoh would stop to say goodnight before making his way to his own apartment. She rolled over on her side and pulled her lightweight bedcovers up to her chin. After spending the better part of a month in the constant company of Tutankhamun, she now missed him when he was otherwise occupied.

I'm so in love with him, she thought, and that amused and amazed her at the same time. How strange her life had become, how wonderfully strange.

The door opened and closed, and Jo smiled to herself, but it was not Tutankhamun who pulled the curtains aside and crawled beside her on the bed.

"How did you get in here?" she gasped.

"Shhh," Nekhare whispered. "You'll alert the bodyguards."

"You've got to leave, now!" Jo said. "Tutankhamun—"

"Is still in a meeting with the generals. I've just come from there."

"If he catches you here, he'll have you executed."

"No, he won't. Exiled, maybe, but not executed. Not his boyhood friend." Nekhare laughed harshly.

"What do you want?" Jo asked.

Nekhare moved closer and pinned her to the bed with one leg. "You, of course."

"Well, you can't have me. I'm—"

"Yes, I know, but that doesn't mean you have to stay with him. I have a boat in the harbor waiting to take us to Greece."

"What?" She couldn't believe what she was hearing.

"A boat. To Greece. And I have secured a place for us to live. We will be happy there, just you and me." He tried to kiss her, but she managed to turn her face away from him in time to avoid it.

"I'm not going anywhere with you."

"I know you love me. Don't be afraid. We'll be out of the palace and well on our way before Tutankhamun even discovers we are missing."

"No."

He paused then, as if it were the first time he had even considered that she wouldn't *want* to go with him.

"Jo, he will let us go. He won't even give chase. He's much too busy with plans for battle. We'll be safe, I promise."

"No."

"You don't think he will ever love you, do you? He married you for what you could do for him. If you don't produce sons, he'll discard you like he did Ankesenamun. I'm the one who loves you. Come with me, Jo."

She could feel the anger rising in him. "I love him."

He paused. "This is all about Ankesenamun and me, isn't it?" He sounded desperate.

"What?"

"She told you, didn't she? It's not what you think … it was for our kingdom, our king. She had to have a healthy baby—"

"You? It was you?"

"Yes. But it is you I love. Only you." He still had her pinned to the bed.

A door slammed, and Nekhare jumped. "Pharaoh's bodyguards have come to check his apartment for his arrival," Jo said. "They'll come in here next."

Nekhare slid off the bed. "This isn't over." And then he was gone, over the balcony railings, she supposed, leaving behind the heavy aroma of his bath oils.

Jo panicked. Certainly Tutankhamun would recognize Nekhare's distinctive scent. She jumped out of bed and pulled on a soft tunic, just as the door opened and the pharaoh entered. She met him at the door, determined to keep him away from her bed, fearful of what might happen if the pharaoh discovered that Nekhare had been in her room.

"I thought you might be asleep already," he said. "Our discussion went overly long, as usual."

"No, I couldn't sleep. Your Highness, who is on guard outside my door tonight?"

"Why?" Tutankhamun asked. Jo could see him tense even in the dim light. "They haven't bothered you, have they?"

"Not at all, but one of them has a cough, I think. He is keeping me awake."

"I'll have Nankti replace them both immediately." She thought she heard surprise in his voice; it was unlike her to complain.

"Good night, then," Jo said.

He paused, now looking truly surprised at the disinvitation. "Good night," he said, and then he left the room.

They boarded the ships again and set sail out of the Nile and into the Mediterranean Sea. Sailing along the northern coast of the Sinai, they finally docked at the city of Gaza. From here they would make the journey on horseback and in chariots, the infantry following behind them on foot.

Jo was summoned to Tutankhamun's tent on the night before the march was to begin.

"The enemy has established outposts in this region," he told her. "We don't expect much difficulty in taking them; however, I want to be prepared for any eventuality." He paused. "I have decided that you will ride behind the retainers, and I have selected two bodyguards to protect you at all times. They have orders to retreat with you if we encounter any real resistance."

"But—" she began.

"No arguments," Tutankhamun interrupted. "I agreed to let you travel with me, but I certainly won't have you involved in combat."

"I can handle myself," Jo insisted.

"On the practice field, perhaps. But this is not practice. Don't assume for a moment that Hittite warriors will have any sympathy for a woman on the battlefield. No, they will think of you as a special prize. I do not care for the idea of your head upon some Hittite spear."

She gulped.

"Or perhaps they might make a prisoner of you, take you home with them for a while before they torture and kill you. Can you not imagine what they might do with a beautiful blonde queen, given the chance?"

"But I came with you to help protect you, not to retreat at the first sign of trouble."

"You'll have to rely on my men to protect me. They've been training for battle all of their lives," Tutankhamun replied.

But I'm not sure that's long enough, she thought to herself.

CHAPTER 21

They set off across the sandy wasteland in a choking cloud of dust, the trumpeters leading the way. Behind them followed the charioteers and Tutankhamun himself. Jo and her bodyguards brought up the rear of that division. The rest of the infantry traveled with them, followed by the supply train. This territory was still under Kemetan rule, but bands of Hittites had infiltrated and set up bases from which to aid others who would follow.

Over the next few days, as they moved northward, they encountered several meager outposts that the enemy held. At the sight of the huge Kemetan army, these forts surrendered without hesitation, and Jo hoped that the entire campaign would be equally bloodless. The forts were disarmed, and Tutankhamun sent the captured soldiers back to Memphis under heavy guard.

It took them eleven days to reach Yehem, a city that still paid tribute to the pharaoh. It was smaller than both Waset and Memphis but well situated at the fork of a river. The entire Kemetan army, twenty thousand strong, camped on the broad plain before the city gates. The landscape was dotted with tents, and the smoke from cook fires spiraled into the sky.

This was a time for regrouping, mending equipment, restocking supplies, and resting the horses. Each man knew his tasks, and the hastily assembled camp ran as smoothly as the pharaoh's palace in Waset. All too soon, they received word from the scouts that the enemy was encamped at Megiddo, about four days' march to the north. On the tenth day after their arrival in Yehem, they marched northward.

Soon the flat land gave way to rolling hills, and on the horizon, Jo could see a range of mountain peaks. A strange feeling grew inside her, part dread and part excitement. The mountains fascinated her, and Tutankhamun had mentioned that they might actually encounter rain in the more moderate climate they were entering. *Rain.* How long had it been since she'd felt the rain? The Nile River valley was virtually rain-free, and suddenly Jo felt herself longing for a Florida-style downpour.

Tutankhamun and his generals knew that the most direct route to the enemy encampment would take them through Aruna, the city that guarded a narrow mountain pass to Megiddo. Tutankhamun's advisers recommended that he use an alternate route, one that would take more time but would not require the army to march through the treacherous pass, which was so narrow that it allowed only two or three chariots through at a time. Their spies reported no enemy soldiers on the other side of the pass; still, Tutankhamun and his advisers realized that the charioteers would be easy targets as they moved through the pass if indeed Suppliminus sent troops southward to intercept them.

The pharaoh decided on a complicated plan: he sent one division to the east and one to the west. These divisions would circle around and protect the charioteers and the retainers as they thrust their way through the pass.

Once again, Jo found herself camped outside the gates of a city. This time, however, they would stay just long enough to give the infantry a head start. In the end, they were there just three days, and Jo was glad for it. With fewer of the pharaoh's men camped with them, she felt vulnerable and nervous. She found herself watching the horizon, always aware of how few men guarded the pharaoh: five hundred at best.

She was relieved when they broke camp and set out again, now moving quickly toward the Megiddo pass, anxious to meet up again with the Kemetan army.

Unfortunately, scouts had failed to report the presence of an enemy battalion lurking in the rocks on the other side—although how the scouts managed to miss a thousand men, Jo would never understand.

The day was windy and almost cool, and most of the chariot units had made their pass through—Tutankhamun and the retainers in the lead—when Tutankhamun's unit was attacked and effectively cut off from the infantry. The topography was rugged and rocky here, and soon the pharaoh's men were divided. A large group of perhaps two hundred chariots, each with driver and archer, pressed northward with Horemheb in command. The rest stayed behind with Tutankhamun and Nankti to defend the rear. Word came that the infantry was engaged with a larger enemy force to the north of the pass.

Immediately, Jo was surrounded by a ring of chariots and dragged from her horse—Tutankhamun's plan to ensure her safety. Her bodyguards pinned her to the ground, and all she could see was the legs of the horses. Of course, she lost sight of Pharaoh's standard.

She fought with all her strength to get away, but Tutankhamun had managed to find the two heaviest men in the unit and assign them to Jo, or so it seemed to her. She heard the sounds of the battle all around her—the clashing of metal, the stomping of horses' hooves, and the occasional scream of a wounded soldier—but she could see nothing.

It went on for what seemed like hours, until Jo heard one of her bodyguards say, "Let's get her out of here while we can."

They picked her up by her elbows and carried her through the ring of chariots, her feet never touching the ground. She searched in vain for Tutankhamun's banner. All around were bodies, some of them gushing blood, some missing arms or legs or heads. Somehow, the Kemetan army had pushed the Hittites back, Jo thought. Still, she could think only of finding Tutankhamun.

The guards set her down between them but continued to clasp her elbows. "We'll have you out of here in no time, Your Highness," said one of them.

"I'm not going anywhere," replied Jo.

"Your Highness, we are under orders—"

"Well, *I'm* ordering you to—"

She heard the unmistakable *thwack* of an arrow, and the guard on her left fell to his knees, the arrow buried in his shoulder. She screamed, and the remaining guard covered her mouth with his huge hand.

Up ahead, on top of a small, grassy hill, Jo could make out the standard of the king, and beneath the flag was Tutankhamun. Beside him stood the hulking Nankti. Together, they were driving back a small group of the enemy, long swords flashing in the summer sun. Jo buried her teeth in the guard's fingers and at the same time twisted just enough to knee him in the groin. He was surprised enough to loosen his grip for just a second or two, which was all the time it took for her to escape his grasp.

He recovered promptly and gave chase, but where he was big and bulky, Jo was nimble and fast. She had covered half the distance to the pharaoh, vaguely aware of a sharp pain in her leg, when she saw a man—a Kemetan, one of her own men—fall to the ground with an arrow through his neck. His bow bounced out of his hands, the arrow still nocked. Jo scooped it up as she ran, faster now, toward the hill and Tutankhamun.

Suddenly a tall, bloody Hittite warrior broke free from the battle and approached Tutankhamun and Nankti from the right. Nankti turned just in time to hold off the Hittite, and Tutankhamun stepped toward them to aid his comrade. Just as he did so, another Hittite warrior approached from behind the pharaoh with his sword held high in both hands.

"*No!*" Jo screamed. Without thinking, she pulled back the bowstring and let the arrow fly.

It found its mark right between the shoulder blades of the enemy.

He didn't fall right away. Instead he turned, slowly, and when he dropped to his knees, his eyes reflected those of a slender warrior, her blonde hair, having escaped its braid, loose and blowing in the breeze.

He fell face-first into the dirt.

Around her, the battle died, and Jo was vaguely aware that the eyes of many men had turned in her direction. She approached the fallen soldier with the odd thought of retrieving the arrow.

Blood oozed from where her arrow had buried itself in his back. Her stomach wrenched, and her legs wobbled. She clasped the arrow with both hands, and for some reason unknown even to herself, attempted to pull it free. It remained lodged in the enemy's back. She gazed down at her hands and saw that they were red with blood. She was aware of a warm trickle that ran down her face, neck, and chest. Her own blood, from a wound that she'd received when her two guards had pulled her from her horse, mixed with that of the enemy's.

Just then, a startled Tutankhamun turned in time to see Jo sink to her knees.

Nankti hurried to her side and succeeded in breaking the arrow at the point at which it had entered the enemy's back. With his boot, he rolled the dead man over.

Nekhare.

CHAPTER 22

Jo awoke wrapped in a light blanket on a cot in a hastily erected tent. The stench of battle hung heavy in the air. Tutankhamun sat by her side on a low stool, holding her hand. He smiled weakly and smoothed her hair away from her eyes with his free hand.

She tried to stifle a sob. "Nekhare?"

"We buried him," said the king in a low voice.

"I ... don't ... understand."

"He would have killed me. At least a dozen of my men saw the whole thing, but none of them acted as quickly as you. If not for you, it would be me in that shallow grave, and my kingdom would have no king. You saved me—again."

"The Hittite gear?"

"He took it off a fallen soldier, no doubt."

For a long time, she couldn't say anything at all; the enormity of what she had done so overwhelmed her. She replayed the scene over and over again in her head, trying to comprehend everything that had happened. Tears ran down her cheeks, and when she looked up again at Tutankhamun, she saw tears in his eyes as well.

"He made the decision, Jo ..."

"Because of me."

"He had many reasons to want me out of the way. You are only one of them. Who knows when he decided to do what he did? Perhaps a long time ago. I told you that there were traitors among us. There always are."

"I am so confused by all of this. Who is conspiring with whom?"

"I'm sure there are many plots. But many will see your defense of your pharaoh as the favor of the gods. Some of those who plot against me will now fear the wrath of Amun. All of them will fear *you*." He smiled.

"What about Suppliminus?"

"Dead at the battle just south of Megiddo. His hand is among those that lie in the pile outside this tent. So far, the scribes have counted more than ten thousand of the enemy dead."

"What will I tell Meritaken?"

"You will tell her nothing. She will be told simply that her brother died in battle. She need not know anything else. But the entire kingdom will know that you saved my life. My death would have resulted in a huge disturbance in the divine order, and Kemet would have been sent into chaos. You may have been born in another land, but you reacted like any loyal subject. My people and I are forever grateful that you chose to defend me."

"There was no decision to be made. I saw your life in danger, and I reacted."

"Precisely my point. Your destiny has finally been determined. You are Kemetan."

Jo nodded, and neither spoke for a few minutes. Tutankhamun turned as if to leave, and that's when Jo noticed the blood on the back of his head and neck.

"Wait. You have blood on you," she said.

He turned back to Jo. "I was hit in the back of my head. Don't worry—it's nothing. You have a badly sprained ankle and lots of bumps and bruises. What happened to you out there, before you saved my life?"

"Your guards almost killed me trying to keep me safe."

He smiled and leaned over and kissed her. "We'll leave that part out when we write all this down. Wouldn't be good for your warrior-queen image," he teased. "I'll leave you to the doctors now. I'm sure they will want to prod and poke you a bit now that you are awake."

"But there is more I want to discuss …"

"All that can wait," he said. "By the way, it's raining." He turned to leave.

"Wait! I have to feel the rain …"

He returned to her side, bent low and scooped her into his arms, and carried her outside. The rain fell heavily. Still in his arms, her arms wrapped around his neck, she closed her eyes and turned her face to the sky.

CHAPTER 23

Four soldiers carried Jo from Aruna to Gaza. Around her, dust flew from the horses' hooves, but she rode above it all in a palanquin lined with silk pillows and shaded by a colorful awning. Tutankhamun rode with the chariot corps, occasionally dropping back to check on her. Fifteen days later, when they boarded *The Wild Bull*, the pain in her leg had dulled. When they docked in Memphis, she was almost as good as new, at least physically.

The emotional wounds were more difficult to heal. It would take more than a rainstorm to cleanse her of the guilt she felt. She tried not to think about him, but Nekhare crept into her thoughts at the most unexpected moments. She knew he always would.

Twisted versions of the moment he died showed up in her nightmares. Once she dreamed that he lived long enough to ask her how she could betray him. Another time it was Tutankhamun who died when she let go of the arrow.

Jo felt angry, sad, betrayed, guilty, proud, and elated all at the same time. Her split-second decision on the battlefield scared the hell out of her. Where had that come from, the ability to take another person's life? Would she do it again? Would the next person deserve it less? *What else am I capable of doing?*

Just before nightfall one evening in Memphis, Jo and Tutankhamun were relaxing on the spacious balcony outside her bedroom. Jo sat with her journal on the table before her, while Tutankhamun rested his elbows on the low wall at the edge and watched the activity on the river far below.

Both of them had fallen silent, and each knew the other was thinking about the same thing.

"Did you finish your poem?" he asked.

"I added a few more lines," she replied.

He crossed the balcony to sit beside her. "Read it to me?"

> *She arrived from a land too distant*
> *to be imagined,*

a fair-haired girl, confused and lonely,
blinded and not yet able to find
the path that lay before her.
He too was born of another time,
When gentle grace was the way of the land.
They thrust upon him the role of God-King,
and he accepted his destiny.
He saw in her a Golden Queen,
and on a brilliantly blue day
they joined hands.
He showed her how duty
can turn to love;
she reminded him that
trust can sometimes be found
where it is least expected.
Together they sailed downriver
to confront those who would
see the kingdom fall.
The Great Pharaoh slew before him ten thousand
of the enemy,
and his queen took down the last
with a single arrow.

He nodded, and his gaze became distant. "Except that Nekhare was not the last of my enemies."

"Have you thought any more about—"

"Why he did it? I can't stop thinking about it. I thought I was prepared for any act of treason..."

"I'm so sorry."

"You cannot blame yourself. You know that. General Nankti and his men are investigating."

"And?"

"It's still not clear."

"Your Highness," she began. "Nekhare came to my room before we left for Megiddo, when I was expecting you instead."

"Ah, yes," the pharaoh nodded. "The night you had me dismiss the guards?"

She nodded.

"It wasn't like you to be upset about a minor disturbance."

"I was in bed, and he trapped me there until the approaching guards scared him off. I was afraid you would recognize the scent of his bath oils, so I made up that excuse about the coughing to get you out of there."

"I see. You were trying to protect him." He leaned back in his chair and crossed his arms.

"No. Yes. I don't know."

Tutankhamun said nothing.

"What would have been his punishment for sneaking into my bedchamber?"

The pharaoh shrugged and still said nothing.

"You would have had him executed—"

"I would have killed him myself."

Startled by his sudden vehemence, she lowered her voice to a whisper. "I was frightened, and I felt guilty about what I had done to him. I never had a chance to explain …"

"You didn't owe him any explanations. You forget that unlike you, Nekhare was born into his position. He understood his duty; he chose to dishonor it. If you had told me, let me handle him, then you wouldn't have had to …"

"I know. I know."

"And you would be spared your nightmares."

"Somehow I don't think so."

Tutankhamun pushed back his chair and went to look out over the river again. Two of Jo's personal servants entered wordlessly, lit the balcony lanterns, and scurried off. The evening settled in around them.

Jo followed her husband to the edge of the balcony. "He tried to convince me to run away with him. He was sure that I would leave immediately for Greece with him—that I was still in love with him."

Tutankhamun nodded. "I guess we need look no further then for his motive."

"But like you said, there are others we need to investigate, I suppose. The assassination attempt before we left home, for example."

"Right." He turned to face Jo, and they stood toe-to-toe. "I will deal with Ankesenamun when we return to Waset. Or maybe I won't. Perhaps I'll send her here to Memphis, make it clear to everyone that she is no longer the Great Royal Wife. Social demotion; now there's a fate far worse than death, at least from her point of view."

True, Jo thought. *And sending her away would be so much safer than interrogating her.* Jo had long ago decided that she would do everything in her power to keep Tutankhamun from finding out that Kiya was not his daughter.

He took both Jo's hands in his. "And what about you?"

"I'm sorry?"

"What would you have done if the guards had not scared Nekhare from your bed? Would you have run with him to Greece?"

He dropped one of her hands and reached out to caress her hair, but she pushed his hand away. She turned to leave, but he still had hold of her hand, so instead she glared at him, refusing to justify his question with an answer.

"I'm sorry," he said finally.

She continued to stare at him.

"It's just that so many people that I once trusted …"

"You told me never to trust anyone."

"I know, but I want to trust you." She let him pull her close, and she laid her head on his shoulder.

Trust. Can I trust him with the whole truth? "Someday, soon, I'd like to tell you more about America, my homeland. When you hear my story, you will understand why you can trust me. For now, you'll just have to believe that I love you, enough to follow you into battle, enough to follow *you* to Greece—or anywhere where we could live in peace."

She paused, and a cool breeze played with the hem of her dress. "Let's just steal a boat and sail far away, somewhere they will never find us."

It was a few minutes before he said anything. Then, finally, he said, "It is our duty to return to Waset."

"*Duty,*" she repeated. "It seems as if we have done our duty."

"Our duty is never—"

"I know," she interrupted. "Our duty is never done." She smiled up at him.

They decided to remain in the northern capital for a while, ostensibly to take care of neglected business there. Both of them were reluctant to face Meritaken, and they were not anxious to return to the palace at Waset, where they knew they would see Nekhare's ghost everywhere they turned.

As long as they stayed in Memphis, they lived the life of newlyweds. They left administrative duties to Pentju, the northern vizier, and escaped to the delta, where they spent lazy afternoons in the sun on the riverbank. They took long walks—guards followed at a safe distance—and Tutankhamun talked endlessly about his past, his family, and their future. When at the palace, they spent afternoons lounging by one of the garden pools and evenings entertaining guests—high ranking officials and wealthy citizens.

Eventually they departed upstream on *The Wild Bull*. Nankti and a small crew of retainers sailed with them, and Ay followed closely behind in *The Power of Amun*. It would be a slow trip, as the seasons had changed again, and the Nile ran high. Little villages that had sat upon the banks of the river as they passed northward the previous spring were now island villages surrounded by flooded cropland. In no hurry, they made frequent stops to explore some of the old temples and tombs. At night, servants set up camp and prepared meals while Jo and Tutankhamun played *senet*. They spent every minute together, and Jo cherished those weeks when he was hers and she was his.

"The engineers are recording record water levels," said Tutankhamun one afternoon, as the two of them watched the countryside slide by from the bow of the boat. "Crops will be exceptional. Amun smiles down upon us."

The previous year, she might have been tempted to explain that the high flood levels were the result of a particularly violent monsoon season in the Indian Ocean. Instead, she said, "It is yet more proof of your greatness, Your Highness."

"Our kingdom prospers. We will live a long and healthy life," he replied.

Jo agreed. She had saved the king, and she had changed history. The two of them would grow old together.

They were still ten days from Waset when Jo noticed, one afternoon, that her husband did not look well. The two of them sat together in the bow of *The Wild Bull*. She had been busy writing in her journal, when she realized that he hadn't spoken for a long while. She glanced over at him. He was pale, and he rested his head against the back of his chair.

"Are you all right?" she asked.

"It's just a headache," he said. "It will go away—always does."

But the headache did not go away. Over the next hour or so, it grew worse. Jo signaled for the medics; there were three of them aboard the two ships. Within minutes, both barges were anchored, and servants began setting up the usual makeshift bedroom in a shady spot on the river's edge. Tutankhamun disembarked and headed straight for his cot. A hush fell over the camp.

The medics hovered over the king for several hours as Nankti, Ay, and Jo looked on. Looking for some sort of external injury, they shaved Tutankhamun's head. No such injury was found, but the young pharaoh grew more ashen by the minute. The medics remained nearby, but Tutankhamun's illness was beyond the scope of their training. Jo tried to quell her panic.

"Perhaps the doctors in Waset will know what to do," said one of the medics.

For the first time in many months, Jo found herself thinking about the twenty-first century, wishing she could leap ahead in time just long enough to grab medication or a doctor or anything that could relieve her husband's pain. But, of course, she couldn't do that, and as hard as she tried, she couldn't think of anything that she could do to help him, other than to keep him hydrated and take him home.

"Let's get him to Waset," Jo said; Nankti and Ay nodded. The three of them stood huddled outside the pharaoh's tent, and Jo couldn't help notice that Ay looked much older than he had the night before.

"I have a plan," Jo continued. "Leave *The Power of Amun* behind with minimal crew. We'll need as many men as possible to take shifts rowing."

"That is a good idea," agreed Nankti. "If we combine both crews, we will have forty or more to row. I'll set up a rotation."

Ay frowned. "I agree. We need to row night and day and get him back to Waset as soon as possible. But I think we need to send a few men back downriver."

It was Jo's turn to frown. "I don't understand."

"Ay is right," interjected Nankti. "Horemheb is behind us—somewhere. We need to know exactly where he is."

"Do you think he's that dangerous?" asked Jo.

They both nodded, and Jo turned to enter the tent.

"Your Highness?" Ay's voice stopped her.

"Yes?"

"We need an official order to break camp and send a group of the retainers downstream."

"So ordered," replied Jo, and she stepped inside the tent.

Tutankhamun lay on the cot, his head newly shaved, his eyes closed. Jo sat carefully beside him and took his hand in hers.

He opened his eyes and attempted to smile.

"I am here, Your Highness. We need not talk. Rest."

Having made all the necessary arrangements, they sailed on, but the trip that had once been leisurely was now agonizingly slow. The river ran against them, the wind was all wrong, and the ship was undermanned for nonstop rowing, despite Nankti's best efforts. *If I only had a motor for this boat,* Jo thought, *or better yet, a helicopter.*

Tutankhamun grew weaker. Servants had erected an awning in the bow of the boat, and Tutankhamun lay under it on his cot, barely able to move. Jo sat beside him and studied his face, trying to impress him on her memory forever. Fear threatened to completely immobilize her. She tried to push it away and convince herself that he would be all right. She told herself that there was just no way he could die now. Not after everything they'd been through. Not when their lives together showed so much promise.

It would be a twist of fate too cruel.

But deep down inside, she knew. She just knew. Hadn't she known all along?

They traveled all night. In the morning, Tutankhamun requested a private conference with Ay. Jo watched from a short distance while the two of them conferred. Ay sat on a stool and bent low to hear the pharaoh's weak voice.

Jo couldn't help thinking about Ay, about how he had been adviser, father, grandfather—all of those things—for his pharaoh. She knew how much he must be suffering.

After half an hour or so, he kissed Tutankhamun on the forehead and beckoned to Jo. "He wants to speak with you now."

Ay left, and Jo sat beside her husband. She held a cup to his lips so he could drink a little water. It was a long while before he spoke.

"If I die ... *when* I die—"

"You will not die. You are Pharaoh," she said, the tears welling in her eyes.

"Listen. Please. You must take Kiya … Meritaken … even Ankesenamun. Leave Kemet forever."

"No! I cannot."

"You will all be in grave danger. Ay will try to hold him off, but Horemheb is breathing down our backs. I imagine that he is but a few days behind." He paused for a moment. "He wants the throne. You are … opponents."

"But Ankesenamun—"

"Is the mother of my daughter. Please take care of them both."

Jo nodded and choked back tears. *I must be strong*, she ordered herself.

"Ay will try to delay the news of my death—to buy time. You must get to a safe place."

"Yes," she whispered.

"The Temple at Luxor. There are those who will help you."

"Who?"

He paused. "I cannot say." Jo waited while he gathered the strength to speak again. "Do you trust me?"

"You know I do," Jo whispered.

"Then you will do this for me?"

"Yes. I will if I must."

He paused again. "Don't cry, my darling. We will see each other again in the afterworld." He closed his eyes. "We will be … together … in eternity, and it will be peaceful."

He didn't speak for a long time; finally he said, "Jo?"

"I'm right here."

"I love you, Queen Johenamun."

"I love you, too," she whispered.

They arrived in Waset under the cover of night and entered the palace with no fanfare, having determined that the best strategy would be to keep the pharaoh's arrival a secret for as long as possible. Tutankhamun, the God-King who had just conquered the Hittites, had to be carried to his chambers, where he lay in silence.

Jo sent the medics away, and she and her advisers, Ay and Nankti, gathered at the bedside. The three of them had traveled thousands of miles to defend their king and their kingdom. They had counseled the young pharaoh in his most difficult hours, and they had been his closet allies. Now the three of them would watch him die.

Tutankhamun had not moved voluntarily or uttered a sound in several hours. Jo wondered whether he had slipped into a coma.

"Your Highness, would you like for us to wake Ankesenamun?" asked Ay

"No. Let's let her sleep for now," Jo replied. "But alert the palace doctors immediately."

"I will do that," said Nankti. He left, and Jo and Ay sat in silence for a few minutes.

"You will assume the throne?" Jo asked.

Ay nodded. "I will hold Horemheb off as long as possible. Scouts report he is still en route from Memphis; that will buy us some time before—"

Jo interrupted, "Ay, Tutankhamun asked me to take Ankesenamun, Kiya, and Meritaken to Luxor."

"I think it's a good plan. If I'm able to hold off Horemheb—convince him that Ankesenamun should become regent while the heir, Kiya, is still young—then I will track you down."

"He won't like that plan."

"No, he won't."

Jo looked across Tutankhamun's wide bed and into the eyes of the man who had been his closest ally, and she knew what he was thinking. *There will be no return to Waset.*

The palace doctors arrived, followed by Nankti, but they had nothing to add to what the medics had already said. They could find no sign of injury and no reason for the pharaoh's grave illness. In the end, they determined that the illness was "internal." No amount of Kemetan medicine would cure Tutankhamun.

They left after being sworn to secrecy by Nankti.

The three continued their vigil. They gathered around Tutankhamun's bed and spoke in low whispers. They talked about how much they loved their pharaoh and how unfair it was for the gods to take him while his work was still unfinished. Nankti and Ay spoke of Tutankhamun's youth and his life at Akhetaten. They discussed how to best contain the chaos that would ensue upon the death of the pharaoh.

Just before sunrise, while the palace was still shrouded in darkness, Tut-ankhamun exhaled a long, last sigh.

"He's gone," said Ay quietly.

They sat in silence for a few minutes more.

"I'll summon the priests," said Nankti.

The two men said their final good-byes and left, but Jo stayed. There was no reason to hold back tears any longer. When the priests arrived, Jo remained by her husband's side, his hand in hers, her head resting on the bed beside him. One of the priests—Jo wasn't sure which—tried to convince her to leave the room, but Jo could not bring herself to say good-bye.

Finally they sent for Nankti. When he arrived, he found Jo in that same position; she had cried enough tears to flood the Nile.

"It is time to leave," he said gently. "The priests must begin their work."

Jo gave her husband one last kiss on the forehead, and then she allowed Nankti to escort her to her room.

CHAPTER 24

Late in the day, Jo awoke to see Meritaken sitting in a chair by her bed. Meritaken's hair hung straight and uncombed, and she wore only a simple shift. She had been crying, and a line of black *kohl* dripped down her cheek. The two friends met in the middle of the room and embraced.

"I'm glad you are home," said Meritaken, finally.

They sat on the edge of Jo's bed. Meritaken continued. "Messengers informed me of my brother's death weeks ago—and now—this." She began to cry again.

"We have much to talk about," Jo said, wondering what she would say when Meritaken pressed her for details. She slid her arm around her friend's shoulders. Jo knew from conversations with Tutankhamun that Meritaken had not been given the details of her brother's death. Meritaken knew only that Nekhare had died in battle.

"Yes, we do. I want to know everything. And I've been talking with Ay this morning." She began sobbing heavily. "I don't under … understand. He says we have to leave. I … I … I don't want to go anywhere!"

"I know," said Jo. "Neither do I. This is my home now, and if I could, I would stay here forever. But Tutankhamun asked me to keep you safe, and he said the only way to do that was to take you to Luxor. I have to honor his wish. Ay and Nankti agree. Horemheb—"

"Is a mean old man, but, Jo, do you think he would … kill us?"

"I don't know, but I can't take that chance. The others seem to think so, and don't they know more about all this than we do? I have to think about Kiya and Ankesenamun. When we leave, do you really want to stay behind?"

Meritaken shook her head.

"I didn't think so." Jo paused. "Maybe we will come back someday."

The two of them sat in silence for a minute, and Jo thought about what that might be like—living there in the palace without Tutankhamun or Nekhare. It would be lonely, but Kemet was her home, and it was where she wanted to stay.

Finally, Meritaken said, "Ankesenamun wants to see us. She asked that I bring you as soon as you woke up."

They found Ankesenamun on the balcony in her room. The afternoon was warm, but a breeze blew through the garden and ruffled the queen's unkempt hair. She turned as Jo and Meritaken entered, but she did not smile.

"At least *you* have returned home unharmed." Her tone was sad and sarcastic, and Jo couldn't tell—at least not immediately—whether Ankesenamun was relieved to see her.

She's lost them both, Jo thought, and she decided then that Ankesenamun was innocent—at least until proven guilty.

"I've been talking with Ay," said the queen. "He has told me much about your trip, and the battle, and your service to your kingdom," she spoke directly to Jo. "I am forever grateful for your devotion to Tutankhamun."

He was my husband, Jo thought. "I loved him," she said.

Ankesenamun nodded. "Ay has been very forthright. He told me of the assassination attempt, and he told me that you intercepted a note to me from Suppliminus. All these months you have no doubt believed that I plotted against Tutankhamun, but you have to believe me, I was not involved in that evil plan."

"I didn't know what to think."

"Suppliminus contacted me and tried to convince me that a marriage between the two of us could unite our respective kingdoms, but I turned him down. I sent a missive to him—if only I'd had you write it! Instead, I trusted one of his men to transcribe for me. I should have notified Nankti. I made so many mistakes." Ankesenamun shook her head slowly.

"All of that is over," said Jo finally. "We must look ahead—"

"Are you sure about this plan?" asked Ankesenamun. She turned to look out over the garden beneath her balcony, and Jo knew how difficult it was for her to think of leaving this place that she had called home for so many years.

"Yes. It is Tutankhamun's plan," Jo replied.

"I'm frightened," interjected Meritaken.

"We all are," Jo said.

Jo went back to her room and curled up on her bed. Nothing made any sense anymore, and the truth of the matter was that she was scared out of her mind. Tutankhamun had bestowed upon her this great responsibility, and she wasn't sure that she was up to the task.

Why not just stay here on the bed until Horemheb and his men carry me out?

"Go to the Temple at Luxor. There are those there who will help you. ... You will do this for me?"

"Yes. I will if I must."

She had promised Tutankhamun that she would protect Ankesenamun, Meritaken, and Kiya. That was her only purpose in life now. She looked around at her spacious, comfortable room. As if by magic, Smoke appeared out of nowhere to curl up by her side. She decided to gather her things. She would leave for Luxor within the next few days; perhaps she would go the very next day.

What to take? She began placing a few precious items into a basket ... her snake armbands and her journals. She saw the book, Foster's book, under the corner of the bed. A remnant of her old life.

She took the book, sat on the edge of the bed, and opened it up to the last readable page. She ran her hand over the next wrinkled page. The magic, or whatever it was, was back.

YEARS OF CHAOS

Although it's not clear how Pharaoh Tutankhamun died, it is known that his death sent Egypt into one hundred years of political instability. The young pharaoh's burial chamber, although packed with artifacts that would one day be priceless, was hastily prepared. What were officials trying to hide? Records indicate that the next pharaoh was Ay, an old man who had been adviser to Tutankhamun, but his reign was very short. Next in line was Horemheb, Tutankhamun's highest-ranking general. But even Horemheb could not hold the kingdom together. Egypt was attacked from the north by the Hittites and from the south by the Nubians. It would be many years before the kingdom would be reunited under the leadership of Ramses the Great.

Suddenly it occurred to Jo: *It's my fault! I sent Kemet into a century of chaos when I killed Nekhare!*

But she didn't have time to dwell on that thought.

Run! The word almost jumped off the page.

She continued to stare at the book. It had sometimes been silent, but it had never been wrong. As she watched, the letters grew larger and turned bright red.

Run!

She threw the book into the basket and flew to the nursery where she found Ankesenamun, the baby, and thankfully, Meritaken.

"We must go now!"

"Now? Are you crazy? Ay said we had time—"

"No, you must *trust me*. We must go now."

Taking with them only what Jo had in her basket and the clothing they were wearing, they fled through the streets of Waset. It was much like the night Jo arrived in Kemet: dark, quiet, and ominous. This time, she had no one to guide her. Instead, she guided the others, who had rarely been outside the palace and who had never been to this part of the city.

Ankesenamun carried the sleeping Kiya, but when she began to tire, she passed the baby to Meritaken. Soon they saw the temple before them; its great golden domes glittered in the moonlight.

"Go now," Jo said, and she motioned them through the first set of pylons. Jo glanced around to make sure they weren't being followed and then hurried along behind them. They made their way into the inner sanctum and finally down the narrow corridor that led to the priests' quarters. Their presence here was an intrusion, a breaking of sacred protocol.

Ankesenamun and Meritaken slowed with Kiya, unsure of whether they should continue.

"Go!" Jo whispered.

They nodded and continued down the hallway.

That was the last she saw of them.

A strong hand clamped over her mouth, and she was dragged through a doorway to her right. She heard a door close behind them, and her captor let go of her. She whirled around and found herself face-to-face with the bearded man.

"*No!* I will not go with you! Not now, not ever!"

He didn't stop to argue. Instead, he gave her a hard push that sent her reeling backward.

CHAPTER 25

She bounced off the wall in the bathroom of her South Florida apartment and landed in a heap on the floor, still grasping the basket containing the book, the journals, and the armbands. A searing pain shot through her stomach. "No!" she sobbed. "This can't be happening!"

She tore open the book and searched frantically for the page featuring the pyramids of Giza, but there was no bearded, white-haired man in the picture. She flipped the pages wildly to the last page that had been written.

Run, it still said in bright red ink. No new messages. She threw the book up against the wall.

Her stomach continued to lurch, and she thought she might throw up. She crawled toward the toilet.

Oh, please, don't let anyone find me here like this, she thought. She lay across the cold tile of the bathroom floor and passed out.

When she woke up, the nausea was gone—but not her outrage.

Foster. I have to get to her right away. But how? Where would I find her? It's been over a year since she sent me to Kemet.

She opened the bathroom door slowly. "Mom?"

No answer. Again, louder, "Mom?"

Still no answer. She left the bathroom and tiptoed down the hall to her own room. Her school clothes lay right on the floor where she had left them.

The clock on her dresser read 8:30 PM.

In the kitchen, a container of chocolate ice cream lay on the counter, melting. *No, this is too much.*

She glanced at the calendar; it read September 2005.

No way. No time has passed at all? I've been in Kemet for over a year, but it's still September 2005?

She went back to her bedroom, took off her dress, and hid it and the rest of her Kemetan existence in a box under the bed. She crawled between the sheets and cried herself to sleep.

"Johanna Wilson, are you still awake?"

Her mother stuck her head through the door, and a light glowed behind her in the hallway.

"Is that you, Mom?"

"No, it's Santa Claus. Of course it's me. What is it with all the sand all over the bathroom?"

"Oh … I forgot. I'm sorry. Can I clean it up in the morning?"

"Are you feeling okay?"

"No. Well, just a little tired."

"Okay, just don't forget. I have an early shift in the morning, so I won't see you till tomorrow night."

"You knew, didn't you?"

Jo dropped the huge book on Foster's desk; it landed with a heavy thud.

She had arrived at school well before any other students, somehow sensing that Foster would be waiting for her.

"Yes."

"Then send me back. Now!" Jo demanded.

"I can't." Foster didn't even look up.

"You have to. I've got to get back to Kemet and help my family to safety. But I bet you know all about that."

"I can't send you back."

"Why?" Jo was frantic. "You certainly sent me to Kemet easily enough. I am a Kemetan, and I am the wife of Pharaoh Tutankhamun. I *order* you to send me back to my home."

"Jo …"

"It's *Johenamun*. Send me home—now."

"Jo, you are home. You know that. I can't send you back. Your journey to Egypt was a … an accident, really. I never intended you to go there for any length of time. And David and I are in deep trouble for sending you."

"An *accident*? It was all an *accident*?"

"Yes. You were supposed to take a tour of the Great Pyramid and then return home with a new respect—"

"The Great Pyramid?" Jo asked, stunned.

"Yes, that's where I sent you. But then you went running out of there. And you didn't have the book with you, so how were you supposed to get back?"

"The book …"

"Is your portal key."

"Portal key?"

"I'll tell you all about that later. Anyway, as I was saying, we sent the book along behind you, but that caused some sort of realignment … or hiccup … or something. You jumped through time again. That's how you ended up in the Eighteenth Dynasty. Jo, if you had just stayed put, not run out of the pyramid … Well, I wouldn't be in all the trouble I'm in now."

"You're in trouble with who? No, wait, that doesn't matter. The only thing that matters is that I return to Kemet *right now*. My family is in grave danger; I have to help them."

"I know, I know. But I have no power to send you anywhere. My power has been revoked."

"I don't understand …"

"You were only supposed to have a little tour of the Great Pyramid. We had no idea where you went, and when we finally found you, you'd been brainwashed into thinking you belonged there."

"*Brainwashed*?" Jo couldn't believe her ears. "I was not brainwashed—"

"And I hear we got you out just in time," interrupted Foster. "You're welcome, by the way."

"You think I should thank you? Thank you for ruining my life? Now I have to go through the rest of my life wondering what happened to my family. Did they live or die? Do they think I betrayed them?" She continued to rage, not caring whether she was making sense or not. "You want me to *thank you*?"

"I'm sorry … I didn't realize—"

"No, you didn't. But now you do, so help me find a way back!"

"I can't, Jo. I'm sorry."

Jo's shoulders sagged; Foster was obviously telling the truth. "So now what?"

"Now nothing. You must not tell anyone about what has happened to you. You have a special talent—not just time travel; do you know how few people are born with language assimilation?"

"Language assimilation?"

"And you need coaching in order to use your talents to their best advantage. But believe me, you cannot tell a soul."

"Yeah, right. Like I'm going to go home and tell my mother that I married Tutankhamun. She'd have me locked away before I could say *I'm an Egyptian queen*. That's it? How do I find out what happened to my family?"

"You might try a library …"

Jo turned to leave the room, completely exasperated. She knew she'd have to find a way back to Egypt, back home, but Foster would be no help. She was on her own.

"Jo?"

"What?"

"You'll be needing this, eventually." Foster held out the big book. She gave Jo a strange look as she handed her the "portal key," and once again Jo lugged the book home.

She didn't go to school the next day. Instead, she convinced her mother that she was sick and spent three days lying in bed with her door locked, rereading her journals over and over again.

She couldn't move, didn't want to move. Nothing mattered anymore.

She wrote the last lines of the poem she had started for Tutankhamun:

> *But fate was their greatest enemy,*
> *the one love couldn't conquer.*
> *Too short was their time together;*
> *He left this world, and she was powerless*
> *to save him,*
> *for in the end, she was*
> *just an ordinary girl.*

On the afternoon of the third day, her mother delivered an ultimatum: go to school the next day, or go to the doctor.

Jo went to school.

Of course, nothing had changed at Southglades High. Foster's social studies class debated whether Tutankhamun was murdered or died of natural causes. Foster kept staring at Jo over those glasses of hers, like she was warning her, silently, not to spill the beans—as if it mattered. Jo didn't even really know whether the king, her husband, had been murdered. Did someone poison the wine when they weren't looking? Did he have a brain tumor? Or did it have something to do with the blow to his head at Megiddo?

All she knew was that she missed him with every inch of her being.

The rest of the madness—everyday life at Southglades—slid right by her. It was as if she'd become immune to it all—like she was nothing more than a spectator at a low-budget movie. Events happened all around her, but they were neither funny nor sad. She didn't really give a damn if Tommy Nystrom called her every name under the sun. He was just a punk, after all, and she was Queen of Egypt.

Teachers were like flies, always buzzing in Jo's ear, annoying her, but never making any sense. She sat through the classes and lectures, but she didn't hear a word they said. Her grades hit rock bottom, and her mother was called for a conference.

"We're really worried about her," she heard one of her teachers say. Foster just sat there, staring at her, silently warning her to keep her mouth shut. "She's in a dangerous downward spiral."

"Yes, I agree," replied Jo's mother. "It just happened ... overnight. I don't know what's going on. All of a sudden all she wants to do is schlep around in her bathrobe ..."

I hate my clothes. Jo wanted to scream. Everything was too restrictive, too tight. She wanted her loose, flowing Kemetan dresses or her made-to-order battle gear. She longed for the heavy beer from the palace brewery.

"... and all she wants to eat is *dried fruit*," her mother continued. "I mean, what's that all about? She's always been such a junk-food junkie."

They continued to talk as if she wasn't even there. "Well, the high-school years are trying times," said Mrs. Whiteson, Jo's math teacher. "They go through so many changes."

"I guess," Mrs. Wilson replied. "All of a sudden she's two inches taller, and just look at the way her body is filling out! And it's not just physical. It's like she's a whole different person ... and I don't even know how to talk to her anymore."

"Perhaps a little family counseling wouldn't hurt," replied Mrs. Whiteson.

Jo went to school early the next day and caught Foster in her room alone. "Send me back, *please*," she begged again.

"Jo, I just can't. But why don't you join our group? Maybe if you spent time with others who are like you—"

"I told you, I'm not coming to your freak meetings."

Foster been bugging Jo to join the travel club that met every Monday night at the local bookstore. Apparently there was a whole group of people with the same gift Jo had, and they met frequently to talk about places they had been and problems they had encountered. It was a support group.

"If you just gave us a chance. You have a special gift."

"Yeah, right."

Jo didn't bother to hang around for first period. Instead she went back home. Her mom was at work, so she went to her room and pulled out the box that held her Kemetan dress, her journals, and her armbands.

CHAPTER 26

The next day she was taken completely by surprise when Tommy Nystrom plunked himself down beside her at lunch. She had taken to eating by herself, at a table in the back of the cafeteria, where no one else ventured.

"We need to talk," Tommy said.

"Well, the thing is, I really don't like to talk much. Especially to you."

"Too bad. I figure you and I are two of a kind."

"I doubt that," Jo said.

"No, really." He pushed himself closer and lowered his voice to a whisper. "I'm one of *them*, too. I just found out."

"I have no idea what you're talking about," she said. She stood, picking up her lunch tray. He caught her by the wrist, and her milk cartoon teetered on the edge of her tray.

"No, wait. We've got to talk. I heard all about it. You went to Egypt, right?"

"You *heard* about me?"

"Yes, at the meetings these last few weeks. I'd really like to talk to you about your trip—"

"No," she said, pulling away. "No way." She dumped her lunch tray and took refuge in math class.

But when the three o'clock bell rang, there was Tommy, waiting outside Jo's last class, his long, lanky frame propped up against a pair of lockers. "Can I walk you home?" he asked.

"No." She walked right by him.

"I can get you back to Egypt," he said. Jo stopped dead in her tracks.

"What did you say?"

"I can get you back to Egypt," he repeated, a little less confidently this time. "I mean, I can't get you there right this minute, but I have a plan."

"Start talking," Jo said.

"Well, Foster's been after you to come to the weekly meetings, right?"

"Yeah."

"Well, do you know what they do at those weekly meetings?"

"Sit around and creep each other out?"

"Well, yes." He laughed. "They're a strange bunch, I'll admit. But, they also talk about all their travels, and they discuss who's going where and when and how. They're kind of like *training* sessions."

"Go on."

"I know they won't let you go back to Egypt. They're afraid you'll screw up history or something—"

"I already screwed up history."

"I don't get why you say that. Nothing much changed after you went there; Tutankhamun still died."

"You don't get it, like you said."

"Anyway, they won't let you go back there, but they are willing to teach us both how to get around in time. That's why Foster is here, you know, at South-glades. She's supposed to be mentoring you and me."

"Great job she's doing," Jo said sarcastically.

"No doubt. She took some serious heat for your fiasco. Anyway, I figure if we go to those meetings, eventually we'll learn how to get around. I think I've got some of it figured out already. And then who's to stop us from going any-where we want?"

"Us?"

"Sure, why not?"

Why not? Jo was ready to do anything to get back to Kemet. "Tommy, do you think we could go back to a specific time and place?"

"Yeah, I think so."

"What's in it for you?"

"What?"

"Why are you so anxious to take me back to Egypt?"

"Why not? I figure I'm not going to be gone long. I just think I can help you do this. Besides, there's nothing going on here."

"You got that right. Let's do it."

"Great. We'll go to next Monday's meeting together. They'll be thrilled to see you—the whole group is worried about you. Now, will you tell me all about your trip? Did you really marry King Tut?"

It took about three days to tell Tommy the whole story.

Jo took him to the apartment when her mother was working a night shift, and they dug her treasures out from under her bed.

"Wow," he said when Jo showed him her journals. "You could get a freakin' fortune for these! Talk about your priceless primary source documents."

"You've been studying way too much," she replied. But Jo knew he was right—not that she would ever let anybody get a hold of her journals.

Another night, they went to Tommy's house. He lived with both his parents in a huge house worth about a zillion dollars. They arrived just as his mom, a petite red-haired woman, was on her way out the door for a tennis match.

"Your father's still at the office," she said to Tommy. "Dinner will be late, so if you get hungry, have Cook make you a snack."

They played video games for a while on a huge wide-screen TV.

"I don't get it. Why would you ever want to leave here?" Jo asked.

"It gets old," he said. "I could be gone for days before they discovered I was missing. C'mon, tell me everything. I want to know everything there is to know about Egypt."

As it turned out, David, the old guy with the beard, had blabbed a lot of Jo's adventure. Of course, he only knew what was common knowledge in Egypt: that she had lived in the palace as Princess Johenamun, that the people of Egypt had dubbed her "The Golden Princess," and that she had married Tut-ankhamun.

He didn't know the whole truth, so he couldn't tell it.

Jo did. She told Tommy everything, partly to relieve herself of the burden but also to test him, to see whether he'd still want to hang with her when he found out all about her.

Tommy passed her test. He listened to the whole story and never passed judgment. Every once in a while, he'd say something like "Un-freakin'-believable" or "No freakin' way."

They talked a lot about Nekhare, and Jo tried to find words to explain how that one moment—the second she let that arrow fly—had changed her life forever. *I am capable of killing.* It was a concept she still couldn't handle.

"I hear ya," was Tommy's only comment.

"I wanted so much to save the king, to be that person he could depend on. I failed so miserably."

"No, you didn't. He died knowing that you were completely devoted to him. What happened after you left? Have you looked it up?"

"I tried, but there's not much information out there, and what is available is conflicting. You know from social studies that the debate about Tutankhamun is still going on."

"Yeah, I just assumed you knew the answer."

"Jeez, it's not like there was an autopsy or something."

"Right."

"He got hit on the head during the battle at Megiddo Pass. But then again, it could have been a brain tumor or something like that. The only thing I know for sure is that Ay became pharaoh for about a year, and then Horemheb. No surprise there. Horemheb undoubtedly killed everyone off. Probably even Ankesenamun. She completely disappears from history right after Tutankhamun's death. Queen Johenamun doesn't make it into recorded history at all."

"Hmmm ... that's weird."

"Not really. I've been thinking about it. The pharaohs were the ones who recorded their own successes. That's how we know about them and their accomplishments and their families. Tutankhamun died before he had a chance to tell his story—or mine. Who knows what Nekhare said about me in his official documents? And then there were my own journals. If I'd left them behind ... Well, it doesn't matter. A few years later, Horemheb erased every record of Tutankhamun's rule. That's why the modern world didn't know anything about Tutankhamun until his tomb was discovered."

"What are you going to do when you get back there?" he asked. "Are you going back for Ankesenamun and Meritaken, or are you going to go back further ... redo the battle at Megiddo?"

"I haven't figured that out yet," she said. "It's all so complex. But I can't help wondering whether Nekhare was supposed to have lived to become pharaoh. And I miss Tutankhamun more every day." She closed her eyes and leaned her head against the sofa.

Finally she whispered, "When I close my eyes it's so easy to imagine that I'm back on the balcony in Memphis. I feel the cool breeze from the river and Tutankhamun's arms around me."

She paused and sat up again. "And then I open my eyes and it's all ... gone ... like it never even happened."

"And all you got left is me. That's pretty freakin' pathetic." Tommy smiled.

On the following Monday, Tommy went to Jo's house, and they walked to the bookstore together. It was not the nationally known mega-store but the little mom-and-pop place on Main Street.

Tommy led Jo through the building to a door at the rear. A sign there read "Travel Club: By Invitation Only." He opened the door to another world.

The first person to notice them was an older man with a long white beard. He wore loose-fitting cotton pants and a white tunic. Jo recognized him immediately. He held his hand out to her; she took it reluctantly.

"Jo," he said, "I'm David. So glad to see you here. I'm glad you've decided to come."

"I might not have if I'd known you'd be here," she said, never one to hold back.

He laughed. "I expected that you'd still be quite upset with me. I was, after all, part of Ms. Foster's scheme to send you to Egypt."

"What I'm really ticked off about is the fact that you brought me back when you knew I wanted to stay."

"Yes … well … it had to happen. That was a nasty little trick you pulled on me out there in the Valley of the Dead."

"And a nasty little trick you pulled on me at Luxor."

"Let's call it even, then," he said, smiling.

"Hardly." They would never be even. "How did you know I would be at the temple that night?"

"I didn't. I knew something was up at the palace, so I was hanging around, hoping to get a chance to see you."

"I don't understand."

"I was living on the grounds of the temple, hoping that the pharaoh would send you to me."

"The pharaoh?"

"Pharaoh Tutankhamun saved your life, Jo. I assume he was the one who sent you to the temple at Luxor?"

"Yes," she said, but she still didn't understand what he meant.

"Of course. You see, before you went to Syria, I sent him a note. I explained that I was waiting at the temple for you and that if he should need to send you to safety, I would be there. I guaranteed him that I would keep you safe."

She stared back. "You told him that I was from the twenty-first century?"

"No, of course not. He would have never sent you to me if I'd said that. He would have thought I was crazy. I just told him that I was waiting to take you home. When he realized that he was dying, he remembered my note, and he sent you to safety."

"But that night … how did you know I would turn up then?"

"I didn't. I got lucky. I was just returning from my evening walk when I looked up, and there you were, tearing down the hallway of the temple. I didn't even stop to think. I knew the portal was open, and I shoved you through it."

"But the book … how were you able to write in the book?"

"Oh, how interesting! Do you mean my message came through? I'll have to talk to the Council about that. All these years they've insisted that would never work. The book …"

He lowered his voice and glanced around the room to make sure no one was listening in on their conversation. "The book is a special kind of magic, not a topic for all ears. Come. Let's sit."

He led Jo and Tommy to the back of the room and motioned for them to sit on an overstuffed sofa. He pulled up a chair.

"So why couldn't it help me when I needed it the most?" Jo demanded. Tommy and David just stared at her. "It wrote for me, told me all about Tutankhamun. But then, before we left for Syria, it had nothing more to say."

"Ah," said David, stroking his beard. "I can only assume that the book didn't know. You were rewriting history at that point, and it can't make predictions. It could tell you what had already happened, but once you started altering the course of history, well—"

"See, I told you so," she said to Tommy.

"Speaking of rewriting history, Jo, the Egyptians were not supposed to have soap for hundreds of years yet. What were you thinking?"

"I was thinking we needed soap!"

"Well, we had to send someone back to fix that."

"Send me," she said. "Look, I believe that Tutankhamun intended for Ankesenamun, Kiya, and Meritaken to come with me. I promised him I would take care of them! It was cruel of you to leave them there. Who knows what their fate was? They probably died thinking that I had deserted them."

"I see your point, but certainly you understand that I couldn't bring those three back to this century?"

"Why not? Seems like they'd fit right in here." She glanced around the room. "You could have sent them somewhere else later. I could have had a chance to explain—"

"I didn't have time to think about all of that. I had to get you out of Egypt before the portal closed. What matters now is that you are here, safe and sound."

"Maybe that's what matters to you," she replied.

"Look, you're just going to have to be patient. Both of you. You're not traveling until you fully understand what you're doing, not until you can prove that you understand the consequences of interfering with events as they are supposed to happen. As for you, Jo, you must never go back to Tutankhamun's lifetime again."

Who's going to stop me?

David continued, "Come. I'll introduce you around."

"Wait," Jo stopped him. "There's one more thing. How do you guys—you and Foster and the rest of these people—know another time traveler when you see one?"

"By the aura, of course."

Jo and Tommy just stared. "The aura?" she finally asked.

"Yes. All time travelers emit a slightly purple aura. You can't see it yet; you're too young. You'll pick up on it eventually."

Jo and Tommy left the Travel Club meeting and walked home, not talking much until they were only a block or so from Jo's house. The night was humid, and Jo could smell jasmine in the air. They stopped to sit on a bus stop bench, the glow from a streetlight bathing them in yellow.

"You're upset," said Tommy finally.

Jo didn't respond right away. "You know how David said that time travelers have a purple aura?"

"Yeah."

"Well, I think Tutankhamun was a time traveler."

"What?"

"I saw his aura once. We were out on the cliffs at Meretsega. The sun had just come up, and it was the most amazing thing I've ever seen—the way the sun's rays seemed to converge on him. I swear to God, he *glowed*. And then all of a sudden, there was this purple haze."

"Jo …"

"I know, I know. It sounds impossible, but we're *freakin'* time travelers, Tommy. What's any weirder than that? If there's one thing I've learned lately, it's that nothing is too weird to be true."

"So, are you thinking you are going back to Egypt to steal Tutankhamun away, bring him back to the twenty-first century with you?"

"Where doctors can cure him, perhaps?" She paused. "It's certainly tempting. And probably doable, if my hunch is correct. Perhaps it's another reason we had this incredible connection. Like minds, you know."

"But Jo, you heard what David said about going back there."

"You told me you could do it," she replied.

"I *thought* I could, but now I'm not so sure."

"C'mon. You have to try. You owe it to me after all the years you've tortured me."

"I know."

"Besides, the whole Egypt thing—it was all your fault."

"*My* fault? How do you figure?"

"You ticked me off and set off a chain reaction that sent me to Egypt."

"Where you fell in love and became queen. Or maybe it was the other way around?"

Jo gave him a playful shove.

"I think you should be thanking me." Tommy grinned.

"Right. Just figure it out, and I'll forgive you for every last piece of drivel that has ever come out of your mouth. Even that last part that you said just now."

CHAPTER 27

And so what had begun with Tommy ended with Tommy.

Just a few days later, Jo found herself sitting with him on the sofa in her living room. She was dressed in her Kemetan dress and her gold armbands, and her long hair was braided and heavily adorned. Black eyeliner ringed her eyes. In her lap were Foster's book—Jo's portal key—and the journals, all tucked in a canvas bag.

"Are you sure you know what you're doing?" she asked.

"No," replied Tommy. "I'm not at all sure."

He sat beside Jo on the sofa, and anyone who might have walked in on them would have thought they both looked ridiculous. Tommy wore only a kilt—actually it was half a sheet wrapped around his waist—and heavy eyeliner.

"But I figure not much can go wrong," he continued. "The portal is open; I know that from eavesdropping on the right conversations. We have your portal key and the artifacts we need." He pointed to her armbands. "What's the worst that can happen?"

She shrugged.

"If it doesn't work, we've just ruined your mother's sheet. No big loss, right?" He grinned. "Now all we need to do is concentrate. Try focusing on the date. Say it out loud."

Jo looked at him suspiciously, finding it hard to believe time travel could be as simple as that. "Thirteen twenty-five," she said.

"No, no. Close your eyes. Concentrate. Say it out loud, over and over." He reached out and grabbed her hand, and with his other hand, he held on to the drawstring bag that held the scrolls and the book.

What are we going to do with all those blond curls? He's not going to pass for a Kemetan. She closed her eyes. "Thirteen twenty-five. One, three, two, five. One … three … two … five … One … three … two … five …"

Her stomach lurched, and her eyes popped open.

"Yes. I felt it, too. Keep going ..."

"One ... three ... two ... five ..."

That was when Tommy realized that something was wrong.

Jo, say B.C., Before Christ.

But it was too late. Before he could get the words out of his mouth, the room went black, and Tommy suddenly felt as though he'd been picked up by a tornado or a hurricane or some other massive force—natural or unnatural—and he knew he was hurtling not through space but through time.

Cool, he thought. But then he realized he had lost his grip on Jo's hand. Soon after that, he thought he heard her scream his name.

And then for a long time there was nothing but blackness.

As for Jo, she sensed from the very beginning that something was very wrong, that this time travel was different from her first. She felt as though she were falling into a deep abyss, one from which she might never return. She lost hold of Tommy's hand, and she thought she heard herself scream. Then there was nothing to do but wait and hope and pray that when it was all over, she'd be in Kemet.

But somehow she didn't think so.

Author's Notes

Despite the masses of riches found in Tutankhamun's tomb, we know surprisingly little about the man, or boy, himself. Recent scientific studies of his mummified remains do not tell us much more than we already knew, although they confirm that Tutankhamun was not murdered with a blow to the head, as some had conjectured.

Almost all we can say for sure is that he lived and that he was pharaoh for a short time. He would have been trained for battle, and he was married to Ankesenamun, who may have been his sister—but even that is hard to say with any confidence, because the ancient Egyptians tended to call all women "sister." We are not sure of Tutankhamun's parentage, but Ay and Horemheb were definitely major players in the young pharaoh's life. The times were chaotic, and they would become even more so after Tutankhamun's death.

Meritaken, Nekhare, Nankti, and Kiya are fictional characters. Evidence suggests that Ankesenamun may have had two stillborn children, but this has not been confirmed.

After the young pharaoh died, there was a hasty funeral. The vizier Ay ruled briefly (he may have married Ankesenamun), and then Horemheb took the throne. Upon his coronation, Horemheb began systematically erasing every record of Tutankhamun, his family, and their accomplishments. Very little is left to give us any clues about how King Tut lived or what he was like. We also know very little about the fate of Ankesenamun; after the death of Ay, she disappears from history.

Some think that King Tut was physically frail, perhaps even handicapped or deformed. They hypothesize that the young man was an ineffective pharaoh, too weak to exert much influence. I prefer to think differently—or, at least, I like to imagine what might have been. After all, how much can we know about a person whose whole life story was obliterated? How much can we really know about events that took place four thousand years ago?

Bibliography

For those interested in learning more about King Tut and the Eighteenth Dynasty, I recommend the following, all of which were valuable to me in my research:

Brier, Bob. *The Murder of Tutankhamen.* New York: Putnam Publishing, 1998.

Brier, Bob, and Hoyt Hobbs. *Daily Life of the Ancient Egyptians.* New York: Greenwood Press, 1998.

Desroches-Noblecourt, Christiane. *Tutankhamen: Life and Death of a Pharaoh.* New York: Penguin Books, 1989.

Reeves, Nicholas. *Akhenaten: Egypt's False Prophet.* London: Thames & Hudson, 2005.

Editors of Time-Life Books. *What Life Was Like on the Banks of the Nile.* New York: Time Life Books, 1997.

978-1-58348-477-7
1-58348-477-9

Breinigsville, PA USA
28 June 2010
240696BV00002B/2/A